Blame *the* Beignets

Books by Ginger Bolton

SURVIVAL OF THE FRITTERS

GOODBYE CRULLER WORLD

JEALOUSY FILLED DONUTS

BOSTON SCREAM MURDER

BEYOND A REASONABLE DONUT

DECK THE DONUTS

CINNAMON TWISTED

DOUBLE GRUDGE DONUTS

BLAME THE BEIGNETS

Published by Kensington Publishing Corp.

Blame *the* Beignets

GINGER BOLTON

Kensington Publishing Corp.
kensingtonbooks.com

KENSINGTON BOOKS are published by

Kensington Publishing Corp.
900 Third Avenue
New York, NY 10022

Special book excerpts or customized printings can also be created to fit specific needs. For details, write or phone the office of the Kensington Sales Manager: Kensington Publishing Corp., 900 Third Avenue, New York, NY 10022. Attn. Sales Department. Phone: 1-800-221-2647.

ISBN: 978-1-4967-4961-1
ISBN: 978-1-4967-4962-8 (ebook)

First Kensington Trade Paperback Printing: December 2024

10 9 8 7 6 5 4 3 2 1

Printed in the United States of America

Acknowledgments

The best part of writing—as in life—is the people we meet, either in person, or through various forms of correspondence, and I thank you all for your time, your patience, your kindness, and for generally being wonderful people.

That includes my writer friends Catherine Astolfo, Allison Brook, Melodie Campbell, Laurie Cass, Krista Davis, Daryl Wood Gerber, Kaye George, and all of the writers I've met in person and over the internet.

And then there are my agent John Talbot and my editor John Scognamiglio, who keep Emily and her friends (and Dep!) at Deputy Donut alive.

What can I say about the team at Kensington Publishing Corp.? Everyone is helpful and so very, very nice. Larissa Ackerman puts together the mini cozy conventions where authors and readers have great fun. Carly Sommerstein designs and keeps tabs on my manuscripts as they go through all the production stages toward publication. Kristine Mills designs the covers, and Mary Ann Lasher creates the delightful artwork (and Dep!).

What would those of us who love books do without booksellers and librarians?

I salute my family and friends, who understand the dreaded word "deadline" and put up with my not being there even when I am.

And then there are the people who hold this book in their hands. Thank you for coming along with Emily on this adventure. You have made my lifelong dream of being a novelist come true.

Chapter 1

Behind me, dishes and glasses collided. I turned around. In our dining area, Hannah, our new assistant at Deputy Donut, grimaced and balanced a tray of dishes. Nothing broke or landed on any of the day's last customers lingering in our café.

Blushing, Hannah threw me a rueful grin. The lanky college sophomore looked younger than ever, partly because her Deputy Donut hat, a fake police hat with a plush donut where a real police officer's badge would be, was crooked. Wisps of long blond hair had escaped from both the hat and her ponytail. She brought the tray into the kitchen where her older sister Olivia and I were.

Olivia cautioned, "Careful."

"I know." Hannah stomped past us into the storeroom. I couldn't see her, but I heard dishes being loaded more forcefully than necessary into the dishwasher.

Olivia sighed. "Emily, I'm sorry I told you she was looking for a job." Olivia's luxurious, wavy brown hair was still neatly tied back, her hat was on straight, and her Deputy Donut apron, embroidered with the silhouette of a cat wearing a Deputy Donut hat, was nearly pristine. Like her much younger sister, Olivia towered over me.

In addition to the hats and aprons, we wore white shirts

embroidered with the same logo, and black jeans or knee-length shorts. Hannah and I were wearing shorts that day. Olivia's jeans showed hardly any specks of frosting, dough, sprinkles, or sugar.

My apron seemed to have attracted some of the powdered sugar that I was practically dumping onto warm beignets, and my shorts hadn't fared much better. I was never sure if my Deputy Donut hat was on straight. My nearly black curly hair had a mind of its own, and it often seemed to tilt my hat by itself. "You shouldn't be sorry, Olivia. Tom and I are glad we hired her."

Olivia carefully wrapped a ball of dough for the next day. "She almost dropped a tray of dishes."

"She caught it in time."

Hannah returned from the storeroom. "Emily, what do you want me to do next to help close up shop?" Before I could answer, she gasped and stared in something like horror toward the window between the kitchen and our office, where my cat Dep stayed while I was at work.

My sometimes mischievous tortoiseshell tabby was behaving herself, more or less. She was standing on the back of the office couch. Although short-haired and smaller than the average cat, she looked enormous. She had puffed up her fur and arched her back. Her suddenly huge plume of a tail twitched back and forth. Her mouth open in a hiss we couldn't hear on the kitchen side of the glass, she glowered toward the door leading to the parking lot behind our building.

One of us must have neglected to lock our back door.

Two strange men were in our office.

The tall, clean-shaven man in the aviator sunglasses and black leather jacket ran his fingers through his tousled dark brown hair, making the waves even more unruly. He removed the sunglasses and peered toward Olivia, Hannah, and me. Licking his lips, he gave us a jaunty wave. His boyishly crooked grin would have added to his appeal if he hadn't been inside our office, where he definitely did not belong. I had never before seen him or the bearded guy in the blue plaid shirt and the worn, tan canvas jacket.

The bearded guy glanced toward us and then let his longish light brown hair fall forward, hiding most of the side of his face.

He was too close to my precious kitty.

Chapter 2

✣

Fearing that the two men might be trying to kidnap Dep, I could suddenly move. Yelling, "Call 911," I skidded around the end of the half wall. Mentally willing Dep to leap to one of her narrow stairways and trot up to the safety of the catwalks and tunnels that Tom and I had built for her near the ceiling, I turned and stormed between the half wall and our serving counter toward the office door. A dog yapped.

A dog?

The handsome man in the leather jacket opened the office door. Smiling, he strode into the dining area.

Ears back, fur still puffy, Dep streaked out of the office, closely followed by . . . I wasn't sure what. I squeezed my eyes shut and opened them again.

It was a dog, a tiny one. She—I assumed it was a she—was wearing a miniature, lace-trimmed white satin gown. A white tulle veil was attached to the brown ponytail sprouting from the top of her silky head. The garments were probably slowing her down.

Nothing, apparently, was going to slow Dep.

The bearded man ran out of the office, pausing only long enough to close the door that his accomplice had opened.

Dep leaped onto a woman's lap and then onto the woman's table. The woman yelped, pushed her chair back, and stood up, brushing at the front of her jeans. Neither she nor Dep spilled anything.

Apologizing to the woman and darting an angry glare at the man in the leather jacket, I dashed to the table and reached for Dep. The canine mini-bride barked shrilly, pranced on her back feet, and pawed at my bare shins.

Dep flew to the next table, an unoccupied one. As if she'd planned it all ahead of time, she gracefully slid across the glass top to the far side, touched down momentarily on one of our leather-upholstered dining chairs, landed on the floor, and sprinted toward the glass front door.

Olivia, Hannah, the bearded man, and I all ran toward my kitty. The bearded man must have learned Dep's name. He was calling her along with the rest of us. Some of the other diners jumped up and were trying to help corral the animals.

A grumpy-looking trio in the corner near one of our large front windows didn't seem to notice anything except their own argument.

The handsome interloper in the black leather jacket stood off to one side, observing the chaos as if we were putting on a show just for him.

Frantically trying to catch Dep before someone opened the door and let her escape into the dangers of downtown Fallingbrook, Wisconsin, I didn't have time to ask Olivia and Hannah if they had called 911.

Dep hesitated near the front door, looking out through the glass. Closing in on her, the yapping dog risked having her elegant gown and veil torn if my almost cornered kitty decided to defend herself.

The bearded man scooted between Dep and me, stooped, and reached for my cat.

I couldn't help it. I screamed. It came out like a pathetic wail, one that would never frighten an attacker.

The man turned around, holding Dep in his arms and cooing, "It's okay, kitty. I've got you."

Olivia brushed past me. "Zachary! What are you doing here?"

"Herding cats, I guess." His smile was sheepish, and his bluish-gray eyes seemed considerate, but I wasn't about to be fooled by these intruders, no matter how attractive they might have looked in less frightening circumstances. The man—Zachary—extended Dep toward Olivia. "Is she yours, Olivia?"

To my amazement, Dep lowered her hackles and unpuffed her tail. She wriggled, climbed to Zachary's shoulders, wrapped herself around his neck, and rubbed her chin on the side of his beard. I had to stop my mouth from dropping open. Dep was an affectionate cat, but she seldom warmed that quickly to strangers.

Again dancing on her hind legs, the furball in the wedding gown and flowing veil pawed at one leg of Zachary's jeans. Hollering to make myself heard over the dog, I managed a curt, "She's mine." Unceremoniously, I reached up and tried to pluck Dep off Zachary's shoulders.

My head barely came up to her level. She must have known that allowing me to take her from Zachary would bring her closer to the dog. She dug her claws into Zachary's jacket. Bending and twisting, Zachary helped me reach her and unlatch her claws. They hadn't penetrated the thick canvas. Maybe that was a good thing, but I would not have minded if Zachary and his friend decided that visiting Deputy Donut wasn't good for them or their clothing.

Frowning, feeling like my annoyance at the two men and the mess they'd created might be causing steam to rise through my curls and seep around the edges of my Deputy Donut cap, I cradled Dep in my arms.

The dog jumped and yapped.

Hannah picked her up, smoothed her gown around her little body, and made shushing noises. The dog stopped barking, but with an almost laughable attempt at a growl, she pointed her muzzle toward Dep, thinned her lips, and displayed a set of tiny teeth.

I carried my unintimidated kitty to the office. She was not purring. I locked the back door, set Dep down, and closed her inside the office. Still inwardly fuming, I returned to the group near the front door.

Looking totally comfy in Hannah's arms, the little dog panted. I could have sworn she was wearing a triumphant smile.

Hannah repeated her sister's question. "What are you doing here, Zachary?" Her usually soft voice had gained a knifelike edge.

"Research," Zachary answered, "for my master's thesis."

"Oh." Despite returning the little dog's kisses, Hannah managed to sound totally bored. "Mushrooms."

Zachary nodded toward the other man. "And Joshua came along."

Joshua gave Hannah a warm smile. "Actually, I hoped to see you, Hannah." Was that his normal voice or was he deepening it to what he thought might be a sexy drawl?

Hannah dismissed both men. "I'm working."

Olivia contributed, "And she'd better get back to it. Why did the two of you come in through the back, and why did you bring your dog?"

Zachary reached out, and Hannah eased the tiny bride into his hands. Zachary held the dog up at face level and stared into her eyes. "She's not mine. Or Joshua's. She was at the door back there, wanting to come in. We figured she belonged here, so we let her in and followed her."

Olivia was apologizing to the woman whose lap and table Dep had invaded. Zachary cuddled the dog, who still seemed perfectly content, as if she'd planned all along to have Hannah pick her up and Zachary snuggle her against him. Joshua watched Hannah make a show of thoroughly cleaning the table that Dep had skidded across.

A woman's voice carried from the sidewalk out front. "Gigi!"

In a billowing yellow ball gown, the woman put her hands to her mouth like a megaphone. "Gigi! Gigi!"

I pointed to her. "That's Madame Monique. She owns the bridal salon in the building on the other side of the alley. She probably knows whose dog that is."

Still holding the little dog, Zachary opened our front door. "I'll check." He went outside and called, "Madame Monique?" The door closed behind him.

Madame Monique turned around. With a teary-looking smile, she trundled in yellow satin kitten-heeled shoes toward Zachary and held her arms out. "Gigi!" Zachary tenderly placed the little dog in Madame Monique's arms.

Joshua beamed down at Hannah. "Sorry about that." Was he apologizing for Zachary? I suspected that he was as much to blame as Zachary was for barging in through the back door, and Joshua was definitely responsible for opening the office door and letting animals into Deputy Donut's dining area.

As far as I could tell, the sour-looking couple and the man conferring in the corner had not looked up during the commotion. Their muttered syllables quick and hissing, they continued their apparent argument. The man who didn't appear to be part of a couple leaned forward, his hands in fists on either side of the plate of beignets he'd barely touched. The other man shoved his glasses higher on his nose. They immediately slipped down. Frowning, he pushed at the nosepiece with his middle finger. I couldn't tell if the gesture was a habit or if he meant to be rude to the man across the table from him.

Customers who had tried to help catch the animals sat down. They laughed and talked as if the pets' interruption had been a special treat.

Although it was warm for early October, we'd already

closed our front patio and put the chairs, tables, and umbrellas away for the season. Zachary stopped on the patio, brushed his jacket and pants with his hands, and then came back inside. He explained, "Madame Monique adopted Gigi only today. Gigi must have gotten out of Madame Monique's shop and lost track of which door was hers. Sorry, Hannah, Olivia, and . . ." He gave me a questioning look.

Olivia folded her arms and rapped out in a tart voice, "Emily. She's our boss."

Zachary blushed. "And Emily. Sorry for the disruption. We'll buy some donuts or something and then get out of your way."

Joshua tilted his head at Hannah. A laughing invitation lit his brown eyes.

Hannah turned her back on the two men and flounced toward our serving counter. "Come to the display case and choose what you'd like."

Joshua followed her, peeked in through the glass, and called back, "Hey, Zachary, come see these. They look more like your mushrooms than like donuts."

"That's impossible," Hannah retorted. "Which ones?"

"Those puffy things with white powdery stuff all over them. The card says, what? Beige nets? Being et? Bag nets?"

Hannah rolled her eyes in more of a flirtatious than a sarcastic way. "They don't look a thing like mushrooms, and they have nothing in common with them. You pronounce it *benYAYS*. Beignets are originally French, but the ones we're making are more like the beignets in New Orleans. They're really good, especially fresh like these are." I had to admire her. Our beignets were good, and they were fresh, but time was the enemy of all donuts, and beignets were best fresh and warm. Hannah knew what she was doing. We wouldn't be able to sell them the next day, and there were too many for the three of us to take home, even though I hoped that Brent, my recently acquired husband, would eat some of them.

At the thought of Brent, I couldn't help a little smile. In less than two hours, I should be with him, out in the country in the home he'd owned since before we married, and I'd find out what he'd been doing there all week when he wasn't in our Fallingbrook home with me. He'd had the week off from his job as Fallingbrook's detective.

Joshua seemed happy to flirt back at Hannah. "They all look good, Hannah. We'll have to stick around in the area for a long time to try them all."

Behind him, Olivia asked, "Where will you two be staying?" Her chilly tone clearly stated that she wasn't going to let the two men sleep on the floor in the small apartment that she and Hannah shared.

Joshua tossed off, "We'll find a place."

Olivia pointed north. "Keep going up Wisconsin Street, and eventually you'll come to motels."

Joshua stared toward Hannah's averted face. "Okay."

Zachary told her quietly, "I'd like to try a beignet. And a coffee."

Joshua shrugged. "I guess that's what I'll have, too."

Hannah asked, "For here, or to go?"

Joshua answered promptly, "Here."

Olivia waved a hand toward our menu board. "What coffee would you like? We always serve a medium roast Colombian. Today's special coffee is similar—a mild, slightly fruity medium roast from Santo Domingo."

I added, "And we're also serving chicory coffee like they serve in New Orleans. It's delicious with the beignets. It's extra strong, and you can have it black or half coffee, half steamed milk. Café noir or café au lait. And sugar's on the table if you want to add some."

"Colombian," Joshua said.

Zachary glanced around the nearly empty dining room. "Not many people order coffee at this time of the afternoon. Are you going to need to make a fresh pot just for us?"

Hannah seemed to be avoiding looking at Zachary. "I'll make you each whatever you want. We use a French press for single cups."

Zachary gazed toward a painting hanging on our peach-tinted white walls. "I'd like to try the chicory coffee. Au lait, please, unless steaming the milk is too much bother." The painting was of ferns growing next to the base of a tree. No wonder Zachary found the painting interesting. A trio of mushrooms peeked out from underneath the ferns.

Hannah told him, "Steaming the milk's no bother. Choose a table, and I'll bring you the coffee and beignets."

At a table for four in the middle of our dining room, Zachary and Joshua pulled out chairs and sat down.

Olivia and I helped plate the beignets and make the coffee. I told Hannah that since we weren't very busy, she could sit with her two friends.

Hannah picked up the tray and thanked me.

Olivia reminded her, "But if we do get busy—"

Hannah interrupted. "Don't worry. I'll pitch in." With exaggerated care, Hannah carried the tray to Joshua and Zachary's table.

Olivia watched Hannah set everything down without spilling, and then confided to me, "I like Zachary. He and Hannah were dating, and I think their breakup had something to do with Hannah deciding not to go back to college this semester."

"He must be older, if he's working on his master's degree."

"He is. That could be part of the problem—he could be more ready to commit to a relationship than she is. And it doesn't help that the other guy, Joshua, is turning on the charm, and she's falling for it."

"Have you met Joshua before?"

"No, so I don't know more about him except what I've observed just now, but from the way he acts, I'm wishing even harder that she'll go back to Zachary."

I hoped Olivia wouldn't say that to her sister. Hannah would be sure to fall for Joshua. I reminded Olivia, "Hannah has a good head on her shoulders."

Olivia snorted. "I'm not so sure. I bet she's the one who forgot to lock the back door. I locked it when I came in, and I know you wouldn't forget."

"I could have." I didn't think I had, but I didn't want to blame Hannah.

Olivia had more complaints. "She's ignoring Zachary and flirting with Joshua. How could anyone choose that playboy type over Zachary? Did you see how caring Zachary was with Dep and the little dog?"

"Yes, and they were immediately comfortable around him. That would have been enough to win me over, but I'm not Hannah. Or her age."

Olivia cleaned one of our marble rolling pins. "Me neither, but Joshua just stood around and sort of sneered. Besides, Joshua was the culprit who opened the door and let the animals into the dining room." She set the rolling pin down with a thump on the marble counter.

I tried to hide my wince at the sound of stone hitting stone. "I'm sure he didn't do it on purpose." Both the rolling pin and the counter appeared to be unscathed.

"I'm not." Olivia glared at the table where the three college-aged kids sat chatting.

Hannah's laugh rang out. It sounded brittle and forced.

I had chosen a good man when I was not much older than Hannah. Alec, my first husband, had become a detective shortly before he was killed. Brent had been Alec's best friend and work partner. It took us a long time, but Brent and I had each stopped blaming ourselves for Alec's death. Although Brent had been present, he could not have saved Alec. I'd been a 911 dispatcher, but had taken that evening off. Brent and I had finally convinced each other that neither of us could have gotten help for Alec in time to save him. Both of us would always miss Alec, but now we were finally, after several years of avoiding each other, crazy-happy together.

I was glad I was past Hannah's angst-ridden age.

A man came inside. He appeared to be in his fifties and was wearing a navy-blue blazer over a white polo shirt and khakis. His unscuffed, pointy-toed leather shoes were in a shade that might be considered tan but was not quite brown and not quite orange. He headed straight for the table where Hannah sat with her friends.

The newcomer must have said something to the three young people. Barely glancing at him, they shook their heads.

Olivia put the French press she'd just cleaned away. "Who's that, Emily?"

I tried not to make my scrutiny of the man obvious. "His careful grooming, extra-short hair, new clothes, and exaggerated, shoulders-back-and-chest-out posture are giving me salesman vibes. I'll go take his order."

Chapter 3

I arrived at the table in time to hear the man tell Hannah and her friends, "This investment is a guaranteed winner."

A guaranteed winning investment. There was no such thing. I braced myself to intervene.

I didn't need to. Hannah, Zachary, and Joshua again shook their heads. Zachary stared at his plate, Hannah placed her palms flat on the table and studied the backs of her hands, and Joshua gazed at the side of her downturned face. She blushed as if wishing she could pull out her hairclips and let more of her long blond hair slip out of her ponytail and hide her face.

Waving my hand toward the mostly empty room, I told the newcomer, "Choose any table you'd like."

He smiled down toward Hannah, Joshua, and Zachary. "I thought I'd sit with these three young folks, if they'll let me."

His pushiness stunned me into momentary silence.

Zachary, however, stood up. "We were just leaving."

Joshua unfolded himself from his seat. "See you later, Hannah."

Without looking at any of the three men, Hannah picked up the tray. "Yeah." She started loading dishes onto it.

I regained my ability to speak, though my smile was far from genuine. I pointed at a small table in a corner near the office. "How about over there? That table's cleared and ready."

"Okay." However, the man in the navy blazer didn't accept my suggestion. He went to the table next to the three people who had been arguing in whispers and sat down almost back-to-back with the woman. I followed him to take his order.

The woman behind him made an exasperated-sounding sigh and thrust her chair away from the table so swiftly that it rammed into the back of the newcomer's chair. She marched out, slapping the soles of her sandals against the floor's gleaming hardwood surface and tugging her yellow floral tunic down until it covered the hips of her bright green capris. Carrying the bag of beignets he'd ordered and shoving the nosepiece of his glasses higher again, the man who'd been sitting beside her caught up with her on the patio. His jeans were loose, and his dingy, no-longer-white T-shirt appeared due for a one-way trip to the rag bag.

I asked the man in the blazer, "What would you like? We have fresh beignets today." I explained what beignets were.

"I'll take two of those. And just water to drink. Tap water."

In the kitchen, Olivia was putting clean coffee carafes in a row on a shelf. Judging by the sounds, Hannah was tidying our storeroom next to the kitchen. I placed a couple of sugar-covered beignets on a plate, filled a glass with ice, and added water.

The newcomer had turned in his chair and was gazing out the front window at Zachary and Joshua, now on the sidewalk with the couple who had just left. The man in the ancient T-shirt was talking, pointing north with the hand holding the bag of beignets, and waving his other arm. Zachary nodded. Joshua stared toward our front windows as if studying his reflection or trying to see Hannah.

The newcomer faced his own table again. With a doleful

expression, he shook his head. "Young people. They should be investing, putting money aside for their old age."

I set his plate and glass in front of him. "They probably have educational debts."

"All the more reason for them to grab a sure thing when they see it. They could pay their bills and then some." He focused on my face. "Now, you. You're older and wiser."

I laughed. "Not that much older!"

"But you're waitressing. Wouldn't you like to free yourself from this dead-end job? You should be getting ready for your own retirement, buying stocks that are sure to quadruple or more in the next few years. Next few months, probably."

"I've got it covered, thanks."

He sputtered, "But you can't!" He handed me a business card. FORREST CALLIC, it read, INVESTMENT EXPERT. And there was a phone number, but nothing else.

At the next table, the man who'd been arguing with the couple beckoned to me. Shoving Forrest Callic's card into my apron pocket, I fled the self-proclaimed investment expert and went to the other customer.

Unlike the argumentative man who had just deserted his table, this man wore new-looking jeans, but one sleeve of his heathery gray T-shirt had a three-cornered tear. His scuffed, tan leather work boots were streaked in green—grass stains, I guessed. He pointed at the four people conversing on the sidewalk. "Bring me the bill for me and the couple who were with me. And I'll pay for the bag of beignets he ordered but didn't pay for, too. This isn't the first time those two have walked out and left me to pay the bill, but it's definitely the last." He looked up at me then and added with a half grin, "I was in business with that man. He didn't do his share, so during the past half hour, I dissolved our partnership." He rolled his shoulders and let out a big sigh. "Feels good."

Outside, the allegedly freeloading couple walked north. Zachary and Joshua headed south. Maybe they were returning to the alley between Deputy Donut and Madame Mo-nique's bridal boutique, and from there to the parking lot be-hind our shop. I was glad I'd locked the back door.

The man whose tablemates had deserted him explained, "We operate—I mean *operated*—a home improvement and lawncare service, but my ex-partner never did his share. He and his wife supposedly act as hosts, whatever that means, in a state forest campground. To make matters worse, she owns a gift shop, so instead of spending the days doing the renova-tions I lined up for him, he was in the campground making sure no one overstayed their allocated time or dropped a piece of litter or failed to extinguish a fire." The man scowled.

Lawncare. I didn't like our customers to be unhappy, even when their bad mood might have had nothing to do with Deputy Donut. Maybe I could cheer him by asking for ad-vice. "You might be the right person to tell me what I can do about my lawn mower. It's the old-fashioned kind that has no motor, and the blades roll with the wheels. I don't know whether I'm getting weak or what. That mower used to do a great job in my tiny yard, but lately it's a struggle to force it to move at all, and it seems to be tearing the grass, not cut-ting it."

"We call them reel, R-E-E-L, mowers. They're great if the blades are sharp. When did you last sharpen them?"

"Um . . . is it difficult?"

He smiled for the first time, which made him look younger and less stressed. "No. Did the mower come with a sharpen-ing kit?"

"Not that I know of. The mower was in the shed when we bought the house, several years ago." I didn't explain that by "we," I meant my late husband and me.

"Bring it to me, or I can pick it up if you don't have a ve-hicle."

"I think I can shorten the handle enough to fit it inside my compact SUV."

"Perfect." He pulled a card out of his wallet. "The map to my place is on the back."

I read, KEVIN LUNNION, LUNNION'S LAWNS AND ORDER. I turned the card over. "I know where this is." I could take a slight detour on the way to Brent's and my house on Chicory Lake. "I can drop the mower off in a couple of hours, if that works for you."

"I'll be there."

I handed him his bill and thanked him. Wondering if the campground his ex-partner hosted was in the state forest bordering Chicory Lake and almost surrounding Brent's and my country property, I headed back toward the kitchen.

Behind me, a chair screeched against the wooden floor, and Forrest Callic said in a cajoling voice, "Mind if I join you? I couldn't help hearing what you were saying about your previous partner, and I can tell you from my own experience that your money problems could be over."

I was tempted to turn around and inform Forrest that Deputy Donut didn't want to provide him with a supply of suckers eager to lose money on "guaranteed" winning investments, but I didn't feel like arguing. I hoped that after his experience with his ex-partner, Kevin Lunnion would be cautious.

I went into the kitchen and helped Olivia and Hannah tidy.

Out on Wisconsin Street, a motorcycle roared north past the front of Deputy Donut. I frowned. I was certain that Joshua was exceeding Fallingbrook's speed limit.

Olivia warned, "Hannah, don't be tempted to go on that motorcycle with your friend. Motorcycles aren't safe."

Hannah snapped. "I'm not likely to be invited to ride on one."

Olivia reminded her, "You can use my car any time you want to."

"I know." Hannah sounded weary.

"Bye, ladies, see you later!" The chummy call came from near the front door. Forrest held the door open for Kevin and touched him on the back of one shoulder, encouraging Kevin to go outside first.

Beyond them on the sunlit street, an old black pickup truck with a camper cap nestled in the pickup's bed drove north.

Olivia folded her arms. "I'm glad Zachary hasn't exchanged his truck for a motorcycle."

And I was glad that Zachary was not speeding.

Forrest walked south with Kevin.

They were our last customers of the day, and it was closing time, four thirty. I went to the front door and peered southward. Gesticulating as if he were doing most of the talking, Forrest was still with Kevin. The two men went out of sight. I locked the door, hung up the COME BACK TOMORROW sign, and returned to the kitchen.

Hannah asked, "Do you know those two men, Emily?"

"I met them for the first time this afternoon, so, no."

She shuddered. "I never met them before, either. The one who was arguing with his grumpy friends seemed okay, but that guy in the blue blazer is a slimeball. Don't trust him, Emily. Don't give him any money."

I swallowed a laugh. I hadn't needed to worry about Hannah believing the con man. "I agree completely. Do you think Joshua and Zachary were interested in what he had to say?"

Hannah shook her head. "Not at all. We all know there are no guaranteed winning stocks."

Olivia asked, "Is that what that man was talking to you about?" She didn't wait for an answer. "Who needs the aggravation? I hope he doesn't come back. Did he at least pay you for the beignets, Emily?"

"Yes." I added, "Tom will be working tomorrow." In addition to being my business partner, Tom was the father of my late husband, Alec. I still considered him my father-in-law. "If that man comes in and starts spouting off about questionable investment schemes, Tom will give him the stink eye, and that man will slither back underneath his rock." Before he retired at a relatively young age and opened Deputy Donut with me, Tom had been Fallingbrook's police chief.

The two sisters laughed.

Still grinning, Olivia asked me, "Do you get to go back to your and Brent's chalet this afternoon?"

I held both thumbs up. "Yes, as long as he doesn't get a last-minute call to work."

"I hope he doesn't. What do you think Brent's surprise for you is?"

"I don't know, something that takes a week to do. Maybe he's been cutting a new trail through the woods. I'm excited to find out." My smirk probably rivaled Olivia's.

She teased, "I never thought you could stay away from him for an entire week."

"I didn't stay away from Brent. I just didn't go out to Chicory Lake. Whenever he wasn't out there doing whatever the surprise is, we stayed in town." We still owned both homes we'd had before our wedding. The one with the small lawn and old-fashioned lawn mower was conveniently close to our jobs, while the lakeside chalet out in the country was fun. We hadn't decided what to do about the extravagance. Maybe we'd sell one or rent them out from time to time. For now, we enjoyed both of them.

Olivia flapped her hands in shooing motions. "You can go now, Emily. Hannah and I can finish here."

Hannah added, "I'd be glad to."

Smiling, I thanked them. "I can't. I promised not to arrive out at the lake before six."

Chapter 4

By five, our shop was ready for the Jolly Cops Cleaning Crew. The four retired policemen usually came in around one in the morning and made everything, including the deep fryers, spotless.

In the office, I coaxed Dep down from her catwalk and put her harness and leash on her. Olivia, Hannah, and I gave her hugs and pats.

We set the alarms, went outside, and locked the back door. The sisters' apartment was only a few blocks away. They didn't mind Dep's occasional dawdling, so we walked together down the alley between our building and Madame Monique's bridal boutique, and then south on Wisconsin until Dep and I turned west on Maple Street.

My neighborhood was Victorian. The larger, older homes were near Wisconsin Street, and the newer ones were farther west, not that they were very new. My adorable two-story cottage, yellow brick with cream-colored gingerbread trim, was built in 1889.

Dep and I climbed to the front porch. The white wicker chairs and table were protected by the porch roof, so I had not yet put them or the cheerful yellow-and-white striped chair cushions away. Bronze and yellow mums bloomed in window boxes hanging from the front railing.

Inside, the house was as inviting as the porch, but I didn't take time to admire the white living room with its jewel-toned furnishings and stained glass window or the white, chrome, and glass dining room, or even the dream kitchen that Alec and I had designed. I checked that doors and windows were still secured and nothing was out of place, and then I retrieved a paint-spotted drop cloth from the basement. Leaving Dep, still wearing her harness but not her leash, in the living room, I went out to the side yard and backed my SUV out of the detached garage.

I spread the drop cloth in the SUV's back hatch. Shortening the mower's handle turned out to be easy, and after one false start, maneuvering the mower into the rear of the car was, too.

Next came the hardest part of packing the car. Although Dep was shut inside the house, she could hear me opening and closing car doors, and she knew what that might mean for her.

Dep did not like riding in cars.

I returned to the house. Dep was still in the living room. I swooped down and grabbed the handle of her harness. Cuddling her, I climbed the two steps to the lower landing and opened the closet door. She wriggled. With one foot, I pulled out her dreaded carrier. Despite her suddenly stretched-out legs, I managed to tuck her into the carrier and zip it closed.

She yowled.

I took her outside, locked the door, slid her carrier into the car's rear seat, latched the seat belt into place, and tethered the carrier to the carabiner I kept on the seat belt.

Trying not to focus on her objections, I drove out of our neighborhood and headed north. Outside Fallingbrook, Wisconsin Street became County Road C. After a mile, I turned left onto a narrower road. It curved, and then the sign for Lunnion's Lawns and Order was on the right.

At the back of a short, wide driveway, a white stucco

building appeared to house an apartment above a two-bay garage with extra-large overhead doors. The doors were rolled up, and Kevin was bent over a riding mower in front of them.

I pulled into the driveway, got out, and opened the back hatch. Dep reminded me that she was still in the car. I lifted my mower out of the car and set it on the crumbling asphalt. Wiping his hands on a rag, Kevin joined me. Dep became suddenly quiet.

Kevin fiddled with the mower's wheels and studied the blades. "This won't take long. You can pick it up tomorrow. If you don't hear from me, just come here about this time tomorrow." He quoted a reasonable price.

I agreed to it, and then apologized, "I'm sorry about that man who left Deputy Donut with you. I hope he didn't bother you. His investment statements sounded too good to be true."

"They did to me, too."

Good.

In the woods behind Kevin's building, something shrieked.

I tried not to look startled, but Kevin only grinned. "The peacocks' coop is back there. The male is reminding me that it's dinnertime."

The peacock cried again.

Dep made a noise between a growl and a chirp. I glanced toward her. "I'd better go before my cat decides that the peacock should be her dinner."

"He wouldn't let her near him."

"She's definitely staying in the car." I closed the hatch, slid into the driver's seat, waved, and drove off. Dep's complaints reached new heights. I warned her that someone might mistake her for a peacock. She didn't seem to care.

I returned to the familiar county road. It wound through forests, up and down rocky hills, and past streams and lakes. Above, the sky was pure blue, contrasting with the reds, greens, oranges, and yellows of the trees. Reaching the summit of the last hill on the trip, I told Dep, "It's all downhill from here."

She howled, maybe because she'd heard that cliché and had complained about it nearly every time we passed that point.

The road curved and swooped downward between dense woods that hid the lake that I still sometimes thought of as "Brent's Lake." Most of the shore was part of the Chicory Lake State Forest, but two private properties bordered the south side of the lake, ours and Chicory Canoe Livery, a boat and horse-and-carriage rental establishment. It had a boat launch and dock and occupied several acres between our property and the road.

I didn't go all the way into the valley. Shortly beyond the top of the hill, a road on the right led into the state forest, and then, farther downhill, I made a sharp right onto our driveway. Running along a plateau above the lake, the driveway was about a quarter mile long and nearly flat. To my left, a wide strip of mown lawn would form the base underneath part of our wintertime cross-country ski trail. Except for the trails that Brent kept groomed for hiking and skiing, dense forest covered the hill all the way down to the lake. Partway up the hill above our chalet, our woods ended, and the state forest began.

What was Brent's surprise?

I didn't notice anything new or different along the driveway or near the chalet and the extra-large garage.

Brent's black SUV was parked close to our welcoming log chalet. I parked behind his car, got out, and opened the rear passenger door next to Dep. She quieted to pitiful mews. Holding her carrier in my arms and cooing, I backed away from the car and closed the door.

Brent came around the far side of the chalet and strode toward me past the chalet's wide front porch. He was dressed comfortably in jeans and an untucked pale blue T-shirt, and his light brown hair flopped onto his forehead. A smile lit his handsome face and those warm gray eyes.

I could hardly wait to find out what his surprise was, but first, I had to hold him tight. He enveloped me, cat in her carrier and all, in his arms.

After what probably seemed like an eon or two to Dep, I became aware of her increasingly plaintive meows.

Laughing, Brent let me go and lifted Dep's carrier out of my arms. "Let's take her inside and let her out of her prison."

At our other house, a high, smooth wall around the rear yard kept Dep safe, but out here, she couldn't be outside among the wildlife unless she was with us, and either leashed or in her carrier.

On the front porch, Brent told me to cover my eyes. With one arm around me, he guided me into the chalet. "Keep your eyes closed." I could tell from Dep's rustling and grumbling that she and her carrier were still in Brent's other arm. He walked me slowly through the great room and, I thought, past the kitchen that occupied one end of that room. He opened the door to the deck on the house's east side. "You can look." I heard the smile and excitement in his voice.

I opened my eyes. "Wow!"

He had roofed the deck and surrounded it with heavy-duty, animal-proof screening plus finer screens to keep bugs out. A door could be opened to steps leading down to the lawn in front of the house. Kitty-sized stairways next to the screens led up to platforms.

I gave Brent a big kiss. "You enclosed this deck and made a catio for Dep!"

Brent gestured toward the outdoor kitchen and the table and chairs, all of which had been on that deck since the first summer that Brent owned the chalet. "For all of us. I couldn't have done this by myself in one week. Tom spent his spare time helping me. He left shortly before you arrived. You probably passed him."

The two men had put care into crafting perfect details. One of Tom's hobbies was woodworking, and both he and Brent were experts at it. "I love it." I eased the carrier from Brent, set it on the deck, and opened it. "You will, too, Dep." She stalked out, lifting each foot high and shaking it before setting it down carefully, as if she feared that the deck's floorboards might harbor puddles or unseen critters.

Brent gestured toward the barbecue. "I bought shish kebabs to grill and made a salad."

I flung myself into his arms and kissed him again. "What a great homecoming!"

By the time we sat down to eat, Dep had ventured up a kitty stairway to a platform. Front paws tucked underneath her chest, she stared past the side yard toward woods descending to a stream. Farther away, hills were covered in a patchwork of fall colors.

Brent laughed at my description of the two strange men letting Dep and a tiny dog wearing a wedding gown into Deputy Donut. I also told Brent about Hannah and Olivia's seemingly difficult relationship. "I understand that they haven't had an easy life, and I admire Olivia for giving up her own education and a career to act as both mother and father to Hannah after their parents died."

"They were young, weren't they?"

I removed deliciously browned cubes of chicken and veggies from the skewer. "Olivia was eighteen, and Hannah was eight. And Olivia did a much better job than some actual parents do. Hannah is confident and competent. Both sisters are great employees and fun to have around, except when Olivia is being critical of Hannah. I feel like Olivia can't let go and doesn't want to give Hannah the freedom that our parents gave us by the time we reached Hannah's age. Olivia doesn't seem to admit to herself that Hannah is old enough to make her own mistakes."

"It must have been a blow to Olivia when Hannah quit

college, even if it's only temporary, in the first semester of her sophomore year."

"Olivia's definitely not happy about that. Olivia is easygoing and has never been overbearing around anyone else, at least not when I'm around, so her attitude surprised me. I wish that she and Hannah could be happy. Maybe I'm being as mother-henlike as Olivia, but I feel like Hannah wants or even needs to reestablish her connection with Fallingbrook after a year of being away. Maybe working at Deputy Donut will help her feel grounded. I like both sisters and hate that they're making each other unhappy. I don't know what I can do or say to help."

Brent covered one of my hands with one of his. "There's probably not much you can do, but they'll probably see how nurturing you are and how much you want to help, and maybe they'll try harder to get along, if only to keep from making you unhappy."

"You have too much faith in me."

He raised his glass and tilted it toward me. "No, I don't." He took a sip of wine.

I tried to smile, but the word *nurturing* had triggered a longing that I was trying to ignore. Both of us wanted children, but I hadn't become pregnant and was afraid I never would. Brent was even older than I was, and a couple of our friends who were my age were expecting their first baby.

The thought of Samantha and Hooligan's impending parenthood cheered me. I glanced around at our newly screened-in deck and said dreamily, "Having this extra, mostly outdoor space will be wonderful for parties, and for Samantha's baby shower on Tuesday. The great room will easily accommodate the guests that Misty and I have invited, but maybe people can help themselves to drinks out here."

Brent got up and flicked a switch beside the door into the house. Fairy lights strung around the top of the screens came on. "Roofing the deck made it easier to install more lighting."

"Nicer ambience, too, than the bright porch lights."

"Those are still there in case we need them."

"It's wonderful."

We finished dinner and managed to coax Dep off her platform and inside the chalet for the night. While Brent and I cleaned the kitchen, I silently resolved to try to help Olivia and Hannah understand each other's wants and needs.

Chapter 5

Driving my indignant cat to work the next morning before Brent was awake, I reminded myself that the friction between Olivia and Hannah had not prevented them from serving customers in a welcoming and friendly way. They were insightful and caring and could work out their differences themselves. If I tried to interfere, I might make things worse. I called over the seatback to Dep, in her securely tethered carrier, "I should stay out of it, right, Dep?"

"Yeow."

"Thanks for the vote of confidence."

I parked beside Tom's SUV at the back of the lot behind Deputy Donut. In our office, Dep raced up ramps and kitty staircases to the catwalks near the ceiling, ran into one end of a tunnel, stuck her head out the other end, and peeked down at me.

Tom was in the kitchen near the deep fryers. He spotted me on the other side of the window between the office and kitchen. A tough and muscular former detective and police chief with distinguished gray flecking his brown hair, Tom didn't seem like a person whose eyes might twinkle, but at that moment, warm humor shone from those dark brown eyes.

I flew out of the office and into the kitchen. Obviously waiting for my reaction, Tom didn't say anything.

I gave him a big hug. "Thank you, Tom! I love the catio. It's perfect for Dep, who definitely agrees, and for us as a screened porch."

"We had fun building it."

Olivia and Hannah joined us in the kitchen. Worry wrinkles between Hannah's eyebrows disappeared when she realized that Tom and I were talking about the surprise Brent had been preparing for me. Why had Hannah looked stressed?

As usual, customers began arriving the moment we opened at seven. By nine, most of the breakfast crowd had left. The two groups of weekday regulars, the retired women who called themselves the Knitpickers and the retired men who didn't call themselves anything, took up residence at our largest tables, beside the front windows. Our front door was centered between those two windows, and the two groups liked to joke and fake-bicker across the aisle.

While Tom was in Deputy Donut, he nearly always did the deep frying. The beignets had been a hit, so he made more and coated them with decadent amounts of powdered sugar. Olivia was the most artistic of us, and although she had long ago overcome her shyness about dealing with people she didn't know, she was still hesitant about socializing with customers. She frosted donuts and topped some with sprinkles, candied walnut pieces, assortments of other goodies, or loops of contrasting frostings. Hannah and I made coffee and tea, took orders, served people, gave them their bills, and processed their payments. If customers wanted to chat and we had time, we joined their conversations.

Halfway through the morning, Hannah started toward the kitchen to fill an order. I needed another pot of the day's special coffee, a rich, low-acid medium roast from the slopes of Mt. Kilimanjaro in Tanzania, so I followed her.

Although Hannah's back was to me, I heard her long, loud yawn.

Olivia looked up from piping autumn-colored icing into leaf shapes on the tops of old-fashioned pumpkin spice donuts and frowned at Hannah. "You got in late last night for someone who starts work at six thirty in the morning."

Tom grinned at the two sisters. "Oh, to be young!"

I winked at Tom and asked Hannah, "Did you see your friends Joshua and Zachary?"

Hannah placed cinnamon-raisin cake donuts topped with cinnamon glaze onto plates. "I went to their campsite. Zachary plays guitar. We had a campfire and sang."

I could honestly be enthusiastic. "I love doing that. Only, I can't sing. My parents play guitar and banjo, and they can both sing. I almost always end up staying later than I planned."

Tom nodded. He'd also enjoyed evenings at the campground south of town, where my parents spent their summers. He gave Hannah an encouraging smile.

Hannah ducked her head. "When I noticed how late it was, I was about to leave, but I couldn't because this guy who called himself a security guard but was really, Joshua said, a volunteer campground host, came and yelled at us to stop making so much noise. Then he spotted me and Lulabelle and said that the campsite was only to be occupied by two people and two vehicles, and I had to take Lulabelle and leave."

I asked, "Who's Lulabelle?"

Hannah picked up two plates of donuts. "Olivia's car. It's her first one, ever, and I thought it deserved a name."

Olivia squeezed orange icing out of a piping bag. "Did you shout back at him, Hannah?"

"Of course not." Hannah's tone was icy.

Olivia persisted. "Did Zachary?"

Another curt answer from Hannah. "No."

Olivia moved the piping bag to the next donut. "How about Joshua?"

Hannah braced her shoulders and lifted her chin. "He stood up for the rest of us, but the campground host shouted over him."

Olivia's piping bag slipped, giving the leaf she was making an odd lump. "Did you get mad at the man for making you leave?"

"Of course not." I wasn't sure if Hannah's exasperation was due to Olivia or to the man. "I would have already left if that man hadn't come along and started haranguing us."

"Tell me something, Hannah," Tom said. "Had your music been louder than the campground host's yelling?"

"No way. Our singing and Zachary's guitar were pretty quiet."

Tom lifted a basket of beignets out of the hot oil. "How did I know that?"

Hannah started toward the dining area but turned toward us. "And you'll never guess who the campground's volunteer host was. Well, Tom, you won't. You weren't here yesterday. But Emily, remember those three angry-looking people arguing in the corner?"

Although Hannah had pointedly left Olivia out of her question, Olivia answered. "Yes."

I added, "They'd be hard to forget, the way they didn't seem to notice Dep and little Gigi racing around."

Tom raised an eyebrow. "Who is little Gigi?"

After the three of us explained, I told Hannah, "I think I know who the campground host was. He was the man in glasses who left with his wife."

"You're right. He told Zachary and Joshua where they could camp. And then after they paid for their site, he turned on them."

I made another educated guess. "Is the campground in Chicory Lake State Forest?"

Hannah started toward her customers again. "Yes. It would be a nice place except for that man." She headed for the Knitpickers' table.

Tom turned toward Olivia. "She's a good kid, Olivia."

Olivia sighed. "I know. I just worry."

Tom's voice softened. "Parents do. For good reasons."

And Tom's only child, who had been my husband at the time, had been killed. I felt like a cannonball dropped into my stomach. From the appalled widening of Olivia's eyes, she felt the same way. She knew about Alec.

I turned my back on both of them and started the coffee grinder. Listening to it roar, I wondered if Brent and I should reconsider wanting children. We were already concerned about Samantha's pregnancy, though it was going well. Maybe loving Samantha and Hooligan's child would provide enough worrying and possible anxiety for us. More than enough.

After their morning of knitting, sipping coffee and tea, eating donuts and beignets, and catching up on the news since the day before, the Knitpickers and the retired men left. We served lunch customers and took turns eating. I went into the office with a plate of radish and cucumber salad and marinated, fried halloumi cheese. Hannah had finished her lunch and was on the couch, cuddling Dep.

I closed the office door and smiled down at the two of them. "She purrs that loudly only when she really likes someone."

"I really like her, too. Emily, can I talk to you?"

"Of course."

"Sorry for being short-tempered."

I sat in the desk chair and turned it to face her. "You're not."

"I am. Olivia's getting to me. She acts like I'm a child."

"Olivia loves you. She worries about you."

"Yeah, but she goes overboard. She wants me to go back to school and date Zachary again. I like him, but as a friend. He's nice, but . . . mushrooms!" Her smile was a little watery.

I teased, "Maybe calling him a mycologist will sound better. What do you think of Joshua?"

"I barely know him, but he's more excite—I mean, he's fun to be around."

I could understand that. Brent was sturdily reliable, but he was also exciting. I suspected that Zachary was, too, but maybe Hannah was too young to recognize and appreciate it. She kissed the orange-striped patch on Dep's head. "I guess I should get back to work. I'll try not to let my feelings about Olivia's helicopter-parenting show."

"You're both great employees, and Tom and I would like you—both of you—to stay here as long as you'd like."

"Thanks, Emily." She put Dep down on the couch. "And thanks for listening."

"Any time."

She left, and I ate my lunch. For the sake of our tranquil existence at Deputy Donut, I wished that Zachary and Joshua would go away and leave Hannah alone. I couldn't help a wistful smile, though. Hannah probably missed the friends she'd made while she was away at college, and maybe, contrary to what I'd been thinking the day before, her high school friends had gone on to new lives, and she didn't have much of a social life in Fallingbrook.

That afternoon, Hannah seemed more charming than ever around our guests, as if she were trying to show us all, especially Olivia, what a good employee she was.

I thought I detected Olivia's skepticism and wariness as she watched her sister laugh and joke with customers.

Maybe Hannah's bubbly enthusiasm was forced, as if she were trying to hide that something was bothering her.

But maybe something was exciting her.

At almost four thirty, when we were about to close for the day, Zachary and Joshua came in.

Chapter 6

This time, Joshua and Zachary used the front door, and they didn't bring any lost pets. The day was warm for early October. I thought Joshua might be too hot in his black leather jacket, T-shirt, and jeans. Zachary looked more comfortable, dressed almost the same way but without a jacket. Zachary came to the display counter.

Joshua sidled up to the serving counter and perched on a stool. "Hey, Hannah!"

She walked over to him. "Hey, yourself."

Olivia hurried to Zachary. "See anything you'd like?"

Zachary pointed into the display counter. "More beignets! We were hoping you'd still have some. They're amazing."

She asked, "How many would you like?"

"Every single one you have left, unless they're spoken for."

"Box or bag?"

"Bag."

I looked a question at Tom. He nodded, so I told Zachary, "Those are best fresh and warm, so they're half price at this time of day."

Zachary told me quietly, "I'm glad we came when we did." He winked. "Maybe we can heat them on sticks over the campfire."

How could Hannah think that a man who smiled that way wasn't exciting enough?

Hannah probably didn't see Zachary's smile or hear his teasing. Facing her, Joshua said loudly, "Actually, we came at your closing time to see if you wanted to go hiking with us this afternoon."

Hannah blushed. "We clean up after our customers leave."

I handed Zachary the bag of beignets.

Joshua slid off the stool. "We can wait." He pointed toward the back. "We're parked out there. You can come explore the Clifftop Trail with us."

Beside me, Olivia stiffened and drew in a deep breath.

Throwing an almost horrified glance at Olivia, Hannah backed up a step. "Not that trail. It's too . . . too dangerous."

Joshua coaxed, "It's not all that dangerous. Supposedly, it doesn't follow the top of the cliffs, it just goes to a lookout where there's a view of Chicory Lake, and there's a railing to keep people from falling off the edge. We wouldn't go close to the edge or even to the railing. And you don't have to climb on that big boulder perched on top of the cliffs beside the lookout."

Tom intervened. "No one is supposed to climb on that boulder, and for good reason. Signs warning against it should be taken seriously."

The paper bag in Zachary's hand crinkled. He clutched it so tightly that his knuckles turned white. He obviously knew what Tom and I did—Olivia and Hannah's parents' death had been due to a rock-climbing accident, and Olivia was terrified that something similar might happen to Hannah. Still frowning, Zachary suggested, "Actually, I was thinking of taking the Cornflower Trail. It's down near the lake and almost totally flat."

Hannah looked up at him and screwed her mouth into something like dismay. "Let me guess, there are no cornflowers on that trail, only—"

Zachary smiled again, but the smile was strained. Sympathy for him shot through me. He finished for Hannah, "Only the mushrooms I'm studying." He turned to Olivia, Tom, and me. "They're called bluing or, as Hannah has probably heard too many times, cornflower boletes. They're white and shaped"—he held up the bag of beignets—"well, not quite like these squarish beignets, more like fritters."

Her face mottled pink, Hannah scowled.

Zachary blushed, too. "Well, they'd be shaped like fritters if fritters had stems. When cornflower boletes are cut or bruised, they turn amazing shades of blue. And unlike some other boletes, they're edible."

Joshua's laugh was scornful. "Some magic mushrooms also turn blue."

Zachary reddened more. "I'm not studying magic mushrooms."

Olivia warned, "Whatever you're studying, don't eat them."

Zachary didn't make any promises but went on as if Olivia hadn't spoken. "Supposedly, bluing boletes can be found near the Cornflower Trail, at the edge of the woods near a bog."

Hannah lifted her chin. "I already have plans. Olivia's fixing us a nice dinner, and I need to shop for last-minute ingredients. But thanks. Besides, is it legal to pick things in state forests?"

Zachary turned toward the front door. "It's not legal, and I won't pick any. I'll take pictures and record the conditions around them." He led the way out. Behind him, the soles of Joshua's motorcycle boots resounded on the hardwood floor.

Our other customers left, too, and we locked the door and quickly put things away.

Olivia, Hannah, and Tom tried to help me cajole Dep down from her catwalks. She stared at us. Hoping she'd come down if she was afraid she might be left behind, I went out to the parking lot with the other three.

Zachary was nowhere in sight. Wearing a helmet, Joshua stood beside a gleaming black and chrome motorcycle. He called out, "Are you sure you don't want to change your mind, Hannah?"

Olivia clamped her lips together.

Head high, Hannah marched past Joshua. "I'm sure."

Together, the two sisters headed down the alleyway. From the back, dressed in their knee-length black shorts and white polo shirts, they looked almost identical, except that Olivia's hair was a rich, almost mahogany brown and wavy while Hannah's was blond and straight.

I risked a glance through the office window. Dep was slowly descending one of her kitty staircases.

I waited until she started yowling about being abandoned, and then I went back inside. "Are you ready to come with me now?" I scooped her into my arms and kissed the tip of a cute little ear. It twitched, tickling my lips. Carefully, I placed her in her carrier. Probably now understanding that she was not going to have to spend the night alone in the office after all, she didn't complain too loudly when I fastened her carrier inside the car.

Joshua was still standing beside his motorcycle. He didn't look up. Staring down at his phone, he rapidly tapped his thumbs on the screen.

I drove to the house on Maple Street, did the security tour and picked up the mail, and then I took Dep north.

At Lunnion's Lawns and Order, both of the oversized garage doors were rolled down tight to the pavement. No vehicles were in the driveway.

I opened the car windows slightly for Dep's sake and got out. A note taped beside a button close to the garage doors said RING FOR SERVICE. I pushed it. A bell rang inside, but no one came.

From the woods behind the building, a peacock screeched.

I tried the doorbell for the second-floor residence. A buzzer was audible, but again, there was no answer.

I walked back to the car and gazed toward the woods behind the building. If Kevin Lunnion was back there feeding his peacocks, they might not have been squawking. I called, "Kevin?"

The only response was the scream-like cry of the peacock.

Hadn't Kevin told me to come for the lawn mower unless he told me not to?

I didn't want to honk my horn, and I also didn't want to trespass to look for Kevin. Besides, wearing shorts, I wasn't about to attempt to brush past thorny wild raspberry canes nearly blocking the narrow pathway that I guessed led to the peacock coop.

I walked across the parking apron to the far side of the building and beyond that to a normal-sized garage with a normal-sized overhead door. That door was also pulled down to the pavement. Half expecting to see more lawn mowers and yard equipment, I stood on tiptoe and peeked through a small lozenge-shaped window near the top of the door. Shelves of paint cans, tools, and the usual stuff people keep in garages lined the sides and back of the garage, but most of the concrete floor was bare except for a few stains. I guessed that this was where Kevin usually parked his vehicle. Maybe he'd forgotten I was coming.

In my car, Dep seemed to be attempting to imitate a peacock's shrieks.

I backed out of the driveway onto the road, stopped, and studied what I could see of Lunnion's Lawns and Order. There was no sign of any living creatures besides the squawking peacock. I headed back to County Road C.

Turning north, I heaved a sigh. "Brent won't be home for dinner, Dep. He has to attend a meeting."

Dep's complaints about her predicament became louder.

"But you and I can enjoy your new catio."

That promise failed to appease her.

Getting closer to our chalet, I couldn't help lifting my foot off the gas, and it wasn't only because the fall colors were even more flamboyant than they'd been the day before.

In a way, I didn't want to arrive home.

I loved our large country property when Brent was with me. I hadn't told him I felt uneasy about being there alone.

I couldn't help comparing this near-wilderness with the cottagelike Victorian home where I'd lived for years, where the garden was safely walled, and where neighbors might hear the tiniest squeak for help.

I pulled onto our driveway. Although I knew I was being ridiculous, I scanned the woods beyond the strips of lawn lining the driveway.

Everything seemed peaceful, and no other vehicles were in sight. I parked, got out, and listened. No noises besides breezes rustling leaves and pine boughs.

Except for Dep.

Apologizing for leaving her in the car ten seconds longer than necessary, I pulled her carrier out of the car. She muttered until I took her up onto the front porch, and then she must have known she was about to be freed. She became suddenly quiet. I stood unmoving, barely breathing. On the hill above me, probably on the nearest road in the state forest, a motorcycle downshifted. I unlocked the door, took Dep inside, and let her out.

I didn't change out of my Deputy Donut shorts and shirt. In the kitchen, I fed Dep. For myself, I poured a glass of skim milk and then spread a mixture of chopped, hard-boiled egg and black olive tapenade on a slice of dense rye bread and topped it with leaves of baby spinach and a second slice of bread.

We both finished our suppers. Sunset would be in about forty minutes, so we still had over an hour before complete darkness. What was I going to do, lock myself inside the house and wish that Brent was with me? I was going to have to teach myself to be brave when I was alone.

Besides, Chicory Lake was a short walk away, down a wooded trail, and my kayak was in our boathouse. Kayaking season would soon be over. Why waste it?

Dep, who was used to her harness, did not mind wearing a kitty life jacket. To Brent's and my surprise, she actually put up with riding in a kayak as long as she could sit on my lap and I didn't splash. Maybe she even liked kayaking. Or maybe she simply hated being left behind.

I fastened each of us into our life jackets and attached Dep's leash to the loop on hers.

If I let her walk down the trail through the woods, she would probably stop and snuffle underneath every fallen leaf and twig, and we wouldn't be in my kayak before dark. I carried her past fragrant pines and the murmuring brook to our small, sandy beach. I looped her leash over one of the posts on the dock and then unlocked the boathouse, pulled my kayak out, and set it on the beach with its bow in the water.

Getting myself, my paddle, and my cat into the kayak while it was buoyant enough to let me push off was tricky. For extra safety, I hooked the handle of Dep's leash to my own life jacket. I plunked down onto the kayak's seat, and Dep perched on my lap and peered over the kayak's bow like the princess she was. The seat was low, allowing my legs to stretch out almost flat, and I didn't have to worry about Dep trying not to slide by digging claws into my bare thighs.

The sun had set, but the sky was still bright. Although Brent had owned this place for a couple of years, I had not explored the entire lake. In the mood for exercise, I paddled quickly away from our shore, and then I headed east. The shore curved south and then east several times, and I was in a bay that I'd never seen before. Ahead, rocky bluffs rose almost straight up from a treed ledge near the lake's surface.

Pines crowned the cliffs, and a squarish boulder with rounded corners perched, seemingly precariously, in front of the pines.

Above me, the sky was pale and streaked in wisps of pinkish, post-sunset clouds. If I wanted to return to the chalet before darkness completely descended, I needed to start back. Steering my kayak away from the cliffs, I looked down at the tortoiseshell tabby cat stretched on my thighs. "Maybe the Clifftop Trail that Joshua mentioned is up there behind us."

Someone screamed, a short scream that ended suddenly.

Chapter 7

With that cut-off scream echoing and jangling in my brain, I tried to pivot my kayak to face the cliffs, but my kayaking skills abandoned me, and I clumsily splashed through the water instead of paddling cleanly.

I finally managed to turn the kayak to face the cliff. At its top, I caught sight of a weathered, peeled-log railing, the kind that was often placed on trails to guide hikers away from precipices.

Something near the oddly shaped boulder on top of the cliff moved. Or was it someone? A person in dark clothing, backing away from the boulder, the railing, and the edge of the cliff?

Whatever I'd seen, or had possibly imagined in my heightened state of alarm, disappeared, and all I could make out beyond the railing were shadows, trees, and brush.

I called, "Hello?" My voice, distorted and tinny, bounced back from rock.

I lifted my paddle and held it parallel to the water. My grasp tightening on the shaft connecting the paddle's two blades, I listened. Water dripped off the ends of the paddle. Somewhere behind me, crows carried on a cheerful discussion.

Dep shifted on my lap. "Mrrp?"

Who had screamed? Why were there no other human sounds?

My kayak drifted, turning me away from the bluffs again. I dipped my paddle into the lake and pushed until I could again see the cliffs.

No one was in sight.

The rustic railing and huge boulder near the edge of the cliffs confirmed my earlier guess. I was staring up at a section of the Clifftop Trail.

Hannah had rejected Joshua and Zachary's invitation to hike with them on that trail. She had said she was going grocery shopping.

During the almost two hours since I'd last seen Hannah, I had gone to Lunnion's Lawns and Order, spent a few minutes there, driven to our chalet on the lake, made and eaten a sandwich, taken our trail down to the lake, and paddled to this spot. While I'd been doing all of that, Hannah could have had time to buy a few things, eat with Olivia, and then drive to the state forest to join her friends.

Had they then gone for a walk on the less-treacherous trail that Zachary had suggested, or had they hiked along the top of the forbidding cliffs in front of me?

When I left Deputy Donut, Joshua had been concentrating on his phone. Maybe he'd been texting Hannah, encouraging her to lie to Olivia and attempt the Clifftop Trail.

I murmured, "Who screamed, Dep? Was it a man or a woman?"

Dep sat up straighter.

I was almost positive that my thudding heart was shaking the kayak.

Could it have been Hannah who screamed?

I forced my little vessel away from the eerily quiet bay. Alternately dipping the paddle's blades into the lake, I skimmed over the water as fast as I could. Far behind me, did branches snap? I hesitated and took a quick glance over my left shoulder. I could no longer see the railing guarding the lookout on the Clifftop Trail, and even the boulder beside the trail was out of sight behind another rock bluff. I plowed my way toward home. Dep settled down on my knees, her ears tucked down and back as if she were trying to streamline herself to increase our speed. Or as if she were also unnerved and listening for sounds behind the headlands we'd passed.

Finally, after rounding several stony and wooded peninsulas, I saw our dock and beach.

Was Hannah all right?

My arm muscles burned, but I didn't slow down. Paddling as hard as I could, I ran the kayak's port side up onto the beach. I scooped Dep into my arms, clambered out onto the sand, dropped my paddle into the kayak, and pulled the little boat all the way out of the water.

Straightening, I glanced out at the lake, although I wouldn't be able to see the cliffs I'd been near when I'd heard that scream.

The far shore sloped gently up toward the hills beyond it. A canoe near that shore was too far away for me to see who was in it. Chicory Canoe Livery seemed to own mostly unpainted aluminum canoes, but I didn't want to take time to figure out what kind of canoe this was or to paddle out into the lake, attempt to intercept the canoer, and then . . . what? Ask for help tracking down a person who might have screamed?

I waved, but no one waved back. The canoe didn't seem to be moving. Maybe a fisherman was hoping that fish would rise to whatever insects might still be biting as the sky darkened.

My phone was in my pocket, but this valley had no phone reception. I would have to go up the hill to the grassy plateau near our house. Clutching Dep more tightly than she probably wanted me to, I raced up the trail.

But when, gasping for breath, I reached the lawn in front

of our chalet, I didn't know who, if anyone, to call. The person who had screamed could have been yelling as part of a game or a prank. Or at the sheer joy of seeing the view. I tried to replay the scream in my mind. Had the scream been as shrill with terror as I'd thought?

I was sure that it had ended abruptly, as if someone had been forcibly silenced.

If Hannah had been hurt or worse, Olivia would be devastated.

I had to know.

Still carrying Dep, I ran into the house for my car keys. I didn't want to take time to remove Dep's life jacket or try to squeeze out the door without her. Her life jacket worked as a harness, so I carried her out to the car and attached the tiny jacket to the carabiner on the seat belt.

Her yowl was so loud that I almost didn't hear the motorcycle roar into higher gears up on the hill. Again, I guessed that the sound was coming from the nearest road in the state forest. Both the yowl and the roar diminished.

I hopped into the driver's seat and turned on the headlights. "This isn't as bad as being zipped inside your carrier, now, is it Dep?"

"*AAAAAOW!*"

"I could have left you at home."

"*OWR!*"

The state forest that surrounded most of Chicory Lake also covered acres and acres of nearby hills. The most likely road to take me to the Clifftop Trail might be the closest state forest road, the one near the top of the hill, the road where I thought I'd heard a motorcycle twice during the past two hours. I sped out of our driveway and up that hill faster than I should have.

With a cringeworthy squeal of tires, I turned left into the state forest. I followed signs and my sense of direction and zigzagged, probably faster than I should have in the darkening woods, along gravel and dirt roads toward where I thought the boulder-topped cliff was.

As I'd hoped, a narrow dirt road ended at a small parking area, where a wooden sign marked the start of the Clifftop Trail. The only other vehicle there was a pickup truck. Even though it had a camper cap on the back, I didn't think it was Zachary's truck. This one was older, dusty as if it had been parked there for a long time, and rusted in places. I didn't see anyone else, which wasn't surprising. Dense forest surrounded the parking area.

Who had screamed?

I lowered the driver's window but heard nothing besides my car's quiet engine and a squirrel scolding in an oak or pine.

Joshua's motorcycle, Zachary's truck, and Olivia's car weren't there, but I couldn't be certain that Hannah wasn't lying injured somewhere on or near the Clifftop Trail.

I needed to check.

I closed the car window, shut off the engine, got out, and released Dep from her seat belt. I reattached her leash to her life jacket. "It's your lucky day," I told her. "We're going hiking." Hugging her against me, I backed out of the car. Above a loosely woven roof of leaf-covered branches, the sky was fading toward indigo. That and the shadowed forest floor reminded me that dusk was closing in. I amended my statement. "It's your lucky evening." I set Dep on the ground and studied the sign's wooden map. The trail, marked in a yellow-painted groove carved into the wood, was an almost perfect circle. I asked Dep, "Why didn't they call this the 'Donut Trail'?"

"Mrrp."

I ran a forefinger along the glossy yellow groove. "Here's a lookout." The information below the map said that the circular trail was about a mile long, which meant that the lookout was about a quarter of a mile from where Dep and I were. I explained to Dep, "Heading left will take us to the lookout faster than bearing to the right."

Like Dep, I was still wearing my life jacket. I was too panicky about Hannah to take time to remove it.

Dep, however, was not in a hurry. We took about ten steps, and she stopped to sniff something whitish on the ground next to the trail. A broken-off mushroom? Maybe it was one of the ones Zachary was studying, the kind he said turned blue when they were bruised or torn.

Making certain that Dep couldn't get close enough to take a bite, as if she would even condescend to taste anything besides her favorite kitty foods and treats, I bent for a closer look.

It wasn't a mushroom.

It was a rather large chunk of pastry, liberally coated in powdered sugar. Startled, I straightened and demanded aloud, "Part of one of our beignets?"

"Mewp."

Disdainful, tail up, Dep started along the trail. Maybe we could make it to the lookout before total darkness.

But hadn't I spotted something blue sticking out from underneath that piece of beignet? Grasping my end of Dep's leash tightly and preventing her from going farther, I bent over the blue object.

It was a hairclip, similar to or perhaps identical to the ones that had peeked out from underneath Hannah's hat the past couple of days in Deputy Donut.

Had Hannah been here? More importantly, was she all right?

I picked Dep up, clutched her against my life jacket, and ran. Fortunately, the trail was almost flat and not as treacherous as Olivia must have feared, but I had to watch for stones and tree roots. I didn't stop or slow down to inspect other things that resembled pastry crumbs or specks of confectioners' sugar.

Hannah was fine, I told myself. She had to be. Blue hairclips were not unusual.

Five minutes later, I spotted the clifftop boulder, the first time I'd seen it from this side. It was shaped like a slightly puffy and bumpy square, balanced on one side. Beignets were on my mind, so of course I told Dep, "From now on, I'm calling that boulder The Beignet."

Dep didn't respond. She could probably tell that I was merely trying to distract myself from my anxiety.

Where was Hannah?

A sign warned against going near the railing or climbing on the boulder. No one was doing either of those things, and I wasn't about to. Birds chattered nearby, and across the lake, a vehicle with a noisy engine chugged up a hill, probably on the road that passed the end of Brent's and my driveway.

Between the trail and the edge of the cliff, the lookout bellied out toward the lake. About a dozen sightseers could have lined up along the railing and enjoyed the view together, but as far as I could tell, no one else was around. Still holding Dep, I crossed flattish stone dotted with dirt-filled indentations until I stood at the railing beside The Beignet. A few of this year's colorful leaves had drifted down onto mats of last year's leaves, now brown, damp, and disintegrating.

Below me, the lake spread out, bare of boats and reflecting the steel blue of the sky.

Dep wriggled in my arms and made a funny, almost growling noise. Instead of gazing out at the lake like I was, she was looking almost straight down.

"Sorry," I said. "Are we too close?" Dep could scramble up the stairways and ramps in Deputy Donut's office and in her new catio, but she had learned when she was a kitten that climbing trees involved coming down. She hadn't figured out how to do it then, at least not gracefully, and she had never been willing to try again. "Are we up too high?" I asked her. "Are these tree trunks on the other side of the railing worrying you? We don't have to climb down them."

But Dep wasn't looking at tree trunks. Peering almost

straight down from The Beignet, she made another of her weird little chirps, the kind she made from a second-story window when she saw birds in nearby trees.

I craned my neck to follow her gaze. Far below The Beignet and close to the lake, the wooded ledge I'd seen from my kayak jutted over the water.

Because of the leaves still nodding on trees between me and the ledge, I almost didn't see the worn-out sneaker next to the ragged hem of a blue denim pantleg.

Chapter 8

✳

I inhaled sharply and called down in a voice suddenly raspy with dread, "Hello?"

No one answered. Neither the shoe nor the pantleg moved.

Had someone thrown jeans and shoes down there? Maybe during the summer, someone had climbed down, removed their clothing, and gone for a swim but had not returned for their pants and at least one sneaker.

A leaf dropped from a tree above me, drifted down, and settled on the hem of the jeans where the person's ankle would be. If the clothes had been lying on that ledge for months, wouldn't more leaves and other plant debris be on them?

And then there was the position of the shoe relative to the pantleg and the way the pantleg was humped over something that could have been an ankle. I wanted to ignore those things. I couldn't.

Someone could have fallen recently, maybe when I'd heard that scream, and that person could be too injured to speak.

Who?

I'd come to the Clifftop Trail because Zachary and Joshua had invited Hannah to hike here with them, and I'd been terrified that the person who screamed could have been Hannah.

Staring downward, I tried to talk myself out of believing

that the person lying many yards below me, if there was a person, could have been Hannah or one of her friends.

Blue jeans. Both Zachary and Joshua had been wearing them when I last saw them, and Hannah could have changed into a pair.

A shoe. I couldn't be certain, but I thought that it was large, a man's. When I last saw Joshua, he had been wearing motorcycle boots, not sneakers.

The person down there was probably neither Hannah nor Joshua.

If it was Zachary, where was Joshua?

And where was Hannah? Had the blue hairclip near the beginning of the trail been hers?

I'd heard a motorcycle a half hour or so after that scream.

Maybe the person on the ledge below me was Zachary, and Joshua had roared off, with Hannah behind him on the bike, to get help. But where was Zachary's truck? Was I right that the one in the parking area wasn't his? I'd never gotten a good look at his truck.

I turned on my phone's light and shined it downward, but it only illuminated leaves above the shoe and pantleg, hiding the clothing among shadows.

Dep chirped again, and I tried to reassure her. "Don't worry, Dep, we're not going to climb down an almost sheer cliff."

Maybe no one had gone for help, and if there was to be a rescue, it was up to me to begin organizing it.

I started to set the wiggly cat down but quickly changed my mind. Part of the soggy mat of last year's leaves in one of the indentations in the bedrock's surface had been over-turned, and there was at least one partial footprint in dust near the railing, probably of a sneaker around the size of the one lying unmoving on the stone ledge.

Shuddering, I held Dep more tightly and backed away from the signs of a possible scuffle. On a less-disturbed part of the trail, I set my still-leashed cat down beside a withering fern. She sniffed at the needle-thin, silvery trail of a snail or a slug.

I tapped a nine and two ones into my phone and told the emergency dispatcher where I was and that I believed someone might have fallen from the lookout.

"Are they bleeding?"

"I can't tell. He's too far down, and I saw only a shoe and part of a pantleg."

"Is he breathing?" Static broke into her voice. I hoped I wouldn't lose the connection.

"I don't know."

She must have had trouble understanding me, too. She asked, "Does he have a pulse?"

"I can't get near him." I undoubtedly sounded as frantic as I felt. "Or her. The cliffs here are nearly straight down, and the person is close to the base. Maybe rescuers can reach him from Chicory Lake, but to approach from the lookout on the Clifftop Trail, we'll need the fire department's high-angle rescue team." Scott, the fire chief, was one of my friends. If anyone could raise an injured person from the ledge below the lookout, it would be Scott and his volunteers.

"Stay on the line," the dispatcher ordered. "We'll send help."

Suddenly, the whispering of leaves and pine needles high in trees sounded like ambushers plotting to leap out at me. "I'll meet them in the parking area." I gave the dispatcher my car's make, model, and license number. "I'll be in the car." *If I can reach it before someone grabs me.*

Holding the phone in one hand, I picked up Dep with the other. Carrying her almost like a football, a strange one with legs dangling over both sides of my forearm, I ran back along the section of the Clifftop Trail that we'd taken to the lookout. The woods were almost completely dark, and obstacles that had seemed negligible earlier had become almost impossible to see, even with my phone's light shining on the path ahead. I stumbled and had to catch my balance. Ends of pine boughs brushed my sleeves. Twigs threatened my hair, and one slashed, stinging, across my cheek. My lungs burned. That quarter mile felt more like five miles.

The emergency dispatcher might have heard my thumping footsteps, my rough breathing, and Dep's grumbling complaints.

And so would anyone lurking in the woods.

Dimly aware of the white powder, the piece of pastry, and the almost hidden hairclip on the trail, I finally saw the back of the wooden map and the break in trees. Thanks to the tiny amount of light remaining in the sky, the clearing was slightly brighter than the woods. I ran to my car. Juggling the phone and Dep, I fiddled with my key fob.

And that was when I noticed that I'd parked on another vehicle's tire tracks. Aiming my phone's light, I could see where the tracks entered the dirt-paved parking area, and also where the vehicle had left in an apparent hurry. Two narrowish wheels had circled, spewing dirt, before straightening into one line and returning to the little-used lane that led to the web of slightly wider state forest roads.

A motorcycle must have come into this lot, parked about where my car was now, and then raced away. My own tires had partially covered the motorcycle's tracks, and if whoever had ridden that motorcycle had gotten off it, I'd probably parked over their footprints. I pictured the impressions made by one pair of motorcycle boots and one pair of ladies' sneakers.

Hoping that Hannah had never come near here, and if she had, she was now safely far away and had nothing to do with the unmoving person—or whatever it was—on the ledge down near the lake's surface, I dove into the driver's seat. I told the dispatcher that I was in my car, and then I turned off my phone's flashlight and plunked the phone onto the dash.

I locked the doors and sat panting, hugging Dep, and swiveling my head to look out first one window and then another.

The dusty pickup was still where it had been when Dep and I had driven into this parking spot. No other vehicles were in sight. I studied what I could make out of the old truck in the fading light. I was almost positive that it was older and rustier than the pickup I'd seen Zachary driving.

The clearing and the sky above it descended into complete darkness.

In my arms, Dep howled. I tethered her to the passenger seat belt. I didn't know when I'd be allowed to leave the scene, but before I drove away, I would fasten her to one of the seat belts in back, where she would be better protected while we were in motion.

She stopped yowling for a second, and I thought I heard distant sirens. I reached out and petted her soft, warm fur. She turned her back to me. Sitting straight up, she peered toward the passenger window. Ordinarily, petting her was calming and relaxing for both of us, but not this time. She let out another aggrieved shriek.

Naturally, the dispatcher asked, "Who's screaming?"

"My cat." Even after sitting in the car for nearly a half hour, I was still trying to catch my breath. Thanks to Dep, the dispatcher wouldn't be able to hear my hammering heart. I couldn't, either, but I felt it.

Staring toward the trail in the blackness of the woods, I reminded myself that I could drive away if a potential attacker rushed out from between trees toward me. I whispered a silent thank-you to Alec for teaching me how to drive defensively, especially when speeding.

Where was Hannah? I should have programmed her number into my phone when she first started working for us. I could have put the dispatcher on hold—something that would undoubtedly alarm her—and call Olivia, but I didn't want to worry or upset Olivia, and I definitely didn't want to cause more friction between the two sisters.

I no longer heard sirens. Had first responders and their vehicles gone behind a hill? Maybe the sirens had been racing to a different emergency. Or the drivers had silenced the sirens when no vehicles or intersections were ahead of them.

Minutes later, I heard the thrumming of a powerful engine. Red and white lights swept through the clearing. A fire truck and the fire department's search and rescue truck rumbled into the parking area and stopped near my car.

I told the dispatcher that help had arrived, and then I disconnected. Dep's complaints dwindled to mutters. I gave her a pat, scrambled out of the car, and ran to Scott.

My tall blond friend and his high-angle rescue squad wore dark cargo pants and shirts and vests with many pockets and reflective stripes.

Scott bent toward me. "Where's the person you called about, Emily?"

Shining my phone's light again, I led him to the map and traced a finger along the route I'd taken to the lookout. "I leaned over the railing about here, beside a big boulder, and I saw a pantleg—blue jeans, I think—and a sneaker. No one answered when I called. I hope I'm wrong. Maybe no one's there, but it looked like a leg and a foot could have been inside that pantleg and that shoe." I tried to quell my shivering.

Scott nodded. "We'll have a look." Not one to waste time during an emergency, he strode toward his crew. They were donning harnesses and hauling equipment out of the search and rescue truck. I shouted, "Want me to show you?"

Without turning, he waved a dismissive hand. "We'll find it."

I returned to my car and stood beside it. I would jump into it and lock the doors if I had to.

Carrying ropes, lights, and a rigid stretcher that could be lowered and lifted with the help of pulleys, the rescuers started down the trail. They took the left branch, the shorter route to the lookout.

Behind me, tires crunched on the dirt and gravel road. Red and blue lights lit treetops. A marked police car stopped behind one of the fire department's trunks, and then a large, dark SUV eased around the cruiser. I recognized that SUV. It was the one Brent owned.

He parked beside my car and got out. He must have come straight from his meeting. He was still wearing a suit and white shirt. Loosening the knot of his tie with one hand and shining a bright flashlight toward the ground with the other, he strode around his car to me. Glow reflecting from the light exaggerated the way his worries were furrowing his forehead. He grasped my arm. "Are you all right, Em?"

"Yes. I saw a shoe and a pantleg at the base of the cliffs below the lookout, and no one answered my shout." I shuddered. "With any luck, the shrill, cut-off scream I reported to the dispatcher had nothing to do with the clothes, and they were merely things that someone had discarded." I pointed at the beginning of the trail. I couldn't see Scott and his rescue team, but lights gleamed between trees, feet tramped, and someone called out a sharp question. "The trail branches just past that sign. Scott and his rescue team took the left branch. It's fastest."

Two uniformed officers left the cruiser and strode to us— Misty and Hooligan. Like Samantha, Misty was one of my longtime best friends. She was also Scott's wife.

Misty was almost as tall as Brent and Scott. Our auburn-haired, mischievous friend Hooligan was shorter, but like nearly everyone else, taller than I was. He didn't look impish at the moment. His face, like Misty's and Brent's, was serious.

I quickly summarized and added, "After I heard the scream, I thought I saw someone in dark clothing backing away from the railing."

Brent asked, "Which direction did they go?"

"I wasn't positive that I saw anyone, but if I did, he or she was backing toward the trail and was quickly swallowed up in the shadows, so I don't know which direction they might have gone after they reached the trail. Also, when I got to the lookout, I noticed signs of a possible scuffle in the dirt near the railing and beside the boulder that no one's supposed to climb." *Did someone? And they fell off it?*

Misty looked at Brent. "The rescue squad will have trampled the area."

"Take pictures," he told her and Hooligan. "I'll be along after I talk to Emily."

I again gave directions.

Flashlights on, Misty and Hooligan hurried toward the trail.

I showed Brent what remained of the tire tracks that I thought might have been made by a motorcycle.

"I suspect you're right," he said.

"Before Deputy Donut closed this afternoon, Hannah's two friends, the ones I told you about last night, invited Hannah to go hiking with them here. Hannah turned them down, maybe because Olivia was right there, but she could have changed her mind when Olivia wasn't around. One of Hannah's friends rides a motorcycle and was wearing motorcycle boots when he left Deputy Donut, so that's probably not him down on the ledge. I'm not sure what kind of shoes Hannah's other friend was wearing, but he could have been wearing sneakers. He drives a pickup truck, a newer one, I think, than the one parked over there behind the fire trucks. That old pickup was here when I first arrived. It could have been there for days. I don't know who owns it."

"We'll run the plates."

"Hannah's friends, Joshua and Zachary, bought beignets at Deputy Donut before their hike, and Dep found a piece of pastry that might be from one of them." My fingernails dug into my palms, but I couldn't relax and unclench my fists.

"Also, there's a hairclip that's similar to the pair that Hannah was wearing yesterday and today." Some people might not have noticed the tremor in my voice.

I was sure that Brent did. He squeezed my hand and gazed intently down into my face. "That scream you heard—did you recognize the voice?"

"No, and I couldn't tell if it was a man or a woman, but it was high, maybe with fright. I hope it was only teens playing in the woods."

"Did the scream change in tone, like someone coming closer or going farther away?"

"Not that I noticed, maybe because it lasted only about a second."

"What were Hannah and her two friends wearing when you last saw them?"

"Zachary was in blue jeans and a black T-shirt. Joshua was wearing blue jeans and a black leather jacket. Hannah was in her Deputy Donut uniform. She wore the black shorts today, not the black jeans." Brent knew that our uniform shirts were white. "She said she was going grocery shopping and having dinner with Olivia, but she had time to do that plus change into blue jeans and come up here to hike with Zachary and Joshua."

"Can you find the hairclip and the pastry-like thing again and show them to me?"

Shining our lights, we followed the trail. Brent took a picture of the now-flattened chunk of pastry and the hairclip and then put them into an evidence envelope.

Our lights picked out a few specks of the powder that I suspected was sugar. Brent gathered some of it and slipped it, along with bits of soil and leaves, into another evidence envelope. "I'll walk back to your car with you, Em."

"You don't have to."

"We don't know who all might be in these woods." He said it lightly. I tried to hide my shivers.

In the parking area, the vehicles' strobes had been turned off, and everything was dark except for our phones' lights and the dim, greenish lights inside the cabs of the fire trucks. At my car, Brent told me, "You can go home now. Don't wait up."

I opened my driver's door. The interior lights came on, showing Dep buckled into the front seat. Giving Brent an accusing glare, she let out an indignant screech.

He only laughed.

I unfastened her seat belt, pulled her out of the car, and hugged her. Brent gave her a knuckle rub, and then put his arms around both of us and gave me a swift kiss. "Take care, okay, Em?"

"You, too." Our log chalet, even on its isolated acreage, seemed much safer than out here in the woods. I hoped that Brent would soon catch up with the other first responders.

Reminding myself that he was a skilled and experienced police officer who could cope successfully with almost anything, including people with evil intent pouncing out from behind boulders and trees, I opened the car's back door, set Dep on the seat, and fastened the clip on her life jacket to the carabiner on the seat belt.

I straightened and shut the door. I could no longer hear her pitiful cries.

Brent was near the wooden map. He turned around. "Just one more question, Em. I think I understand why Dep is wearing her life jacket, but why are you wearing yours?"

"I follow Dep's fashion trends."

Brent laughed, waved, and headed into the woods. Soon all I could see of him was the light showing the route ahead of his feet, and then I couldn't see even that.

Chapter 9

I got into my car, backed away from the other vehicles, and then braked to a stop so I could stare at the parking area's dirt surface. My headlights showed tire tracks in sharp relief. Between the tracks I'd made when I pulled in and just now, when I backed out, I saw what could have been marks made by a motorcycle's tires and kickstand. And large boot prints also? My shoe prints were probably among the smaller ones closest to where my driver's door had been, and lots of footwear prints were clustered near where I'd talked to Scott, Brent, Misty, and Hooligan.

I swung the car toward the lane leading out of the parking area. My headlights were the only illumination. I passed no other vehicles in that dark forest. Obviously not impressed by the picturesque tunnel of trees arching over the road, Dep moaned. Finally, we reached the paved county road, and I rolled down the windows slightly. The air was still warm for this time of night and smelled fresh and piney with hints of woodsmoke. I wondered if Joshua and Zachary were enjoying another fire at their campsite and possibly again annoying the campground host.

Where was Hannah?

The beginning of our long driveway was also dark, but

closer to the house, timers had turned on lights, and motion detectors lit more.

Dep stopped mumbling after I took her out of the car, but she didn't purr, even when I cuddled her in my arms, carried her into the house, and removed her life jacket. She gave me a baleful look, sat down, and flicked at her shoulders with her tongue. Then she stalked off toward the kitchen and her food and water dishes. I followed, refilled her dishes, and poured myself a large glass of water.

I still didn't want to call Olivia. How could I word my fear that Hannah or one of her friends might be injured or dead? There was no point in scaring Olivia unnecessarily.

Sitting on a couch in the great room, I sipped water and wondered if Brent, Misty, Hooligan, and the other first responders were safe. Would they be able to rescue an injured person, or . . . ? Dep curled up on the other end of the couch. I tried to convince myself that nothing besides clothing had fallen off the lookout.

Finally, after staring at nothing and paying no attention to the passing of time, I set the empty glass on a table and took a deep breath, bracing myself for what I needed to do. Still wearing my life jacket, I grabbed a flashlight that was only slightly smaller than a baseball bat and went outside. Dep didn't look up from her nap. I locked the door.

Shining my light on the trail, I headed down the hill through the woods. Except for sighing pine boughs, the distant whine of a vehicle, and my sneakered feet landing quietly on the earth, I heard nothing.

My kayak was where I'd left it, haphazardly pulled onto the beach. I set my flashlight on the dock to shine on the boathouse, put the kayak and paddle away next to Brent's, and locked the boathouse.

Wavelets rippled onto the beach. Voices carried across the water from the direction of the beignet-like boulder on cliffs hidden beyond other rocky peninsulas. I walked to the end of the dock farthest from the beach and turned off the flashlight. Stars pricked holes in the sky and reflected in the almost flat water, so many stars that I felt like I could almost hear them, as if their buzzing and crackling traveled millions of light years to this nearly silent lake in these nearly silent woods.

An actual noise startled me, an outboard motor sputtering to life somewhere in the direction of the lake below the Clifftop Trail. Chicory Lake wasn't large enough for most motorboats. Smaller ones occasionally ventured onto the lake, usually piloted by people fishing at dawn or dusk.

I couldn't help shivering. The fire department must have borrowed a boat, hauled it to the Chicory Canoe Livery boat launch, and motored to the ledge where I'd seen the pantleg and the shoe. The boat might now be taking an injured—or worse—person away.

I waited. Finally, a headlight, a green starboard light, and a high taillight chugged out from behind the nearest bluff hiding the Clifftop Trail from our dock. Aside from its running lights, the boat was a dark blur, churning across the lake, disturbing the water, and temporarily erasing the reflections of stars. If anyone in that little craft was speaking, I didn't hear them. Slowly, its motor putt-putting, the boat continued west. It went beyond a curve of the wooded shoreline, and although I could still hear it, I could no longer see it. It had to be heading to Chicory Canoe Livery.

I stood still in the darkness, watching the motorboat's wake widen until waves slapped against our dock's underpinnings, washed onto the pebbly sand, and receded, tumbling small stones enough to make them clatter against one another.

Gradually, the lake flattened, reflecting even more brilliant stars. Muted clanks sounded from near the boat launch.

I turned on the flashlight and strode up the trail.

Close to the plateau where our house was, the trail rose

sharply. Near the top, a soft glow from the lights I'd left on illuminated branches above me. I turned off my light and slowed down, picking my way up the steepest part of the trail, and listening.

I stopped at the edge of the woods. The lawn was bare, my car was the only vehicle in sight, and the house appeared undisturbed. Dep sat in one of the great room's tall windows. I ran to the porch and let myself in.

"Mewp." My soft little cat wound around my ankles.

I picked her up. "Do you forgive me for making you ride in the car?"

Silence.

I reminded her, "I could have left you at home alone all evening instead of only during the past half hour."

She wiggled. I set her down. Finally, I removed my life jacket and put it away.

Brent had said not to wait up. It was after nine. Maybe the high-angle rescue team had rappelled down the cliff and other first responders had arrived by boat only to find a heap of clothing, and Brent would be back soon.

Nerves and adrenaline kept me from even considering being sleepy. I went into the kitchen and took bleu cheese and brie out of the fridge. While they softened, I made a batch of savory herb and cheese shortbread dough for Samantha's baby shower. I shaped the dough into long rolls, wrapped the rolls securely, and refrigerated them. We would slice them, bake the slices, and serve them hot. Misty and I had hired Hannah to help with the cooking and serving at Tuesday evening's shower.

Was Hannah all right?

It was ten. We started work at six thirty in the morning. Olivia had probably gone to bed. Reminding myself that I would see her in the morning, I again resisted the urge to call her and ask about Hannah. I took old Wisconsin cheddar from the fridge, grated it, crumbled the blue cheese, cut the brie into wedges, and put the three cheeses, a dollop of sour cream, and a generous splash of golden turmeric into the bowl of my stand mixer. I let the mixer stir until the mixture was nearly smooth and about the shade of the yellow mums in boxes hanging from the porch railing of our Maple Street house. Again, I made long rolls. I coated them with chopped walnuts, wrapped them tightly, and refrigerated them. We would put slices of the cheese logs on crackers for another appetizer at the shower.

Brent wasn't home.

I still wasn't sleepy.

I made a couple of balls of piecrust dough and refrigerated them, too. I closed the fridge door.

At my feet, Dep gazed up at me. "Mew!" Her eyes seemed unusually large.

I picked her up. "It's past your bedtime, too, isn't it, sweetie?"

She purred.

I carried her to one of the couches, sat down with her on my lap, picked up a magazine about hosting baby showers, and flipped to the recipe section.

Quiet footsteps sounded on the porch.

Brent came in. I put the magazine down, clutched Dep, ran to Brent, and threw myself—and Dep—into his arms. He buried his face in my hair and held me tightly for a long time. Finally, he loosened his grip and murmured, "Thanks for calling that in."

"Was he . . . was it a person?"

"It was, now unfortunately deceased."

"Recently?"

"Probably around the time you heard the scream."

Despite the warm arms around me, I shivered. "I should have called for help as soon as I could, instead of taking time to drive over there first."

"That wouldn't have saved him. He was dead before he went over the cliffs."

"He?"

"A man, yes."

I exhaled in relief. *Not Hannah.*

And probably not Joshua. I hoped the deceased man wasn't Zachary, either. And I hoped that those three had been nowhere near that lookout, that they hadn't gone hiking, or if they had, they had hiked somewhere else, like the Cornflower Trail that Zachary had suggested.

And then the rest of what Brent said hit me, and I repeated, "He was dead before he went over the cliffs? Does that mean he fell off the boulder?"

"I don't think so. The signs of a scuffle that you mentioned were still there. The rescue team noticed and avoided them. I suspect that someone pushed his body underneath the railing beside that boulder. He received wounds after his heart stopped. And there's no way he could have died and then simply tumbled off the edge. The railing's a good foot from the edge. I'm calling it suspicious, probably a homicide. We've taped off the trail access and will return in daylight."

"Did someone take his body away by motorboat?"

"Yes. If he'd been alive, the high-angle rescue team would have tried lifting him up the cliff and taking him by ambulance to the hospital, which would have been faster. But there was no rush, and lowering him from that ledge into a boat was safer for the rescue team. Most of them had to climb back up with the help of their ropes. They're good at it, and more practice never hurts."

"I saw the boat cross the lake toward the boat launch, I think, when I was putting away my kayak."

"You could have left that for me."

"I know."

His arms tightened around me again, and he didn't let go for a long time.

Finally, I pulled away. "There was another boat, earlier.

After I heard that scream, I paddled to our beach as fast as I could. Someone was near the other side of the lake in a canoe. I couldn't tell who it was or what type of canoe it was. It could have been from the rental place."

Brent got out his notebook and wrote in it, and then he told me, "Chicory Canoe Livery is open only weekends at this time of year, but that doesn't necessarily mean anything. It's Friday. Maybe Barney opened this evening. Also, people can make appointments to rent one of his boats. I'll ask him if anyone rented a canoe from him this evening."

"Do you know who the deceased man is? Was?"

"The wallet in his pocket belonged to someone named Albert McGoss. Does that sound familiar?"

"No. Poor man."

"He had a few coins in one pocket, and something else. I'm glad you're still awake, because the other thing was a wadded-up paper bag from Deputy Donut, and I wanted to see if you recognize him from the photo on his driver's license."

A wadded-up bag from Deputy Donut . . . I said shakily, "I packaged beignets for Hannah's friends Zachary and Joshua in a Deputy Donut paper bag. And there was that hunk of pastry, some crumbs, and possible powdered sugar on the trail that might have come from beignets. And the hairclip like Hannah's . . ." Miserable at where this could lead, I broke off.

Brent opened an evidence envelope and pulled out a wallet. "There was no cash in this."

"So, someone might have gone out to that isolated spot and robbed the first person he saw, and then killed him?"

"It's a possibility."

I couldn't help shuddering. I was already having trouble feeling secure at our beautiful but lonely woodland property when Brent wasn't with me. The even more isolated Clifftop

Trail was uncomfortably nearby. Had Albert McGoss's killer left the area, or would he continue to prey on people in and near the state forest?

Brent held the man's driver's license by its edges and angled it so I could see the tiny portrait.

It took me a few seconds to recognize him. "That picture must be a few years old. That man was in Deputy Donut yesterday with his wife and another man, and the three of them seemed to be arguing. The man who was with the couple is Kevin Lunnion. He owns Lunnion's Lawns and Order."

Brent made more notes in his book. "I've heard of it."

"Yesterday after work, I took the mower from our Maple Street house to him to sharpen the blades. He said I could pick it up today, but no one was there."

Brent became very still. "When was this?"

"Right after we finished at Deputy Donut, so around five fifteen."

"And you heard the scream when?"

"About one and a half hours after that."

Brent wrote more and then turned to a new blank page. "Can you tell me about the argument you observed in Deputy Donut?"

"All three people were so tense and focused on their dispute that they didn't pay any attention when that little dog chased Dep into our dining room. McGoss and his wife left first, stomping out like they were angry. But then they stood for a while outside talking to Joshua and Zachary, and they no longer looked angry. Lunnion told me that McGoss and Lunnion had been in a partnership, but Lunnion had dissolved the partnership only minutes before, right there in Deputy Donut, because, according to him, McGoss wasn't doing his share."

"It sounds like I need to talk to Lunnion, and not only about where he was this evening when you were supposed to retrieve the mower from him."

I took a deep breath. "There's more, and it might have something to do with Hannah and her friends Zachary and Joshua."

"The hairclip."

I groaned. "Besides the hairclip and the bits of beignet and powdered sugar, too. Yesterday, Kevin Lunnion said that one of the reasons that Albert McGoss didn't do his fair share was because Albert and his wife were hosts at a campground. This morning, Hannah said that Zachary and Joshua were camping in Chicory Lake State Forest, and the campground host was Albert McGoss. Last night, he yelled at her, Zachary, and Joshua for singing. McGoss also sent Hannah away because she and the car she was driving, Olivia's, were not registered to stay in that campground."

"It sounds like several people might have argued with McGoss before his death."

My shoulders slumped. "Yes. I can't imagine Hannah getting herself mixed up in anything like a . . . well, it sounds like at the very least, an attempt to harm Albert McGoss." I brightened. "Albert McGoss also took away a bag of beignets, which Kevin Lunnion paid for, so the bits of pastry on the trail and the crumpled bag in his pocket probably had nothing to do with Hannah and her friends. And the hairclip could be nearly anyone's. Even if Hannah, Joshua, and Zachary were on that trail this evening, it could have been before McGoss was there. Or maybe after. It took me probably over a half hour to paddle back to our beach and drive to the entrance to the trail."

"If they were anywhere nearby, I'll want to talk to all three of them in case they saw or heard something they didn't realize was important. I'm going to have to question everyone in that campground."

"Who owns the old pickup that was near the entrance to the trail?"

Brent put the driver's license away. "Albert McGoss, but

the truck was locked, and we didn't find the keys with his body. We'll search again with metal detectors in the daylight. Did you see what vehicle Lunnion drove to or from Deputy Donut, or was parked at his place when you dropped off the mower?"

"After he left Deputy Donut, he walked south on Wisconsin Street and went out of sight without getting into a vehicle. There were no vehicles besides a riding mower at his place when I tried to pick up the mower. He has two garages. One is oversized with extra-tall doors, and I think he uses that as his workshop. On the other side of that building, which seems to have an upstairs apartment, there's a smaller, detached, one-car garage. I peeked in. Spots on the floor showed where a vehicle parks, but other than the usual stuff being stored, that garage was empty. Do you know the name of Albert McGoss's wife?"

"Not yet, but it should be easy to find, along with information about any vehicle she might own."

I raised a forefinger. "Maybe it's a motorcycle!"

"Maybe. If she returns to Deputy Donut, let me know." He finished writing and closed the notebook. "I'm going to go have a chat with Mr. Lunnion, and then if he can tell me which campground McGoss hosted, I'll go question people there."

"In the middle of the night?"

He smiled. "It's not even eleven yet."

"You'll get backup?"

"I'll get backup at both Lunnion's and the campground. Misty and Hooligan will be on duty all night. Don't worry."

"Easy for you to say."

He kissed me and left. He was still wearing his suit.

Chapter 10

At breakfast the next morning, I asked Brent if he had arrested Lunnion. "Or anyone?"

"No one. Lunnion was watching TV when we arrived. He said he'd been doing yard work for a client in the south end of Fallingbrook. He returned to his place about five forty-five and had been there alone until we arrived. I didn't ask him about the mower, but when it's ready, I'll pick it up. You shouldn't go there again by yourself."

"Not even to see the peacocks?"

"Not even to see the—did you say peacocks?"

"They're in the woods behind his building. I heard them but didn't see them. The pathway from his driveway toward the back is not inviting. It's like he doesn't want people snooping around his place, and I have to wonder why. Not," I added quickly, "that I would snoop around his place. I leave that to you."

Brent grinned. "Thank you."

"Did you go to the campground where McGoss was host?"

"Yes. Lunnion had told us which campground Albert and his wife—her first name's Dawn—hosted. No one was at the McGoss trailer. Hannah was still at her friends' campsite. She looked scared. Misty interviewed her, I interviewed Joshua, and Hooligan talked to Zachary."

"Had they been to the Clifftop Trail?"

Brent paused in a way that meant he was thinking about how to word something, and I thought, *uh-oh*. Finally, he answered. "They all said they hadn't."

I bit my lip. "You don't sound convinced."

"Misty, Hooligan, and I will go over everything more carefully tomorrow."

"Did you get a good look at Joshua's motorcycle at his campsite? Do you think his bike might have been the one that drove into and out of that area?"

"I couldn't rule it out, but a forensics team from the DCI will compare whatever tracks weren't obliterated at the Clifftop Trail parking area to tires in the campground, and also to the tires of Lunnion's van." The Wisconsin Division of Criminal Investigation provided investigative aid to smaller communities.

"Did you find anyone else in the campground who had argued with Albert McGoss?"

Smile wrinkles appeared beside Brent's eyes. "No one who would admit it, though we did hear about his argument with Hannah's friends the night before. We talked to all of the adults in that campground. Several of them had seen Albert McGoss around his own campsite yesterday, but he drove away after about four in the afternoon, and none of them saw him after that."

"You three did a lot."

"We'll need to tackle other campgrounds in the state forest. I hope the detective the DCI sends arrives soon."

I crossed my fingers and held them up where Brent could see them. "And I hope it's Rex Clobar. When he was here before, I thought I glimpsed a romantic spark between him and Summer Peabody-Smith."

My comment caused a few of our own romantic sparks. I had to tear myself away to put Dep into the car and arrive at work on time.

In Deputy Donut, both Olivia and Hannah were quiet. That wasn't unusual for Olivia, but I couldn't help eyeing Hannah and wondering if anything had happened the evening before that was making her less communicative than usual. Instead of wearing hairclips, she had braided her hair along the sides of her head and fastened the braids into a ponytail in back. She often wore her hair that way.

She cheered up when the retired men and the Knitpickers came in. For years, the two groups had spent only weekday mornings in Deputy Donut. Then the Knitpickers started spending Saturday mornings with us, too, for some peace and quiet from the retired men, they claimed, but they also said they needed the additional crafting time to use the yarn they kept buying. It wasn't long before the retired men began taking up their regular table across the aisle from the Knitpickers on Saturday mornings, because they needed good coffee on Saturdays, too, they said. The Knitpickers pretended to be dismayed, but they didn't change their schedule, and they teased the retired men almost as much as the retired men teased them.

Hannah and I took orders from both tables and went into the kitchen. Olivia and Tom started new pots of coffee, and Hannah and I put sweet treats on plates. She and I each carried a tray of plates. The retired men told Hannah she was giving the wrong donuts to everyone.

She tossed her ponytail over her shoulder. "There are no wrong donuts, but I'll return them to the kitchen." She pretended to be about to take Charles's plate. He held onto it, and she laughed. I wondered if I'd only imagined that she'd been distracted earlier.

A motorcycle roared south along Wisconsin Street. I followed Hannah's gaze out the window. Joshua? Hannah blushed, turned to the table of Knitpickers, and asked Priscilla what she was knitting.

Priscilla held up a tiny mint-green sweater knit in a pattern resembling chains of leaves. "It's for Samantha Houlihan's baby. Samantha is one of Fallingbrook's paramedics." Priscilla nodded at me. "She and Emily have known each other since junior high." Hannah smiled. Misty and I had enlisted her to help with Samantha's baby shower. Priscilla explained, "Samantha has come to my aid a few times when I've done something stupid like trip over my own feet. I want to show my appreciation."

Charles scrolled through his phone. He looked up, saw me watching him, and gave me a droll smile. "I'm reading the news." He studied his phone again, and then jumped to his feet faster than I'd ever seen him move. "Gallopin' grasshoppers, would you look at this? The guy who built my deck died!" He showed me the screen.

The article showed a small picture of a very much alive Albert McGoss beside an uncompleted and possibly too-steep wheelchair ramp. The Fallingbrook Fire Department had recovered his body below a large boulder at the lookout on the Clifftop Trail in the Chicory Lake State Forest.

Tom brought a fresh pot of coffee to the men's table and poured the coffee Charles had ordered, a mellow, medium-dark roast from Mexico. Charles showed Tom his phone. "Chief Westhill, did you ever arrest this guy?"

Tom gave Charles that almost neutral but slightly inquisitive detective look. "No."

"That's kind of surprising." Charles let out an uneasy laugh. "Not to speak ill of the dead or anything, but he rebuilt my deck a couple of years ago, and it started falling apart almost the minute he got his money and left. I'd heard good things about Lunnion's Lawns and Order, so that's why

I hired them to do the deck, but maybe they're only good at landscaping. I never saw hide nor hair of Lunnion."

I glanced toward the front door, half expecting Joshua to have parked his motorcycle and be on his way inside. I didn't see him.

Tom refilled another man's mug. "I understand that Kevin Lunnion is good at lawn mowing, small engine repair, and sharpening mower blades, but I've never used him. You're not the only person to say they were disappointed in the handyman part of Lunnion's business."

I bent to peer at Charles's phone. The photo was definitely one of Albert McGoss, probably several years ago. I said, "Albert McGoss was in here Thursday afternoon with his wife and Kevin Lunnion. After Albert and his wife left, Kevin told me he had just broken up his partnership with McGoss because McGoss wasn't doing his share. He was spending too much time at the campground he was hosting in the state forest."

Tom turned around and looked at Hannah from underneath lowered brows. "Is that the man you were telling us about, Hannah? The security guard out at the campground where your friends are staying?"

Hannah was still admiring the tiny sweater Priscilla was knitting. "What man?"

Charles went to the other large table and showed Hannah the screen of his phone.

Her face paled. "I . . . I think it is."

Olivia finished pouring another Knitpicker's coffee and peered over her sister's shoulder. "I'm sure he's one of the two men who were arguing with each other in here on Thursday afternoon." Olivia's voice was harsh and stern. "Did you see him last night, Hannah, when you went out to your friends' campsite?"

"I . . . we didn't see him at the campsite. I guess that's not surprising, if . . ." Her voice dwindled to nothing.

Olivia held the carafe close to her chest. "You see why I told you those trails up there are dangerous?"

Hannah glared. "I know that without anyone telling me."

Olivia demanded, "Did you go there?"

Hannah made a quick intake of breath. "I told you I wasn't going to." *It wasn't exactly a denial.*

Olivia persisted. "Did Joshua and Zachary?"

"If they did, it was early in the evening, before our campfire. I told you where I was going, Olivia."

"And I reminded you that you and my car weren't welcome in that campground."

Hannah's face was becoming red. "Not after midnight, and I didn't plan to stay that long." She glanced at me.

I smiled, knowing that Brent and his team had probably kept Hannah from leaving the campground when she wanted to.

Olivia didn't let it go. "What did you do, park outside the campground and ride Joshua's motorcycle to their site so the security guard wouldn't see my car there?"

"I didn't have to. For one thing, as I said, I wasn't planning to stay past midnight, and for another, if I wanted to catch a ride, I could have asked Zachary." Again, Hannah avoided a direct answer.

Despite my attempts at mentally nudging the bickering sisters away from the retired men and Knitpickers, who seemed too interested in the argument, Olivia accused, "But you weren't home until nearly one, and when you got there, your hair was messed up and one of your hairclips was missing."

"Hair doesn't stay neat all of the time, and my hairclip must be somewhere in your car, like stuck between the driver's seat and the console. I'm always losing things down there." Hannah turned and carried her empty tray back to the kitchen.

I wondered if Olivia was thinking of another reason why a young woman might be out late and her hair could become disheveled. I wasn't about to remind her, but I did wonder which of the two young men might have been running his fingers through Hannah's hair. I was almost certain that the hairclip I'd seen had been Hannah's, and if she'd been making out with one of the men on the trail, it was before I got there. And I knew that Misty's interview with Hannah had caused Hannah to return home late. Maybe Hannah would tell Olivia later, when our customers weren't listening, why she'd stayed at the campground longer than she'd intended.

The Knitpickers and retired men concentrated on their donuts, fritters, and beignets, and soon they were back to hurling silly insults across the aisle between their tables.

I didn't get a chance to talk to Hannah alone until I went into the office for my lunch break. Dep purred in Hannah's lap on the couch. Both of them seemed to have forgotten about Hannah's half-eaten sandwich. Hannah moved Dep to the cushion beside her. "Oops, is my time up?"

"No." Even though Olivia wouldn't be able to hear us through the glass window between the office and the kitchen, I spoke quietly. "You can finish your sandwich. I wanted to talk to you."

"It's okay. I'm not hungry." She picked up her plate and took a step toward the door.

I turned my back on the window into the kitchen in case Olivia could read my lips. Hannah was facing the kitchen. "Let's go out on the porch," I suggested.

"I should get back to work."

"Olivia and Tom can look after everything for the next few minutes."

Bringing her plate, Hannah came outside with me. The day was warm enough that we didn't need jackets, even in the shade of the porch roof. I grasped the railing and looked out over the cars in the parking lot.

Hannah asked in a quiet voice, "Am I in trouble?"

"Not at all."

"Sorry for arguing with Olivia in front of customers this morning."

"I think that man's death upset everyone. I just wanted to ask—are you happy working here, I mean while you decide what you want to do with your life?"

"Yes. Sorry if I gave you the impression I wasn't. You and Tom are so nice, and our customers are, too. The ones who don't go off and die, that is." Finally, I heard a spark of her usual feisty humor.

I again told her, "We hope you'll work here as long as you want to, but if you want to go back to school, we'll understand. Are you closer to a decision about next semester?"

"This semester has barely started, so, no. I don't know what I want to do. Olivia wants me to go back, and I get it. She sacrificed a lot. She gave up going to college so she could look after me and make sure I got into college, but it doesn't seem fair. I feel like she should be the one going to college first."

"Obviously, Olivia doesn't think so."

"She's not the only one who gets to sacrifice and martyr herself." I heard a hint of anger in Hannah's swift retort.

"What if you get your degree, land a decent job, and then help Olivia go to college if she wants to? You earned scholarships. She probably made excellent grades, too, and maybe she could get a break for that or as a mature student."

"I don't know. That's all so iffy."

"What isn't iffy is that you have scholarships now and can continue, and you might lose them if you don't."

"Yeah. Zachary doesn't say anything, but I'm sure he thinks I should go back." Her voice hardened. "But he doesn't get a say in how I live my life just because we went out a few times, and I'm not about to do anything just to please him. Joshua's more easygoing. He thinks I should do whatever I want."

"You know, after a detective from the Wisconsin Division of Criminal Investigation arrives, he'll probably need to talk to everyone who was at Zachary and Joshua's campground last evening, as well as everyone who might have been near where that man fell off a cliff." I hoped my sudden change of subject wasn't too abrasive.

"Your friend Misty questioned me last night, and Brent and the other policeman talked to Joshua and Zachary. As I told Misty, we didn't go on that trail. Well, I'm not sure about Zachary. Joshua met me at the grocery store and picked up dinner for himself and Zachary, then he went back to the campground. I had dinner with Olivia, and drove out there later. I didn't see that campground host at all."

"Do you remember when you arrived at their campsite?"

She gazed up toward the porch roof. "No, but we didn't spend long at dinner. Olivia had prepared most of it the night before, and I only needed to buy some parsley and sour cream for garnishes. Olivia wasn't in the greatest mood, so I didn't stick around. Our apartment can seem constricting. I guess I got to their campsite around six thirty."

I didn't let on that I was hoping that she and Olivia had been together around six forty when I heard that scream. I didn't mention the scream or the timing of it or my having been nearby. I merely warned, "Don't be alarmed if the police want to question all of you again, and the other campers. And tell them the truth. They're good at knowing when people don't."

I didn't turn toward her, but out of the corner of my eye, I saw her hand fly up to where one of her hairclips would have been if she was wearing them. She quickly lowered the hand. "Of course we will."

I pretended not to notice the annoyance that had crept into her voice. "I don't have any siblings, but Misty and Samantha are like sisters to me. If you ever want to talk about problems with Olivia or about anything, like going back to school, I'm willing to listen."

"Okay. I need to get back to work now."

Her shoulders stiff, she marched back inside to the office. I hadn't intended to hurt or anger her, but I was afraid that I had. Less than twenty-four hours before, Hannah had confided in me about coping with her older sister. Now she didn't seem to want to talk to me.

Sighing, I watched her carry her plate and that half-eaten sandwich past Dep and let herself into the dining area.

I went back into the office, sat on the couch, and hugged Dep for a couple of minutes, and then I picked up the backpack I used as a purse and slipped out into the parking lot.

Chapter 11

Ordinarily, I might have walked the ten minutes to the grocery store near Olivia and Hannah's apartment, but I'd driven in from the country that morning, and my car was nicely handy. It took me to the store in about two minutes.

I picked out a spinach, feta, and olive wrap and took it to Laura, a long-faced, fortyish woman. She had started working as a cashier after closing Cheese It, a shop that had carried an exciting variety of cheeses and everything to go with them. Laura's worried frown, uncombed hair, and wrinkled blouse gave me the impression that she felt harassed. My nearly untamable curls probably made people wonder the same thing about me.

Laura rang up the charge for the sandwich. "You're the second person in two days who's come in here wearing a Deputy Donut shirt."

I closed my eyes and touched my fingertips to my temples as if channeling the universe's secrets. "Let me guess. Hannah Kentsen was the other one." I opened my eyes.

Mouth gaping, Laura stared at me. "Are you psychic?"

I grinned. "Only three of us were working at Deputy Donut yesterday. After we closed, Hannah told her sister and me she was coming here."

"Such a lovely pair of girls—young women, I should say. It

was a tragedy when their parents died, but that Olivia, she just pitched in and raised her cute little sister. And no one can tell me that Olivia didn't do a superb job of it."

I paid for my lunch. "I agree. They're both wonderful. Hannah said she came here late yesterday afternoon with a friend, a handsome man in a black leather jacket."

"Hannah has never come in with a man. She was here yesterday, but by herself. She bought a couple of things that Olivia needed for a dinner she was fixing for the two of them. Not that Hannah can't cook. Olivia says she's very good at it."

"Maybe Hannah and the man didn't come in together or check out together."

"No one fitting that description has been here, not while I was working. I'd have noticed." She glanced up and to the side and scrunched her mouth. "Actually, I wasn't feeling well when Hannah was here. I left right after she did. So, maybe the young man came in afterward."

I couldn't help leaning back a little. "I hope you're feeling better now."

"I am. And at least I didn't end up like some." She leaned forward and lowered her voice. "I just found out that Albert McGoss is dead. Not surprising. I bet he was murdered. A lot of people hated him."

I tried for a neutral expression but couldn't help blinking in surprise. I wanted to demand, "Who?" Instead, I squeaked out, "They . . . did?"

Laura continued in confiding tones. "He called himself a handyman, but I heard lots of complaints about him. He didn't show up when he said he would. He worked slowly and took time off. And to make matters worse, he always charged more than he'd estimated, and his work was shoddy. People demanded their money back, and to be fair, his partner, not him, paid them back, but it never covered ripping out everything the man had done and starting over. Murder." She drummed her fingers on the counter beside the cash register. "His partner probably did him in just to get back at him. Or Albert's wife finally got her revenge. For, you know"—Laura clenched her fists and boxed at the air in front of her—"for beating her up. Well, I don't know for sure if he did, but that's the rumor, and I wouldn't put it past him. I've seen Dawn more than once with makeup that didn't quite conceal a black eye, and wearing long sleeves on a hot day. She would come into Cheese It like that."

I tucked my sandwich wrap into my backpack. "I miss Cheese It. I was sorry when you closed it."

She looked down at the counter. "Running a business isn't always easy."

"Right." And I could imagine how much harder it would be if one had to maintain an inventory of expensive, perishable goods like cheese. Making donuts and brewing coffee and tea only minutes before they were consumed kept us from needing to keep an unwieldy amount of food on hand. I waited in case Laura wanted to talk about it.

She looked at the woman hovering nearby and told her, "Here, I can take that."

The woman put a carton of milk onto the counter. "Oh." She sounded unsure, as if she weren't quite done shopping. "Okay."

Calling out a general goodbye, I headed for the door. Laura was talking to the other woman and didn't reply.

I drove back to Deputy Donut and plopped down onto the couch in the office. Not tempted by the feta or anything else in the sandwich, Dep curled up on the couch beside me and snoozed.

I stayed in the office until Tom came in for his lunch break. I told him about hearing a scream while I was kayaking, fearing that Hannah could have been in trouble on the Clifftop Trail, and then investigating and discovering what later turned out to be a body. "I didn't say anything about it to Olivia and

Hannah because, despite what Hannah said this morning, I'm not sure that she and her friends weren't in the area around the time that McGoss fell. I didn't want to cause Olivia more worries than she already has."

Tom shook his head. "You're good at being in the wrong place at the wrong time, aren't you." It wasn't a question.

I groaned. "And I don't have an alibi for when he fell. No one besides Dep was with me, and while she might try to explain, no one would understand her, not even Brent." I became serious again. "Besides, if I did actually see, and not imagine, a person leaving the scene, I can't expect that person to vouch for me. When I got back to our dock, someone was in a canoe near the far shore, but I don't know where they were when McGoss fell, and they probably wouldn't know where I was, either."

Tom warned in ominous tones, "Or they might. Did you tell Brent about the canoe?"

"Yes. And as usual, investigators from the DCI are coming to help. I'm afraid that whoever they send will probably conclude that I must be the killer because I was first on the scene. Which is understandable." I made a tragic face.

Tom laughed, and I went back to work.

Halfway through the afternoon, a tall, slim, muscular man wearing a navy-blue suit, a white shirt, and a green-striped tie came into the shop. He saw me and smiled.

I nearly ran to him. "Rex! I'm glad the DCI sent you." It was no wonder that Summer found the detective from the state intriguing. Those dark eyes held both kindness and warmth.

"Hey, Emily. Do you have a moment?" He looked beyond me and waved toward the kitchen, where Tom and Olivia were. He nodded toward Hannah, who stopped in the middle of talking to a customer and was staring at us as if trying to figure out what was going on.

"We can talk in the office." I started toward the back of the dining area.

Tom came around the half wall, shook Rex's hand, and said, "Today's special coffee is from Mexico. It has chocolatey and almost cinnamon notes, and we've made churros to go with it. I'll bring you some of each."

Rex winked at me. "Sounds good." He was as handsome as ever, with laugh lines around his eyes and mouth and a few more flecks of gray in his dark brown hair. When he'd been here another time, investigating a murder that took place in the lakeside cabin that Summer's parents owned, she had invited him to go kayaking. He'd needed to work that time, but maybe while he was here, he would be able to carve out some leisure time to spend with Summer. For her sake, I hoped he was single.

In the office, he had me read the statement that Brent had prepared for me based on what I'd told him. Tom brought two mugs to Rex. One held coffee. In the other, five sticklike churros, glistening with crystals of sugar, stood on end. The aromas of warm cinnamon and vanilla tempted me, but I didn't nab one.

Rex asked questions while I described everything I could remember about the evening before. I added details of my not-quite-satisfactory discussion with Hannah and told Rex about Hannah's possibly difficult relationship with her sister. "I don't believe that Hannah would have intentionally hurt anyone, but I have a terrible feeling—and it's no more than that, really—that Hannah might know more than she's telling. Maybe she merely doesn't want Olivia to find out that she did something that would frighten Olivia, like hike on a treacherous trail or ride a motorcycle." I also told Rex about my discussion with Laura. "Hannah told me that Joshua went with her to the grocery store, but Laura didn't see a man matching his description. Laura left the store right after

Hannah did, though, so maybe Joshua went in later. But it's funny that Hannah said that Joshua was with her, and Laura said he wasn't."

Without making it obvious, I checked Rex's left ring finger. Still no ring.

I'd have been happier about a possible romance between him and Summer if I hadn't been worried that Hannah, probably thanks to what I'd just told Rex, might have become one of Rex's primary suspects.

He and I went over my statement, making additions, and then I signed it. He said he was heading back to the police station. I let him out the back door close to where he'd parked an unmarked police cruiser.

He'd been gone barely five minutes when Joshua and Zachary came in through the front.

Chapter 12

Zachary gave Hannah the wisp of a smile. Joshua waved and made his way to a table for four in the middle of the room next to the table where Hannah was serving other customers.

Certain that they would prefer to wait until Hannah was available, I returned to the kitchen.

It was close to four thirty, and we weren't busy. Hannah took Zachary's and Joshua's orders and then sat with them while they ate their churros and drank their coffee. They talked quietly together, so I wasn't able to eavesdrop, but I couldn't help watching them for clues about their guilt or innocence. They seemed relaxed, not nervous or upset. Chatting and laughing together, they probably didn't notice Forrest Callic, the investment "expert," peering through the glass front door, opening it, and gazing at them.

I marched toward him. I didn't mean to look unwelcoming, but he must have caught a look at my determined and probably forbidding expression. He turned around and let the door close behind him.

It was almost disappointing. I would have enjoyed enlisting Tom to help me convince Forrest Callic that Deputy Donut should not become his personal sales office.

I turned back toward the kitchen but only made it as far as

the table where Hannah and her friends were when my phone rang.

Ira, one of the Jolly Cops, told me, "I'm not calling about cleaning Deputy Donut, Emily. I'm throwing a party for the kids' football team I coach. Can I order a delivery of six dozen assorted donut bites for Tuesday afternoon?"

Samantha's baby shower was Tuesday evening, and I had Mondays and Tuesdays off. However, I didn't want to turn down an order. I could come in on Tuesday and help make the bites, and then I could do the delivery. "You certainly can. Tell me when and where, and I'll bring the donut bites in our delivery car. Kids like seeing our 1950 Ford with the donut on top."

"These boys would love that. The high school field, Tuesday at three?"

"Great! See you Tuesday at three at the high school field."

I disconnected. Hannah smiled up at me.

I gave her a thumbs-up. "Big order."

In the kitchen, Olivia, Tom, and I discussed flavors and toppings that kids might like. Olivia and Tom said they'd be glad to make the donut bites, and that I didn't need to come in on my day off. I agreed that I wouldn't come in to help in the kitchen unless they called me in desperation, but I insisted on making the delivery. "This place could become too busy for one of you three to leave for even a half hour. Besides, I get a kick out of showing off that car, especially to kids."

Olivia began protesting, but Tom glanced at the ceiling and then back at Olivia. "Emily does have fun with that. Besides, there's no point in arguing with her once she decides to do something."

Zachary, Joshua, and our other customers left. Hannah locked the front door, joined our planning session, and took notes.

Olivia asked her, "Are you going out to their campsite again tonight?"

"Probably. If you need the car, Zachary will pick me up and bring me back."

Olivia paused but said, in a non-sarcastic and nonjudgmental way, "I'm not going anywhere." And then when Hannah made suggestions about the flavors the kids on the football team might like best, Olivia agreed. It was almost praise for Hannah.

Tom and I traded smiles. The sisters were making progress.

Hannah and Tom took her list to the storeroom to check our inventory. For certain, we'd need to order the birthday cake and bubblegum flavoring extracts that Hannah was sure the kids would love.

Olivia and I collected creamers, bowls of sweeteners, and vases of flowers from the tables. I told Olivia that I'd talked to Laura at the grocery store. "She praised you and Hannah."

"That was nice of her. I've always done most of my shopping there. She worked there for years and then quit and started Cheese It. And now she's back at the grocery store."

"I loved Cheese It and was sorry she closed it."

"Poor Laura. One day when I was in the grocery store, she poured her heart out to me about it. Cheese It was going well, so Laura decided to expand and renovate. But there were delays and cost overruns, and then when the remodeling was supposedly finished, the store didn't look anything like Laura's plans. There were gaps between walls and cabinets, corners that stuck out all wrong, and uneven floors. It was not only ugly, Laura told me, it was hazardous. And her landlord thought so, too, and told her she had to have it all ripped out at her own expense."

"That sounds sort of like the story Charles told us about Albert McGoss building his deck." It also resembled Laura's story about the difficulties that unnamed people had experienced with Albert McGoss.

"It certainly does. Not only that, but the renovator had a partner who, I guess, could have been Kevin Lunnion. The partner paid back some of it, but not enough to cover the amount that Laura's landlord demanded for the damage to his building. Laura lost everything and had to close the shop. When she told me about it, she was boiling angry. She had hoped to franchise Cheese It and start a chain, but she ended up losing the shop that was supposed to begin her little empire. She was so angry that I thought she might rant about it every time I saw her, but she hasn't said a word about it since."

Laura had abruptly stopped talking to me about closing Cheese It and had wanted to help the next customer check out, even though that woman hadn't seemed quite ready. If Laura had killed Albert, she probably realized she shouldn't complain about her disastrous renovations in case someone connected them to Albert. Laura had told me she hadn't felt well and had left the grocery store shortly after Hannah shopped there on Friday evening. Did Laura then follow Albert to the Clifftop Trail?

Or did Albert's wife or Kevin Lunnion go to the Clifftop Trail, kill Albert, and push his body off?

Hannah, Joshua, and Zachary might have been in the area when it happened, but I was certain that Hannah would not have killed someone simply because he'd sent her away from a campground when she was about to leave anyway. Zachary seemed like a gentle soul. I wasn't sure about Joshua, but I couldn't imagine any of the three young people risking a possibly promising future by killing someone.

However, killers usually didn't expect to be caught.

After work, I put my poor kitty into her carrier again and drove her to our Maple Street house. Then, although I took her, still inside her carrier, out of the car, I left her inside the carrier while I toured the house and collected the mail. And to make matters even worse for Dep, after I was satisfied that everything in that house was fine, I again buckled her carrier, with her crying inside it, into the car's rear seat and headed north.

Driving out of Fallingbrook, I couldn't help thinking about Albert's murderer. Had the killer fled the Clifftop Trail in a vehicle, and would the investigators find tracks in the sandy soil of the nearby parking area that they could match to tires?

Who had been in the canoe I'd spotted when I returned to the dock after hearing that scream?

It didn't seem likely that it had been the killer, but I continued north past our driveway and went all the way to the bottom of the hill to Chicory Canoe Livery.

The owner, Barney, rose from a red Adirondack chair on his dock. In a rumpled khaki shirt and worn camouflage cargo pants, he ambled toward me as I parked and got out of my car. "Hey, Emily." He pointed with the stem of his pipe. "Like my new sign?"

I turned around and tried to read Barney's new sign. The painting emphasized certain letters of his company name. CHICORY CANOE LIVERY. Not sure what to say, I stared at the strange-looking, almost cryptic lettering.

Barney chuckled. "I'm calling my place Chicanery from now on. Now, can you read the word on the sign?"

"Since you explained it, yes."

"You folks in town have your cutesy company names. I thought I'd go with the flow. The wife says I should act my age, which is nearing eighty, but I won't say which side of eighty. Isn't whatever I do acting my age?"

I grinned. "That works for all of us."

"Precisely. What can Chicanery do for you this fine evening?" I occasionally detected Barney's long-ago Irish roots in his speech.

I gazed out toward the far shore. "Last night around six thirty, I saw someone in a canoe out there, and I couldn't figure out who it was. Had someone rented a canoe from you?"

Luckily he didn't seem to think my question was strange, and he didn't ask why I was being nosy. "It couldn't have been a canoe from here. We're closed this time of year except for weekends and by appointment, like if someone needs horses and carriages. No one reserved anything for yesterday, so I didn't bother coming out here. One of the concessions to advancing age that the wife forced me to make was having a place in town near the hospital and suchlike, staying there most of the time, and letting the kids look after the horses and everything here." He nodded toward the lineup of unpainted aluminum canoes and a couple of blue kayaks overturned on the shore. "My canoes and kayaks are all chained up."

"Are any missing?"

"No, and I can tell without counting. See, the row starts at that stump and ends over there at that rock, and there are no gaps. If I had to be counting boats all the time, I'd never get to do the important things, like sit in my chair there on the dock and ponder all the mysteries of this earth. Like white mushrooms that turn blue if you step on them. I've lived around here all my adult life and never heard of such a thing, but a young chap came out here and said he was studying them. Said they grew over there, about where you're looking." Again the pipestem came out of his mouth. He aimed it toward the Clifftop Trail, though even from where we stood, that trail and the cliffs it was on were hidden behind jutting headlands.

"I think I've met him in Deputy Donut. When did he tell you that?"

"Today. He asked about renting a canoe, but then he didn't do it. And on a day when we're open! Maybe he'll be back tomorrow or next weekend. Or he can reserve a canoe, and

I'll be sure to rent him one when he wants it. Business is business."

I thanked Barney. "I'll let you go back to your pondering."

"I shall do that until time to close for the evening. Wouldn't want to shirk and leave work early. Maybe someone's going to come along and give me some paying business to make all my pondering worth it. Not you. I know that you and Brent have boats of your own." He winked and turned toward the dock. He was wearing leather bedroom slippers.

I'd left windows open in my car for Dep. Her protests were verging on record-high decibel levels. I slid into the car and told her that everything was all right.

But, I muttered to myself, *not everything is quite all right.* If there had been chicanery involving a canoe the night before, the canoe had not, apparently, come from Barney's place.

As I'd expected, Brent's SUV wasn't parked outside the chalet. I lifted Dep out of the car and told her, "He and Rex need to find the killer quickly so that we won't have to be alone so much out here."

"Mew."

"I know, we're not totally isolated. Barney and his wife and their adult children are often down at the bottom of the hill."

"Mew."

"You're right. Misty should be here any minute to help plan Samantha's baby shower." I climbed the porch steps and opened the front door. "Misty probably won't tell us anything that will help us solve this latest murder, but maybe she'll let something slip." I gave Dep a stern look. "You and I will have to do whatever we can to help figure out who killed Albert McGoss. We didn't learn much at the Chicory Canoe Livery."

"Mewp?"

"Chicanery," I corrected myself. That seemed to satisfy my

kitty. I shut the door, took her out of her carrier, and snuggled her in my arms. She purred.

I changed into comfy leggings, a tunic, and flip-flops and returned to the kitchen section of the great room. I popped two twice-baked potatoes into the oven and concocted a fruit punch.

Misty arrived wearing jeans and a red plaid boyfriend shirt. I handed her a glass of punch. "Come see what Tom and Brent made."

She gazed around the inside of the screened-in catio. "Purrfect."

Dep demonstrated that Misty was right by climbing to one of the kitty-sized ledges, sitting down, and purring. We let her stay there while we went into the kitchen and made a leafy salad. I showed Misty the savory shortbread dough and cheese logs that I'd prepared for the shower. "And I made piecrust for mini quiches and other tarts."

"I've started dips for the veggie trays and made the dough for cheese puffs."

By the time our spicy sausages were grilled, the potatoes were ready. We ate out on the catio.

After we finished and cleaned up, we sat on one of the couches with a pile of baby shower magazines between us. I had already bookmarked articles about games.

Neither of us wanted to subject our guests to games involving melted chocolate and diapers. Or to being blindfolded and sniffing anything, even if it was supposedly baby food.

Misty ran a finger down a page. "Here's a cute one. We give each guest a list of animals and a pencil, and they have to write down what the animal baby is called, like owlet for owl and cygnet for swan. The guest with the most correct answers wins a prize. We'd have extra prizes in case of ties."

"I love it."

That was the first and only game on our list. I put the still nearly blank list down, lifted Dep off the pile of magazines, placed her on my lap, and gazed toward the dark woods beyond a window. "What if we put the letters of the alphabet into a baby hat, have people pull out a letter and come up with a name for the baby immediately, before the next person draws? That might be fast. And they wouldn't have to be real names. Depending on how creative people are, it could be fun."

"Add it to your list. Maybe we could all vote on the names, a first name and a middle name, and the people who proposed them win prizes."

"I like that." Dep had oozed off my lap and was now sitting on my list. I put her back onto my lap and wrote down our naming idea. I turned to another magazine article. "And how about a third game, the kind that can be played all evening, like this one—everyone starts out with one clothespin, and if they say the word 'baby' to anyone, that person gets their clothespin. The person with the most clothespins at the end of the day wins the prize." Dep batted at my pen.

Misty put a magazine back onto the pile. "That sounds like fun, and with that, we should have enough games. Everyone will be eating, plus Samantha will need time to open the gifts and ooh and aah over them."

I added the clothespin game to my list.

Misty asked, "Who did we hire to help in the kitchen during the shower?"

I stared at the list in front of me. Misty knew that we had hired Hannah, and Misty never forgot names or faces or any tiny details. I answered, anyway. "Tom's and my new assistant, Hannah."

"Maybe we should think of someone else we could call on if we need to."

I looked up at her, closed my mouth, and succeeded in not pinching my lips together in something like dread. "Brent and Rex don't suspect Hannah, do they?" Based on what Misty had just asked me, it was a silly question.

"They—we—haven't narrowed it down, but it is possible that Hannah and her two friends were in the vicinity at the time."

"So was I."

"Had you argued with the deceased?"

"No. I guess you know that he was in Deputy Donut with his wife Dawn the day before he was killed. They were arguing with Kevin Lunnion. Hannah served them. I didn't talk to Albert or his wife. Brent must have told you that when I went to pick up my lawn mower from Kevin, he wasn't there, even though he'd said he would be. That was an hour and a half before I heard someone scream."

Misty nodded. "Hooligan and I went with Brent as backup when he talked to Kevin. But I'm not sure what Kevin's motive would have been. He had solved his problem with Albert the day before by kicking him out of Lunnion's Lawns and Order."

"We don't know what other resentments might have been boiling under Kevin's skin. Maybe he felt threatened, or Albert knew something that Kevin didn't want made public?" I thought about the scene in Deputy Donut on Thursday afternoon. "But you could be right. Albert seemed to be the angrier of the two. Angriest of the three, I should say. Dawn barely said anything, but she was frowning and glaring, mostly at Kevin. What if Albert attempted to push Kevin over the cliff, and Kevin acted in self-defense? Kevin could have said he was at home all evening, even if he wasn't."

"Brent and Rex are considering all of it."

"Other people besides Kevin Lunnion must have had grievances with Albert McGoss. I'm guessing that Hannah and her friends aren't the only ones who have found Albert difficult at that campground." I told Misty about Charles saying his deck fell apart after Albert rebuilt it and about Laura's allegations that Albert might have abused his wife. I also mentioned Olivia's story about Laura's needing to end the business that she'd loved and hoped to franchise. "Even Tom said that the handyman part of Lunnion's Lawns and Order did not have a good reputation."

Picking up one of the leftover churros I'd brought home for dessert, Misty tilted her head. "Does Brent know what you just told me about Laura?"

"I haven't seen him since I found out about it. I'll tell him tonight if I'm still awake when he comes home."

He arrived shortly after Misty left. We took Dep out to the catio, turned off the lights, sipped wine, and gazed through the screens at the wooded hills, shadowy forms beneath the starlit sky.

I told Brent that Laura said she'd left the grocery store shortly after Hannah was there, and I also told him who I guessed might have been the person whose renovations caused her to give up her dream of franchising a chain of cheese stores. Brent thanked me and added, "I hadn't heard that Albert was the renovator who caused Cheese It to close, though it fits with what other people, including your customer, Charles, have been saying about their experiences with the man's workmanship. We'll look into it. Also, as you know, we always check out the nearest and dearest in homicides, so Dawn McGoss is also on our radar. Obviously, I can't tell you details about domestic disputes, but I should tell you that we have no record of complaints involving Dawn or her late husband."

I didn't point out that people didn't always report assaults. Brent knew that, and besides, he was pulling me close, and I couldn't have said more about the late Albert McGoss, even if I wanted to.

Chapter 13

✿

The next day was Sunday. Deputy Donut opened later than it did the other six days of the week, and ordinarily, Brent would merely be on call, but he and Rex needed to work on the Albert McGoss investigation.

Dep woke up around five thirty every morning, no matter what. Her self-appointed duty as an alarm clock gave us time to enjoy a leisurely breakfast on the catio with her. One of the best things about autumn was wearing sweaters again, and mine kept me cozy even though the sun wouldn't rise for over an hour. The dawn was fresh and lovely, and there were enough birds singing to keep us—and Dep—entertained.

Too soon, especially for her, Brent and I had to pack her into her carrier, belt the carrier inside my car, kiss each other goodbye, and head into town. Since we could never guarantee that we would be ready to go home at the same time, Brent drove to Fallingbrook in his own car. He followed me until he turned toward the police station. I continued down the block and parked behind Deputy Donut.

We weren't as busy as we would have been on a Sunday in summer, but in addition to the usual locals coming in for sweet treats and hot beverages, we had lots of tourists enjoying the activities that northern Wisconsin offered in the early fall—hunting, fishing, hiking, boating, and camping. The rivers, lakes, and waterfalls around Fallingbrook were always big attractions, especially that week, when the trees displayed some of their most vibrant colors.

During my lunch break, I left Dep in the office and walked down to The Craft Croft, the artisans' co-op that Summer managed.

Dressed in a long skirt, pretty blouse, and jacket, Summer was outside, hands on hips, studying the front window display. "Emily! Want a tour of the latest arts and crafts?"

I looked up, way up, into her face. She accentuated her height with stiletto heels. "I'd love it." And if towering over many of us wasn't enough, she piled her ruby red curls on top of her head.

The interior of The Craft Croft was as serene as ever, all white, glass, and brushed nickel, understated to allow the paintings, fabric art, jewelry, and glassware to shine. I groaned. "I should never come in here! I always want to buy nearly everything. Like that darling mobile!" Brightly painted wooden police cars, fire trucks, and even an ambulance dangled from it. "That could be perfect for the child of a police officer and an EMT. Do you know if anyone has bought one for Hooligan and Samantha's baby?"

"No one has. It's handmade and one-of-a-kind."

I got out my charge card. "Guess who's in town."

Those brown eyes radiated warmth similar to Rex's. "I already know. There was a murder, and Rex is here."

I raised my hand for a high-five. "He contacted you although you can't possibly know anything about the murder! That's a great sign."

"I hope so, but the reason he called me might not have anything to do with me. Despite investigating that murder in my parents' cabin, he liked Deepwish Lake, the cabin, and the idea of being able to walk outside and go kayaking. Before he left home this time, he phoned me to ask if the cabin was available for the next week or two. My parents take care of all that, so I gave him their number, and I think he's staying out at Deepwish Lake. I haven't seen him, though."

"He looks as good as ever. No wedding ring."

Again, the laugh rang out. "Maybe there's hope."

I reminded her, "He kept your number."

"He probably keeps every possible suspect's and witness's number, including yours."

"He doesn't need to. He can always reach me through Brent. I hope you get to see him while he's here."

"So do I."

I walked back to Deputy Donut and put the cute baby mobile in my car's front passenger seat.

Hannah went for her lunch, and Misty and Hooligan came in for their break. They asked us to refill their travel mugs with the day's special coffee, a medium roast from the Congo with fruity and floral hints, and they bought two dozen fresh-out-of-the-fryer and heavily sugared beignets to take back to their headquarters. Hooligan winked at me. "If they last that long."

Placing a baker's dozen in each box, I teased, "Maybe you should buy more, just to be sure."

They'd barely left with their purchases when Kevin Lunnion came in. That surprised me. After his interview with Brent, Hooligan, and Misty, I might have expected him to put hundreds of miles between himself and Fallingbrook. But there he was, sitting at a table and staring at me as if he hoped I'd wait on him right away. I would have preferred to go hide in the kitchen and leave him to Olivia or Tom. I reminded myself that I might learn something that I could pass on to Brent.

Hoping that Kevin would be the first to mention his former partner, I merely said, "Welcome back to Deputy Donut."

Kevin's smile was engaging, open, and friendly. "Emily, your mower is ready. I hope you didn't come looking for it Friday evening."

"I did. You weren't there."

"I'm sorry. I planned to make it home before you came, but it took me longer than I thought it would to get back from a job."

I managed a lame response. "That's okay. I can pick it up another time."

"You don't need to. It's in the back of my van. Give me your address, and I'll drop it off."

I wasn't about to tell him either of Brent's and my addresses. I pointed toward the parking lot behind our building. "My car's in back. We can transfer the mower to it." I glanced around the shop. "The other two can cover for me while I go out there. Would you like something to eat and drink first?"

"That would be great."

"What can I get you? How about apple cider donuts with an apple cider glaze? The cider is from a nearby orchard."

"I'd like two."

"Would you like anything to drink? Coffee, tea, milk, cider?"

"Cider sounds wonderful. If I drank coffee this late in the day, I'd never sleep."

I thought, *a guilty conscience might also keep you awake*, but I only said, "Would you like your cider cold, or mulled with cinnamon, ginger, and cloves?"

"Just cold."

When I took him the cider and donuts, he asked me, "Do you remember the couple I was with the last time I was in here?"

In an attempt not to fidget, I folded my hands in front of my Deputy Donut apron. "I saw them but didn't talk to them. I talked to you after they left."

"And I told you that I'd just broken up with my business partner, the man. Did you hear what happened to him?" *So,*

Kevin probably didn't know that my husband was the detective who talked to him in the night.

Or maybe he did.

I managed a slightly strangled question. "I, um, was he the man who died out at Chicory Lake?" Now it was really difficult to hold still and not fidget. Or run away. I didn't want to admit to Kevin that I had probably been nearby when his former partner was killed. But what if Kevin had been near the Clifftop Trail's lookout? He could have been skulking around in the woods or paddling a canoe. He could have seen me in my kayak or later, up near the top of the cliff. By not admitting that I'd been there, I could be informing a murderer that I suspected him, which seemed more dangerous than simply admitting that I had been there.

Luckily, since I'd asked a question, Kevin seemed to think it natural to answer it, and I could stop dithering about how much I dared to say. "Yes," he said.

"I'm sorry. It must be difficult—it is difficult—to lose someone you knew well."

"Thank you for understanding. As I told you the last time I was here, I ended Albert's and my partnership, but that doesn't mean I didn't care about him or what happened to him. In fact, I put off what I knew I needed to do simply because I didn't want to hurt him. I warned him a few times and kept hoping he'd improve, but he didn't seem capable of making an effort to do anything well or on time. And then he died only a day after I removed him from my company. I hope no one thinks that my dissolving our partnership had anything to do with his death. I was more hurt by his behavior than angry. If anything, he was angry at me, though if he'd wanted to make our partnership succeed, he should've worked harder. Do you know who might have been angry at him, though?"

"Who?" I tried not to sound breathless and excited.

"His wife. As far as I can tell, Dawn worked much harder

than her husband did, between her gift shop and helping host the campground. When I put an end to the income he got from me for doing basically nothing, who could blame his wife for being angry at him?" Kevin raised a cautioning hand. "I'm not saying that anyone killed Albert. He was careless, and never paid attention to detail, so I can imagine him climbing where he shouldn't, putting a foot in the wrong place, or not watching where he was going, with drastic consequences. Or maybe he and Dawn had an argument near the top of that cliff, and push came to shove, or something." The excuse Kevin was suggesting for Dawn could have applied to anyone, including Kevin himself.

Remembering suggesting a similar scenario to Misty involving Kevin and Albert struggling at the top of the cliff, I merely nodded.

However, Kevin wasn't watching me. He stared toward the front door. "When I was coming up the street, I saw a couple of police officers leaving. Were they questioning anyone in here about Albert's death?" Kevin looked at me then, with a gaze that seemed to pierce my skull.

I found it curious that he didn't admit that the two police officers he'd seen minutes ago had paid him a visit late Friday night. Brent had told me that Misty and Hooligan had gone as backup. Maybe Kevin hadn't gotten a good look at them that time. I gave him the honest answer. "They weren't here to question anyone. They picked up coffee and beignets to take back to the station. Lots of people who work around here come in for breaks."

"But they could have been observing someone in here. And they must have said something about what the police think happened to Albert."

"They didn't."

I wasn't sure that Kevin believed me, but he turned his head toward the kitchen and pointed. "Isn't that man back there Fallingbrook's former police chief?"

"Yes, that's Tom Westhill. He retired a few years ago."

"Betcha the police officers who come in here aren't tight-lipped around Chief Westhill. He probably gets to hear about investigations."

"He works in the kitchen most of the time, and I was the one who served the two officers. They didn't mention the case while they were in here."

"I've always thought that coffee shops must be like bars—good places to, you know, get a grasp on what's going on in the community."

This time, my smile was almost genuine. "I think you're right. People do love to gossip."

"Women gossip. Men discuss." Usually, I trusted people whose eyes twinkled like Kevin's, but I wasn't about to trust him. "Just kidding," he said. He bit into a donut. "Mmm." Chewing, he gave me a thumbs-up. "And this place is even better for donuts than for"—he grinned—"discussion."

I thanked him. "I'll leave you in peace to enjoy your donuts and coffee."

In the kitchen, I mumbled to Tom that the man I'd been talking to was Kevin Lunnion, the former partner of the man who had died. I added, "Before the murder, I dropped a reel mower off at his repair place. When he leaves, I'll go out with him to move the mower to my car. Can you keep—"

Tom interrupted me. "An eye on you? I could, but you're not going outside with him. Give me your car keys, and I'll do it." I agreed and put my key fob on the counter where Tom could reach it when he was ready.

I served other people, and then Kevin signaled for his bill. Paying me, he said, "Albert's death was probably an accident. The police have to investigate any unusual and unexpected death." Kevin still gave me no clue whether or not he knew I was married to Fallingbrook's detective. If he truly did not know, then he probably didn't know that I was spending most of my spare time out near Chicory Lake, and maybe he hadn't seen me kayaking or in the state forest and maybe he couldn't know that I might have caught a glimpse of Albert's killer.

But maybe Kevin was the killer, and he knew that I'd been in the vicinity when Albert died. Maybe Kevin suspected that I hadn't told him I was there because I was afraid of him. Which was true.

Possibly, Kevin was innocent and no danger to me.

His next words did nothing to make me feel safer. "It would be nice if the police let us know if Albert's death was an accident. If it wasn't, some random person might have attacked him, and who knows? We might all be in danger."

Had that comment been a veiled threat? I managed an almost confident reply. "I hope not."

I wasn't sure that Kevin heard me. Shoulders back like someone who had accomplished a mission, he stood up. "Shall we go out and move that mower now?"

What had his mission been? To threaten me into keeping quiet about the argument I'd witnessed between him and Albert? I asked, "What do I owe you?"

"I'll send a bill. Just give me an address."

"You can send it here." I told him the street number.

"Or I'll bring it, and have more of your delicious donuts."

"Great."

Tom had obviously noticed that Kevin was about to leave. He took off his apron, came out of the kitchen, and told Kevin, "Emily said you're about to put her mower into her car. I'll come out with you."

Kevin didn't seem upset by the change in plans. "Great, Chief Westhill." They went out through the front. As the door closed behind them, I heard Kevin say, "You must know a lot about this town and the people in it."

The door closed. I didn't hear Tom's response.

Chapter 14

✲

Tom brought me my key fob. "That man was full of questions, as if I would know everything going on in the police department. I don't trust him, Emily."

I put the fob in my pocket. "I don't, either."

Hannah returned from lunch, and Olivia took her turn. As often happened, Tom was the last of us to take a break. He returned, and most of the customers in the afternoon were tourists who either didn't know about the recent murder in Fallingbrook or had no interest in discussing it.

After we locked the doors and were finishing our tidying, Hannah turned toward Olivia. "Do you need your car tonight?" I wondered if Hannah asked the question in Tom's and my presence to try to avoid an argument.

Olivia took a second to answer. "No, feel free to use it." She sounded genial enough. "As long as your friends are in town, you might as well enjoy them."

Hannah glanced at her from beneath lowered eyelids. The expression could have been skeptical, but she answered in polite tones, "Thanks." Untying her apron, she hurried into the storeroom.

Olivia muttered to me, "As long as she stays off that motorcycle."

I gave Olivia an encouraging smile, but my heart ached for

her. When she'd been Hannah's age, she'd been too busy raising Hannah to have a social life of her own besides being
around the parents of Hannah's friends at school functions. I
didn't think that Olivia had ever had a serious romantic relationship. She would say that looking after her younger sister
was more important to her than anything else, but I wished
she could be even half as happy with someone as I was with
Brent. I mentally sorted through everyone I knew around
Fallingbrook but didn't come up with any possible matches
for Olivia.

Tom, Olivia, and Hannah waved goodbye and left. I put
Dep into her carrier.

Brent phoned. "Sorry, but I'm working late again. Rex and
I will grab something to eat."

I teased, "You'd better solve that case soon!"

"I agree." His voice was warm.

I told Brent about my conversation with Kevin Lunnion
and that the mower was now in my car. "I couldn't help
wondering if he was trying to learn all he could about the investigation so he could adjust whatever he tells you accord-
ingly. He also prodded Tom about what the police might be
doing."

"Does Lunnion know you're married to me, or that you
are often out at Chicory Lake and might have witnessed
some of what happened that night?"

"If he knew, he didn't let on. I didn't tell him any of it."

He asked, "Would you like to stay in town tonight?"

"Would you?"

"I will if you are."

I was sure he wanted to go out to the country property, although he wouldn't be able to be there long before he had to
go back to work. I said, "I'll check on the house here, put the
mower away, and then go out to the lake."

"Okay, see you tonight."

Poor Dep. She wailed all the way to our house in town,

and again, I didn't let her out of the carrier, even after I set it on the living room floor. I told her, "I'll be back for you in a few minutes."

I went outside, removed the mower from the SUV, and tried it out on the pocket-sized front lawn. It worked beautifully, and I quickly cut the grass. I put the mower away in the garage and went back into the house.

Dep grumbled while I hugged her, carrier and all, and walked around the house. Nothing had changed since she and I had checked the evening before. I picked up the mail and buckled Dep's carrier into the rear seat of the car.

She made disapproving remarks until I unzipped her carrier in the great room of the house on Chicory Lake. She sprinted to her basket of toys, pulled out a catnip-stuffed donut, and batted it over the smooth wood floor.

She and I ate a quick dinner in our screened-in catio. The view was great, and Dep, though she stared outside the entire time, was good company.

I missed Brent.

Cleaning up after dinner was quick. I brought Dep inside, set her on the floor, and told her, "I'm going for a drive. You can lounge around here." She ran up the stairs to the loft and peeked down at me between two of the railing's balusters.

Although I'd spent all of my life in Fallingbrook except when I was away at college, I had never explored much of the vast Chicory Lake State Forest. I'd hiked there as a teenager with friends once or twice, and after Brent bought this property on the hill above Chicory Lake, I'd been out in a kayak many times. And on Friday, I had searched for and found the Clifftop Trail. But other than that, I hadn't seen much of the state forest. I wasn't sure I'd ever been to the campground where Zachary and Joshua were staying.

I turned left at the end of our driveway. Near the top of the hill, I turned left again, into the state forest.

On Friday I had driven quickly, following the chain of narrow roads through hills and valleys until I arrived near the east side of Chicory Lake. In my hurry that night, I had ignored signs for other trails—but hadn't I seen signs for at least one campground?

I drove slowly. The road wound around boulders and outcroppings. The sun was low, sending beams slanting between deep green pines and aspens that had turned yellow near their tops. The road curved down to the right. Just before it edged uphill and angled toward the left, a brown wooden sign in the shape of an arrow pointed right. Yellow-painted letters carved into the sign said HERBGROVE LAKE CAMPGROUND. I slowed and turned down the road.

It meandered mostly southeast, down a wooded hill. I half expected to be stopped at a gate or a kiosk. Instead, a tented wooden roof beside the road sheltered a built-in table, a sign with instructions, a box of registration cards, and a drop box for completed cards. A pencil tied to a string dangled from the table. I wasn't registering, so I didn't stop.

On the right, a few yards farther into the campground, a weathered camper trailer, once white but now dotted with mildew, occupied the first campsite. I slowed more but didn't stop. A handprinted sign in the trailer's window said CAMPGROUND HOST. No other vehicles besides the trailer were at the site. The firepit appeared to hold only ashes, and the picnic table was bare except for fallen leaves and piles of small brownish fragments that could have come from chewed acorns and pinecones. Nestled in the woods, the site should have looked peaceful and tranquil, but it was slightly off. It lacked the homey touches of lawn chairs, hammocks, and camp stoves that campers often left outside when they were there or didn't expect to be gone long. Was the site as abandoned as it appeared, or was Dawn inside the trailer, grieving, lonely, and desolated? Wherever she was, I couldn't help a pang of sympathy for her. Reminding myself that she might have murdered her husband, I continued into the campground.

Creeping along, I lowered my window. After my years of spending all or parts of summers with my parents at the Fallingbrook Falls Campground, I relished the nostalgic smell of woodsmoke and the distant sounds of cheerful voices, tent stakes being hammered into the ground, and an axe smacking into wood. Children shrieked with glee.

The campsites were separated by bands of trees, giving the entire place a woodsy feel. People were washing dishes, taking swimsuits and towels off clotheslines, and tending campfires. Toddlers padded around in footed sleepers. Strangers waved. I waved back.

Ahead on the right, I saw Zachary's pickup truck. It had pulled into the site forward, and the door at the back of the camper cap on the truck's bed was open, showing a red plaid sleeping bag and a cartoon-printed pillow on a foam mat. Zachary was sitting in a low, folding chair beside the picnic table. With his legs stretched out in front of him, he was reading. Although the sky was still light, trees caused an early dusk, and an old-fashioned gas camping lantern on the table beside Zachary lit the booklet in his hands. A small tent was near the back of the site.

Neither Joshua nor Hannah was nearby, and I didn't see Joshua's motorcycle or Olivia's car.

I lifted my foot from the gas momentarily but decided to keep going. I was there to see the campground, not to question Zachary or anyone else.

He lifted his head, gave my car an impersonal glance, and then seemed to notice me. He leaped to his feet. An expression of something like fear crossed his face.

I braked and pulled into the site's parking area behind his truck.

I'd barely gotten out of the car before he demanded, "Is Hannah okay?"

"As far as I know, yes. Is she . . . late or something?"

He blushed, "No. I don't even know if she's coming here

tonight, but when I saw you, I thought maybe you'd come because for some reason she couldn't tell me that something was wrong. If something was wrong. And she asked you to find me. You being her boss." His explanation was almost as mangled as the booklet he was crumpling between his hands. Blushing even more, he asked, "Did you come here looking for her?"

"No. I live nearby, but I haven't lived there long, and I thought it was about time to explore the state forest." It was close to the truth. "I don't know where Hannah is. She could be at home with Olivia, but I think she plans to borrow Olivia's car this evening." Maybe I shouldn't have told Zachary that. Hope brightened his eyes and quickly disappeared. I added, "I'm not sure where she planned to drive."

Zachary bit his lip, didn't say anything, and continued rolling the booklet between his hands. Laughter burst from a trailer down the road.

I gazed around Zachary's tidy campsite. "I thought Joshua was staying here, but I don't see his motorcycle."

Zachary turned and pointed at the small tent. "That's his tent. I sleep in my truck. He left a couple of hours ago because he's tired of my cooking. He was going to look for a restaurant."

"Do you think Hannah's with him?"

Zachary lifted one shoulder as if he didn't really care. "Probably."

"Even though she said she's borrowing Olivia's car, I hope she doesn't leave it somewhere and go off with Joshua on his motorcycle."

"It's probably safe, but I get you. That's one battle she doesn't need to pick with Olivia. Those two are close, or they were before Joshua came along. I don't think he cares about Hannah. He just wants to make a conquest. Then he'll go and leave her brokenhearted while he pursues someone else."

I didn't let on that I'd been suspecting similar things.

Zachary looked down toward his hiking boots. "I'll be there for her if she needs me." Again, that one-shouldered shrug, and he met my eyes again. "But maybe she won't want me near her."

"She should."

"Not if she thinks I'm like Joshua."

"I doubt that she does." Hannah had implied that Joshua was more exciting than Zachary. "She must know that you are reliable."

"Reliable. For all the good that does." Like a disappointed child, he kicked at the dirt.

I asked him, "Why are you camping with Joshua? Are you two good friends?"

"I barely know him, but before she left school, Hannah mentioned in his hearing that she was going home, and when he heard that I was driving to the Fallingbrook area for research, he said he'd join me. Luckily—or maybe not—he has his own transportation, and we don't have to stay together all of the time."

"Like Friday evening? Were you three together then? Hannah said she and Joshua went grocery shopping."

Zachary gazed down at the curled-up booklet in his hands. "If that's what she said, that's where she was."

"Didn't you go with them?"

"I wasn't invited. Despite what Joshua might have said, we didn't need groceries, at least not for the meals I make. Joshua's tent was brand new when he got here. He didn't have a clue about setting it up. I doubt that he's ever been camping before."

I stated what I thought was obvious. "And you have."

"All my life. And I hope to do lots more, studying fungi for a career. And probably teaching."

A squirrel chittered in apparent annoyance in the top branches of an oak tree above us. I glanced up, but the squirrel was hidden among leatherlike leaves. "Do you know what Joshua's career goals are?"

"Only that he plans to be wealthy." Zachary gave me a half smile that didn't reach his eyes. "Probably selling snake oil."

"Don't you trust him?"

The smile became more genuine. "Maybe I'm only imagining faults that I hope Hannah will see. But I'm realistic. Even if she doesn't fall for him, she might never come back to me, and I'll have to accept that. I won't chase after her if she doesn't want me near her."

Ouch. Brent and I had spent too much time being afraid of letting each other know how we felt. I hinted, "Maybe she could use a nudge. I'm sure she likes you."

"She did, but she's young. She needs to figure out what she wants in life, whether it's school or something else. She needs to figure out who she is before she can know who she wants to be with. I mean, like for more than a few dates."

"Maybe she'll soon realize that Joshua is not the one for her."

He exhaled. "I might not be, either, but he really isn't."

"I don't think so, either, but why do you say that?"

Zachary smiled at three boys wobbling past on bicycles and shouting about who would win their race. "Sometimes Joshua lets his anger get the better of him. No woman should have to put up with that type of personality."

I agreed. "Unfortunately, lots of women do. I got the impression that Joshua argued more with Albert McGoss the night before Albert was murdered than you and Hannah did."

"Absolutely. I was playing my guitar, and we were singing. The campground host came stomping into our site and yelled at us to stop making noise. Joshua shouted that the host was making more noise with his yelling than we'd been with our singing. It escalated. The host shouted at all of us and told Hannah to leave. The host even became aggressive—you know, thrusting his chin forward, making fists, and getting into Joshua's personal space."

That night, Zachary, Joshua, and Hannah had sung around a campfire. Now, kindling and logs were tented in Joshua and Zachary's firepit. I wondered if Zachary was waiting for Hannah before lighting the fire. The area around the firepit was cramped. A physical brawl between Albert and three people near the fire could have been disastrous. I asked, "Did any of you threaten McGoss either verbally or physically?" I was sounding too much like a detective.

"Yeah. Hannah grabbed Joshua's arm and held him back, so Joshua resorted to a verbal threat. He said he was going to report McGoss to his employers. McGoss scoffed that he wasn't an employee. He hosted this campground as a volunteer and was chosen out of all the other applicants. Hannah stayed between McGoss and Joshua until Joshua started acting less like he was going to let himself be pulled into a fist-fight, and then Hannah got into Olivia's car and drove away. McGoss made rude gestures and stomped back toward his trailer."

"So, McGoss won the argument and got the last word?"

"I suppose. I was worried about Hannah and didn't pay much attention to the other two."

"Was Joshua angry about the argument?"

"I was. More annoyed, really. I think Joshua was simmering, but he didn't say a thing about it after McGoss left. Swearing at his tent's zipper for pinching the nylon or going off its track or something, Joshua managed to close himself inside his tent. I put out the fire and went to bed. I didn't hear another word from Joshua until the next morning. By then, he seemed to have gotten over his anger."

Or, I thought, *he hid his anger until the next evening.* I asked, "Do you think that Joshua could have been hiking alone on the Clifftop Trail on Friday evening, like after he went grocery shopping with Hannah?" If Laura had been telling the truth, Joshua hadn't been in the store, with or without Hannah, that evening. Joshua could have followed

Albert McGoss. The two men could have ended up at the outlook on the Clifftop Trail at the same time.

Zachary didn't exactly answer my question. He merely said, "Joshua's not a bad guy, really. If he pushed anyone off a cliff, it would have been an accident. Your husband and a couple of other police officers came here and questioned the three of us separately, so I told them all of this. I don't think that Joshua actually went out and hurt anyone. I just don't think he's good enough for Hannah." Zachary took a deep breath. "You're trying to protect Hannah, too, aren't you, Emily?"

"Not only from Joshua. I'd like to keep her from being the suspect in a murder investigation. I'm sure that Hannah wouldn't purposely harm anyone."

"Me, too. Also, I'm sure that Joshua would not have gone near that lookout. He wouldn't hike by himself in the woods. He's not really the outdoorsy type, and besides, he likes to be seen being the hero or the he-man or whatever. Also, he's not as wealthy as he plans to be, and that motorcycle is his prize possession." Zachary glanced ruefully toward his old but well-maintained pickup truck. "It's his chick magnet. He wouldn't go far from that motorcycle and leave it alone in a parking area in a remote state forest."

Something must have shown on my face.

Zachary's lips twisted. "You're wondering how I know how far it is from the parking area to the place where Mc-Goss fell. Maps. When you drove up, I was looking at maps of trails in this state forest and trying to guess where I would most likely find the mushrooms I'm studying, the cornflower boletes. Come see." Zachary led me to the picnic table and smoothed the booklet he'd been rumpling. The softly hissing camp lantern shed light on the book's title—*Chicory Lake State Forest*. Zachary turned pages and showed me a map of the part of Chicory Lake adjacent to the cliffs where the lookout was. "That lookout is about a quarter mile from the parking area. And these hills are forested. Joshua's motorcycle would have been out of his sight. He wouldn't have gone to the lookout." Zachary pointed at the map and added, "Here's the Cornflower Trail. That's the one where the cornflower boletes are supposed to be abundant." Zachary's sudden enthusiasm made him seem about twelve years old.

"Haven't you checked?"

"It's accessed by water only. From this map, you might think that the Cornflower Trail comes close to the Clifftop Trail, but you can see from these elevation lines that the Cornflower Trail is at the bottom of the hill, and the Clifftop Trail is actually quite a distance away because it's almost straight up."

Wondering if Zachary would admit to having talked to Barney at Chicanery, I told him, "There's a boat rental place on Chicory Lake."

"It's only open weekends in the fall."

"It's Sunday. You've lost a weekend." I glanced up at the sky. Between tree branches, stars were starting to appear.

"I've been exploring parts of the state forest that I can drive to. I plan to be here next weekend, too. Or the guy at the canoe rental place said I could call and reserve a canoe during the week. I might do that and check out the Cornflower Trail before next weekend, but I'm not in a hurry." His crooked smile was boyish and charming. "I mean, what if there are no cornflower boletes on that trail, after all? That would be a huge disappointment. Also, after I have a look at those, I won't have much of an excuse to stay up here."

I hadn't taken time to put on a sweater over my short-sleeved Deputy Donut polo shirt. I tried to warm my upper arms with my hands. "It's going to turn cold for camping."

"It's been unseasonably warm, so maybe it will hold off." With a wistful smile, he said, "I wonder if it's true that absence makes the heart grow fonder. Probably, in some cases." His vulnerability was endearing.

I lightened the moment by teasing, "Maybe if Olivia told Hannah that she should date Joshua, not you, Hannah would come back to you."

Zachary laughed. "Olivia has already made it plain—to Hannah and to me—that Olivia would like to see us together. Olivia doesn't change her mind easily. If she pretended to, Hannah would know that Olivia was trying reverse psychology. Hannah wouldn't fall for it."

"You're right. You seem to know them both well."

"I do, and I think they're both wonderful."

"So do I. And I agree with Olivia about you."

Zachary thanked me, and I left him to his map booklet, fungus research, and unlit campfire.

Driving along the dirt road looping through the campground, I reminded myself to be cautious. Believing that Zachary was a good person could turn out to be dangerous for Hannah.

And also, possibly, for me.

Chapter 15

I was too willing to like Zachary and believe him. I needed to be more analytical and rational.

Zachary had casually mentioned that if Joshua had pushed Albert McGoss off the cliff, it would have been an accident.

Zachary had also said that Joshua would not have gone all the way to the lookout.

Had Zachary hoped I might conclude that Joshua could have abandoned his motorcycle for a few minutes and had killed Albert, perhaps accidentally?

Why would Zachary hint, in a roundabout way, that Joshua could be the murderer?

Maybe Zachary had said similar things to investigators in the hope that Joshua would be arrested for Albert's murder, and then Hannah might lose interest in Joshua and return to Zachary.

Blaming Joshua could have been a motive for Zachary himself to kill Albert.

I continued to rebel at the thought of Zachary harming anyone. Was I sure that he was a good person, or did I want to believe he was innocent and that he and Hannah could live a long and happy life together? I muttered, "You carry your matchmaking too far, Emily."

As always in a campground, I drove slowly. The sites were

quieter now that darkness had fallen. Firelight lit the faces of people intent on roasting marshmallows. Near the campground's exit, my headlights shined on Albert and Dawn McGoss's trailer and campsite. I slowed for a better look.

With her back to the road, a woman in pink culottes and a matching tunic stood next to the McGoss trailer. She had cupped her hands beside her eyes and appeared to be attempting to peer through one of the trailer's windows. My first thought was that maybe Dawn had locked herself out of her trailer, and then I realized that the woman was much shorter than Dawn.

The woman must have heard my car on the road behind her. She turned, waved, and strode toward me. Sparkly printed seashells spilled across the front of her tunic and culottes, from one shoulder to the opposite knee.

I stopped the car.

She came to my open window. "Are you looking for a campsite? I can help you."

"I—"

She patted her head. "Excuse the curlers. Have you picked out a site?"

I quickly came up with an excuse for snooping. "I wasn't planning to camp. I'm just curious about the campground. Do you recommend it?"

"I certainly do, and it has gotten better recently. Come join Harv and me at our campfire, and we'll tell you all about it."

Even though it was getting late, her offer was too good to refuse. I tried not to appear as eager as I was. "Isn't there a curfew?"

"Not until midnight, and you won't be staying that long. And it wouldn't matter anyway, especially now, when . . . it's a long story. Park your car—the side of the road here will do just fine—and come join us. Careful, don't trip over the tent stakes and guy ropes."

I followed her into a campsite where almost all of the

ground was covered with chairs, tables, screened rooms, and multiple appliances for outdoor cooking, including a deep fryer. Tarpaulins strung between trees and poles provided shelter over most of the site. A ferocious-looking pickup truck guarded the driveway in front of a sizeable trailer.

The woman pointed to a wooden sign on their trailer. The words THE DRIFTERS were burned into the sign. Smaller letters below said HARV AND ESSIE. "We're the Drifters, and that's our real name. I'm Harv." She patted the balding head of the gaunt man sitting on a low armchair and gazing into the fire. "And he's Essie."

The man grunted a laugh. I suspected that this wasn't the first time he'd heard the joke.

I smiled.

The woman patted my arm. "Just kidding. He's Harv, and I'm Essie." She peered expectantly up at me.

Being taller than another adult was unusual for me. "I'm Emily."

"Grab a seat, Emily. Not mine, and especially not Harv's, ha ha."

Harv stared into the fire.

I moved a lawn chair to the fire and sat down.

I didn't have to wait long for Essie to begin the stories she'd promised. "I told you that you didn't need to worry about the curfew anymore. That's because the regular campground hosts are dead."

My "Oh!" came out like a gasp.

Harv grunted.

Essie lifted a hand as if to silence her husband, although he had not yet said a word. "Well, the man is dead. His wife disappeared."

I managed not to gasp again. With what I hoped passed as polite interest, I lifted one eyebrow.

Essie leaned toward me and spoke conspiratorially. "That's why I was over at their trailer just now, wondering if maybe someone had dropped her off, and she was in there, sick or something. We haven't seen her since Thursday night. Her husband, Albert, started a shouting match with campers, and she got into her own car and drove away. I mean, who could blame her? The campers weren't doing anything wrong, but Albert's hollering must have awakened everyone for miles around. And then Albert died from a fall the next night, Friday. Only, we think he was murdered, don't we, Harv?"

"Huh."

Essie turned her attention back to me. "See, detectives and other police officers keep coming around asking everyone where they were Friday evening, and why would a detective go around questioning people if it wasn't a murder?"

Not about to tell her that one of the detectives was my husband and that she was right that he suspected foul play, I didn't say anything.

My silence must have gone unnoticed. Essie continued, "Besides, I'd heard sirens earlier in the evening, and I got Harv to drive me the direction they went. We came to police tape strung across a road. I can tell you that sight gave me instant palpitations! We couldn't drive past that tape, but we could duck underneath."

Harv cleared his throat.

"Well, not go underneath precisely. See underneath, um, beyond it. And there were police cars and fire trucks, including a search and rescue vehicle. They were near the beginning of a trail that runs along the cliffs, so when the detectives and police officers were asking when we'd last seen the campground host, Albert McGoss, I put two and two together, and I just knew that Albert must have fallen from the lookout on the Clifftop Trail, or even from that balancing boulder near it." Essie shuddered. "And early Saturday, a reporter came here asking questions, too, and I told him what I was sure had happened, and where. And the next thing I knew, it was in the papers, thanks to little old me! That was the first time anything I ever said was in the newspapers. Well, they do say that we all get our fifteen minutes of fame. Since then, I've been warning everyone in this campground that the Clifftop Trail, and that boulder, are dangerous. I wouldn't want anyone else to die there. We'd like to believe it was an accident, but here's the thing—Albert wasn't a hiker. Someone must have taken him to the top of the cliff or that boulder and shoved him off."

I didn't have to pretend to be shocked. "Who would do such a thing, and why?"

Essie didn't need to pause to think about it. "We think his wife killed him, don't we, Harv?"

Harv didn't take his gaze away from the fire. "Yup."

Essie explained, "They had fights, like loud arguments, those two, and they didn't seem to realize how much sound comes out of these trailers. Theirs is especially flimsy." She lowered her voice again. "And we're pretty sure he hit her, aren't we, Harv?"

"Yup." Sighing, Harv shook his head. "Horrible."

Essie pointed at her bare arms. "Dawn always wore long sleeves and long pants, even when it was hot and there were hardly any bugs. And sometimes her makeup was extra heavy, like she was trying to cover up a black eye or other bruises. Several times, she claimed she'd walked into a door. At least once, she said she'd tripped over the leg of their picnic table." Essie pointed at the traditional picnic table in the McGoss's campsite. "Those legs are made of thick logs, and they do angle outwards, but still, it's not like a leg could suddenly . . ."

"Jump out and trip her," Harv said.

Essie barely had time to draw another breath. "And Dawn must have had a powerful grudge against her husband. She did all of the work around here while he just lazed around. Not that either one of them exactly did the job they were supposed to do. They were almost never here. They hardly ever cleaned the johns. In fact, just about the only thing that Albert could be counted on doing was enforcing rules, like yelling at campers he didn't like. His friends could make noise, but perfectly nice young people couldn't do anything. Thursday night, I got so upset by Albert's yelling that I crept closer and spied on him yelling at some kids."

Harv cleared his throat.

"Not kids, exactly," Essie said. "Young people."

Harv coughed behind a gnarled hand.

Essie added, "And I wasn't spying, really, it's more like I was there with my phone's camera in case Albert became violent, which I wouldn't put past him. Actually, I think that only the two young men are actually camping here. One's perfectly nice and polite and quiet. The other one drives a motorcycle, so he can't help being noisy. And he was the one shouting back at Albert. I felt sorry for the girl. Albert told her she had to leave. She didn't argue. She got into her car and drove away, but I could tell she was upset at anyone treating her that way. She was close to tears, poor thing." Essie took another breath.

Harv shook his head. "Rules." The word came out like a prediction of doom.

The fire snapped and shot out sparks. Despite having spent many hours sitting next to campfires, I jumped.

Essie waved smoke away from her face. "Right, Albert was a stickler for rules, especially if he didn't have to follow them himself. Like, he and Dawn could keep their trailer in the same spot for the entire season. But the rest of us, no. You can't stay in Wisconsin campsites for more than fourteen days at a time. Most campground hosts—and remember, they're not law enforcement, they're only there to serve the camping public—would let people stay more than two weeks if no one else wanted the site. But not Albert. We had to haul our trailer out of here on the dot after two weeks and stay away at least twenty-four hours before we could return, often to the site we'd just left, this one, usually, since most people prefer being closer to the beach. This entire campground is almost never fully booked." The volume of Essie's voice was rising again. "There was no reason not to let us stay or move to another site if someone reserved ours."

Harv contributed, "All summer."

Essie leaned toward me and spoke quietly again. "Albert and Dawn got to stay here all summer, every year, and we didn't. And it's more than just summer. There's part of spring and fall, too. It doesn't make any sense for people like that, who barely lift a finger, to be able to do that, when other people would be better at looking after everything and everyone. I mean, shouldn't hosts be friendly and gracious instead of antisocial and grumpy? Also, good hosts would stay here all of the time except for grocery runs. That's all we'd do, right Harv? We'd never go away?"

"We don't now. Except—" He yawned.

Essie finished his sentence. "Except when Albert forced us to."

I asked, "Does the campground host have to be a couple?"

Essie sighed. "I doubt that it's an official regulation. One person could do it, but a couple is best. There are more chances for campers to identify with at least one of them and, you know, feel at home." She nudged Harv with an elbow. "And there should be a man to clean the johns."

Harv yawned again.

Essie stretched her legs toward the fire. "We'll apply to host this campground next season in case, you know, Dawn no longer wants the job."

Harv's grunt sounded skeptical.

Essie defended her statement. "She might not. Maybe Albert forced her into hosting. I don't think they have anywhere else to live besides a room behind her gift shop. With him gone, that one-room apartment won't be as crowded, and maybe she'd prefer to stay near her shop and not have to come out here all the time to work another job." Essie gazed into the distance over the dying embers. "It would be really nice to stay here all season. We know so many of the regulars, and I love meeting new people. Plus we already fill in, without being asked, for Albert and Dawn whenever they're not around and campers need help. It's not like we haven't been doing a lot of their job for years. And if we could become hosts here, you wouldn't have to back that trailer into position every couple of weeks, Harv. Or into our driveway, either."

Harv nodded. I wasn't sure if he was agreeing or about to fall asleep. His eyelids drooped, and his yawns were becoming more frequent. The campfire was dying. Essie's hair was in curlers, and despite the glittery seashells, her outfit might have actually been pajamas.

I stood. "Thank you. You've convinced me that this is a nice place to stay."

Essie stood, too, and brushed at the seat of her culottes. "It is. And you should see it in daylight. Come back and check out our beach! Herbgrove Lake is small, no motorboats, and lots of us like it that way. And just listen, now. It hasn't been dark that long, and the place is almost completely quiet. Hold on a second. I'll get a flashlight and walk you to your car."

My car was barely ten feet away, and I could see it in the dwindling firelight, but Essie insisted. Her light was so bright that everything except what it illuminated became a dark blur. She grasped my arm. "Careful, Emily. The ground's uneven."

Neither of us tripped. At my car, I opened the driver's door and thanked Essie again.

She gazed toward the McGoss trailer and lowered her voice. "Albert might have had another enemy besides Dawn. Friday morning, I was cooking bacon." She gestured back toward her trailer. "The stove's by the kitchen window. Albert came stumbling out of his trailer in his pajamas and with his hair going every which way. He went straight to their picnic table, the one you see over there, and picked up a rock. A rock! I thought, *trust him to leave a rock on the picnic table when his wife's not there.* Her car was still gone, so I assumed that she was, too. Then he picked up a small piece of paper from where the rock had been, and stared at the paper, but he wasn't wearing his glasses, so I doubt that he could see what was on it. He stuffed it into the pocket of his pajama top. Then he tossed the rock into the bushes and glared toward the direction where the young men were camping, though I doubt that they were making a noise. At least, I didn't hear anything, but our trailer windows were closed, and you know how much noise bacon can make when it's frying."

"Yes. And how good it smells, especially in a campground."

"You got that right. But since Albert was staring toward those boys' campsite, I'm guessing they left him a note. Maybe an apology?"

I didn't point out that if Albert was staring toward Joshua and Zachary's site, he was also staring toward most of the other sites in the campground. I thought about suggesting that she should call the detectives and tell them about the note, but remembering her pride in being the source for a reporter, I decided that I shouldn't let her guess that the piece of paper could be important to the case. I would tell Brent what she said, and maybe he could interview her before a reporter leaked a possibly important clue to the public. I hoped my next question would not cause her to conclude that the note Albert might have received was newsworthy. "Did you see or hear anyone near Albert's trailer during the night?"

"Not a soul, except I thought I woke up slightly once during the night and heard a car engine, like maybe Dawn coming back, but I didn't get up and look. I had a feeling it was a noisier engine than Dawn's and that it didn't come close to our trailer, so it wasn't really my concern. Besides, I was barely awake, and Harv was snoring enough to vibrate our entire trailer, so I just dozed off again, and I didn't really think about it until now. One of those boys must have left Albert a note apologizing. If they walked to Albert's picnic table, and didn't ride a motorcycle, I wouldn't have heard them come and go." She shook her head. Her curlers rattled. "Poor Albert. You're not to think we're glad he's gone. No one should go before their time, and he was still young. It's sad, even though Dawn might not exactly agree. You take care, now, Emily, and be sure to stop by and see us if you do decide to camp here."

I promised her I would, got into my car, and shut the door. I watched until Essie was back at her trailer door and waved her flashlight in my direction. I couldn't see Harv, but a light had gone on inside the trailer.

I started the car and drove slowly through the state forest.

Like nearly everyone else at that campground, Harv and Essie could have found the means and the opportunity to kill Albert McGoss and shove his body over the cliff, but I wasn't sure that disliking backing a trailer into parking spaces or wanting to take over a volunteer position that involved cleaning outdoor toilets qualified as a motive for murder. Besides, if they were correct that Albert and Dawn's hosting of the campground was far from adequate, anyone else applying for the volunteer position, even if Albert were still alive, probably had a good chance of being accepted. Harv and Essie Drifter, who were, if they were to be believed, already doing a large part of the job, wouldn't have had to murder Albert.

I drove home. Brent's car wasn't there.

Inside, I cuddled Dep on one of the couches, and wondered about Essie, Harv, Joshua, Zachary, and the seemingly pleasant campground where they were all staying.

A familiar step sounded on the porch. With Dep in my

arms, I rushed to open the front door. Brent swept us into a bear hug.

I said into his suit jacket, "Have you eaten?"

"We had sandwiches. You?"

"Same. I could use an apple and some cookies."

We trooped into the kitchen section of the great room and grabbed fruit, cookies, and milk, and then we turned on the fairy lights in the catio and ate outside in the fresh, cool night.

I asked Brent, "How's the investigation going?"

"Rex and I are still asking a lot of people a lot of questions."

"Do you know where Rex is staying?"

Brent's eyes twinkled. "At Summer's parents' cabin on Deepwish Lake. He's hoping to take at least a short vacation there after we complete the investigation."

"Summer told me she'd given him her parents' phone number, but she didn't know if he'd called them. Do you think he might be interested in Summer? She's interested in him."

"I think that's why he's staying south of Fallingbrook instead of near the police station or the scene of the crime. But as you've probably noticed, he hasn't had enough time to start a proper courtship."

"Who said it had to be proper?"

He laughed. "He's probably found time to at least call her by now."

"If nothing else, there must be something about that cabin that needs explaining."

Brent agreed. "By Summer, and not by her parents."

Before we got any cozier, I had to admit, "I went to the Herbgrove Lake Campground this evening."

"Why?"

I fudged a little. "I hoped to be able to get a better idea of what Hannah's two admirers are actually like. I wasn't sure if it was the right campground, but I saw Zachary there. I stopped to talk. I'd have liked to have seen more of how

Hannah interacted with her two admirers so I could get an idea of how to help protect her from them if necessary, but she and Joshua didn't show up. I hope Hannah wasn't riding around on Joshua's motorcycle. Olivia would collapse."

"Olivia needs to remember that her younger sister is practically grown up."

"I know, and I guess I should, too, but it's hard not to want to keep her—or anyone—from being harmed."

"I know the feeling."

"I got waylaid when I tried to leave the campground. By the Drifters, Harv and Essie. Well, really by Essie. That woman likes to talk."

"I noticed. What did you learn from her?"

Brent grinned at my imitations of Essie and her less loquacious husband. Essie had also purposely switched her and Harv's names when she introduced herself to Brent. I told him, "They suspect Dawn. I caught Essie peering into their trailer. She claimed that Dawn had disappeared, and Essie was checking for her. I thought it was her excuse for spying."

"Probably. Dawn might not have been back to the campground recently, but she hasn't disappeared. We've talked to her."

"Later, when Essie had me to herself and we were out of Harv's hearing, she told me she saw Albert come out of his trailer Friday morning, lift a rock off his picnic table, pick up a piece of paper, and then stuff the paper into a pajama pocket. Essie thought she might have heard a noisy engine, noisier than Dawn's, during the night on Thursday, but she wasn't awake enough to be sure. She guessed that Joshua or Zachary walked over from their campsite and left a note apologizing for their behavior earlier in the night. My impression is that Essie tends to put a positive spin on things, except Albert possibly hitting Dawn."

"She didn't tell me about that note."

"She can distract herself and go off on tangents."

Brent fetched his notebook, wrote down what I'd told him, and put the notebook aside. "Rex and I will go back and talk to Essie and anyone we might have missed or who might have remembered something since they first talked to us. Plus we've been following up on the campers who left before or right after the murder, in case they noticed anything, like someone threatening Albert or being threatened by him. We've talked to people in other campgrounds in the state forest. The other campgrounds are farther from the Clifftop Trail."

I sighed. "That's a lot of people."

"Yes. And we haven't gotten anywhere with our questioning. Yet."

"The Drifters seemed to think that Dawn was a likely culprit because they're sure Albert quarreled with her and hit her more than once, and also because she did most of the work at the campground. The Drifters have a motive, being able to stay in one campsite for the entire season, by becoming volunteer hosts, but it doesn't seem strong to me."

"Stranger things have happened. Remember, Em, I need you to stay safe."

"I'm careful. Probably more than you are."

"I'm trained."

"I know." When I could speak again, I said, "I really like Zachary. He seems sweet, and like he'd be a much better match for Hannah than Joshua."

Brent repeated what he'd said earlier. "Hannah is practically grown up. You'll have to trust her to make the right decisions for herself."

I eased over into Brent's lap and stroked his chin. "I know, but shouldn't everyone be as happy as we are?"

"Impossible," he said, and then neither of us spoke for a long time.

Chapter 16

The next morning, Brent and I prepared a substantial breakfast—eggs, sausages, grapes, and muffins—and enjoyed it out on the catio with Dep. Then we packed a submarine sandwich, an apple, and cookies for Brent's lunch. Saying he hoped to be home for dinner, he left for work.

I looked up at Dep, high on one of her shelflike perches in the catio. "Dep, we have two days off from Deputy Donut. What would you like to do?"

Without interrupting her steady gaze out toward trees, she chirped.

I interpreted aloud, "Stay there all day, unless you could go out and play jungle kitty, chasing things? You'll never be allowed to do that, except on a leash."

She chirped again. Leaving the door open between the catio and our great room, I cleared our breakfast table and did the dishes.

A drizzly mist cooled the catio, and Dep came inside. By lunchtime, I was ready for Samantha's shower the next evening, except for shopping for clothespins and a baby hat for our games, decorating the great room, and doing the last-minute finishing touches. I ate a sandwich of toast, smoked gouda, and roasted red peppers and then changed from jeans and T-shirt into navy slacks and a sweater knit in shades of navy and purple.

Dep was curled on a couch. I suggested to her, "You can continue your nap. It's supposed to clear up later. Maybe we can do something outside when I get back."

She opened one eye and closed it. I went to the hallway closet in the section of the chalet beneath the loft. When I came out with a water-resistant jacket, my shiny blue rain boots, and the backpack I carried as a purse, Dep was still lying on her side. Without opening her eyes, she stretched all four legs straight in front of her, and then curled herself into a tighter ball with her front paws covering her face. I patted the soft warm fur on her shoulder, cooed a goodbye, and locked her inside.

Guessing that the windowless gift shop on a side street east of Fallingbrook's village square belonged to Dawn McGoss, I drove there.

The shop had a new-looking sign above the door—PROCEEDS OF CRAFT. On the sign, a whimsical painting depicted a long-nosed fox wearing spectacles and knitting a scarf. The painting gave me hope that the shop offered creative gifts. I already had the mobile and other gifts for Samantha and Hooligan's baby, but I might discover something that I couldn't resist. And maybe I could buy the baby hat we needed for the naming game.

I opened the door. Bells jingled. I took one glance at the cluttered shelves, and my hopes for finding creative gifts evaporated. The "crafts" appeared to have been mass-produced with tiny parts that made them unsuitable for anyone under three years old. Pretending to search for baby gifts might be difficult, and I didn't need party decorations or favors. I took a deep breath. Surely, no shop owner would mind someone browsing. Under the too-bright lighting, the clutter of gaudy packaging made me want to return outside to the soft feel of the cloudy morning. Blinking, I attempted to focus on a shelf of toy airplanes in front of beige-painted concrete blocks that had obviously replaced one of the two bricked-in front windows.

Behind me, a door quietly unlatched and closed, and then a soft voice asked, "Can I help you?"

I turned around. Wearing an apron over her jeans and acid-green turtleneck, Dawn McGoss came out of a back room. She didn't appear to be wearing makeup. Dark circles rimmed her eyes. Fatigue, grief, or bruises?

"May I look around?"

"Of course." She squinted toward me for a second. "You're from Deputy Donut, aren't you?"

"Yes." I waved toward the street. "I love the painting of the fox on your sign outside."

"Thank you." She almost smiled. "I enjoy fooling around with painting and cartoons."

"I wouldn't call it 'fooling around.' You're really good."

"My husband didn't think so. Late husband, I should say. I suppose you heard . . . ?" She brushed at her eyes.

"I did, and I'm sorry for your loss." I'd wanted to sound sympathetic, but I probably sounded trite.

Dawn's shoulders tensed as if she were restraining a shrug. "He was not an easy man to live with. He was never truly happy, and it was like a full-time job, always having to be careful what I said or did. He didn't like being contradicted, even over the tiniest things. I always had to cater to his ego, including when his business partner invited us to Deputy Donut and then proceeded to fire Albert from their partnership. I had to act like I was as angry at Kevin as Albert was, but I could actually see Kevin's point, at least if Albert was as lazy with the jobs he did for Kevin as he was with the job he supposedly did with me." And then, as if she couldn't hold it in any longer, she did shrug. "Albert wasn't that bad, really, just sometimes nerve-racking and tiring." She folded her arms. "But because he was so argumentative, people must have thought he was abusive, but he wasn't, so I always had to fight off that impression he gave people, too. Kept me on my toes. Are you looking for anything in particular?"

"Mostly, I'd like to see what you carry. I have the day off."

"Lucky you. I wouldn't know what a day off was if it bit me. In addition to running this shop, I have to host a campground. I needed to be here in my shop during the day, so Albert covered the hosting during the days whenever he wasn't working as a handyman. And we both worked there at night. Now that he's gone, I have to do that all by myself."

"That must be overwhelming."

"It's exhausting. Not that I've been there recently. I left the place Thursday night. Albert needed to subdue some rowdy campers, and I just couldn't take another fight. I hid in our trailer at first, but I knew he'd come back in a rage, so I got into my car and came here. And I stayed here even after I closed the shop Friday evening. But that night, someone, maybe those rowdy campers, shoved him off a cliff and . . ." She heaved a huge sigh.

I repeated my condolences.

She thanked me. "I never got to say goodbye, and hoo, boy, was my timing ever bad. I decided not to go back to the campground on Friday night in case Albert was still in one of his moods, so I was here alone, and I have no way to prove it, and now the police have questions because they always blame the spouse when something goes wrong. But I'm not like that. I would never have harmed my husband, no matter what."

Not knowing quite what to say, and certainly not about to admit that I was married to one of the police officers asking questions, I made sympathetic sounds.

Fortunately, Dawn was looking down at her hands, and not at my probably too-expressive face. She sighed again. "I haven't been able to face going back to the campground, though I suppose I should. There's this other couple up there who would do anything—and I mean anything—to get the job of hosting the campground. They've probably already crowded their trailer into our space now that Albert's truck and my car are gone. Come have a look at these fun fidget gadgets. They make noises."

"Cute!" But I didn't want to give noisy fidget gadgets to our shower guests unless I shoved them into their hands as they went out the door. Then they could noisily fidget as much as they liked.

"And look at these dog toys. You'll love these. They're shaped like donuts and cupcakes! Do you have a dog?"

"No."

"You must know someone who does. And I know you have a cat in your shop. Cats love these." She guided me to toys that resembled little fishing poles with feathers tied to the ends of the lines.

"She would."

"Here, I'll get you a basket to put things in."

I dutifully placed one of the toys, sporting bright red feathers, into the basket.

Dawn led me to colorful plastic discs with holes in them, like flattened donuts. "Here's for if anyone wants to play a game of toss indoors. You could paint them to look like donuts and give them out in your shop. You know, promotional items."

They looked too small to fling very far. Even so, I wouldn't want anyone throwing them or anything else in Deputy Donut. I admired them but didn't add any to my basket. Instead, I asked, "Do you have anything like diaper pins or clothespins?"

"Not diaper pins, but I think I do have clothespins. Not real ones, not full-sized. They're more for attaching things like greeting cards to ribbons, things like that."

"That might work."

She led me to a box holding packets of small plastic clothespins, the spring-loaded kind. "They come in different colors." She sounded almost apologetic.

They were big enough to clip onto a sweater or a collar. And while many of the packets held only bright colors, several contained pastel pink and blue clothespins. I couldn't help a big smile. "These are perfect, even better than full-sized ones!" Explaining how we planned to use them, I added two packets of pink and two of baby blue to my basket.

"That game sounds like fun." Dawn yawned and then apologized. "Sorry. It's just that I'm so tired. It's hard to sleep, you know?"

I did, but I didn't have a chance to answer.

She went on. "I mean, I've been here all the time since Thursday evening, working, and detectives keep pestering me with questions, like, did Albert have enemies? Well, I'm sure he did, the way he loved telling other people what to do, but I don't know who all they could be. Well, there were those rowdy campers, and he's kicked lots of others out of the campground over the years. And then there's the couple who want our job up there, and now that I'm alone, they might get it for next year. I guess that the hosts are supposed to be a couple, not a single person, but I did all the work up there, and I'll force myself to go back. We don't earn a cent from hosting, but it's a break from this shop and my apartment behind it, and it's free for us. Well, for me, now. But that other couple would really like to camp up there during the entire season. Albert was diligent about enforcing the rules about staying only two weeks at a time, and they resented it." Her voice took on bitter notes. "Maybe they found a way to get their revenge on him. If they're still up there when I go back, I'd better be careful." She tugged at the folded-over neck of her sweater. "One way for them to get that job for sure would be to get rid of me."

"Would they do that?"

"I wouldn't put it past them. Like, who knows exactly

what happened to Albert and who did it? Could have been them." She strode to another corner of her crowded shop. "Come over here and have a look at these cute greeting cards. Some have matching wrapping paper."

I followed her. "Did you ever think of having your own cards printed, with some of your paintings and drawings?"

"Yes, but Albert said it was too expensive and that I wasn't very good."

"Judging by the cute fox outside, you are." I placed cards and wrapping paper in my basket and added gift bags, pens, and notebooks, all of them printed with cute children's toys. The only hats I saw were cone-shaped paper birthday party hats. They might have worked for our baby name game, but I was sure I could do better, even if I had to raid my own supply of stocking caps.

I paid for my purchases. Dawn leaned toward me. For once, her eyes seemed to come alive. "Another thing I thought of, but I haven't told the detectives—my late husband's business partner, that is his ex-business partner, has made some moves on me over the years, and I can't help wondering if he offed Albert in hopes of dating me." She raised her eyebrows. "Not that I'd fall for a trick like that."

Unable to come up with a response, I thanked her.

She handed me my purchases. "Your receipt's in the bag."

Outside, the clouds had blown away, the sky was a fierce shade of October blue, and the day had warmed slightly. Enjoying the fresh air after the stifling atmosphere inside Dawn's gift shop, I walked back to my car.

The Craft Croft probably had a selection of baby hats. I drove there.

Wearing a loose, long-sleeved poplin dress in a shade of ruby that matched her hair, Summer met me at the door.

I asked, "Did you make your dress?"

"I did."

"I love all the pockets."

"They come in handy."

There were other people in the shop. I murmured, "Have you talked to Rex?"

"Not in person."

I grinned. "It's just as well. It must be nice not being a suspect."

Her eyes opened wide. "Don't tell me that you're one."

"I was kayaking on Chicory Lake and heard a scream. I should have just shut my ears and continued paddling around, but I investigated and saw something that turned out to be a body. I think that Brent and Rex believe me that I didn't push Albert McGoss off the cliff."

"I should hope they believe you! Are you looking for more baby gifts? Another handmade mobile came in from the same artisan, with cute animals." She showed it to me.

"It's adorable, but maybe one from me is enough and I don't need gifts for other babies yet, but we can always hope." I was thinking of Misty and Scott, not of Brent and me. Maybe. My face heated, and I asked quickly, "Do you have any baby hats?"

"Bonnets?"

"Unisex."

"We have a few. Knit, sewn, or crocheted?"

"It doesn't matter." I described the naming game.

Summer showed me about a dozen cute hats. Most came as a set with a sweater or mittens. I chose a cheerfully vibrant turquoise knit hat. It had ear flaps, a soft, knitted chin strap that buttoned on the side, and a puffy pompom on top.

Driving home, I mulled over Dawn's suggestion that Kevin Lunnion could have killed Albert in order to date Dawn. When those three had been together in Deputy Donut, they'd all looked and acted cranky. I hadn't watched them the entire time they'd been there, but I hadn't noticed the least bit of flirtatiousness between Kevin and Dawn, which didn't prove anything.

Knowing how people often accused each other of doing what they themselves did, I couldn't help turning the idea inside out. Dawn could have become fed up with Albert and with his verbal and emotional abuse, and although she denied it, possibly also with physical abuse. She might have hoped to upgrade to a partner like Kevin, a presumably harder-working and more successful man, someone who could become the other half of a campground-hosting couple, and then Dawn would have been able to continue enjoying staying up at Herbgrove Lake Campground, and she might not need to work as hard with a new partner to help her.

Chapter 17

At home, I changed into shorts and sneakers and put on a
sunhat. Dep looked up from the couch and spotted me coming toward her with our life jackets. She trotted to me, rubbed
against my ankles, and meowed. I asked, probably needlessly,
"Would you like a ride in a kayak?"

She purred.

Apparently, she didn't blame her life jacket for the car
rides she'd been forced to endure on Friday evening. She
stood almost still and let me snug the flotation device around
her and hook her leash to it. I grabbed a mesh bag containing
my water shoes and let Dep lead the way outside.

Maybe she liked wearing her life jacket because I often put
it on her before a walk through the woods. We strolled down
the trail, and I let her examine fallen leaves and pounce on
beetles. I didn't let her go near mushrooms.

Finally, we made it to the shore. I slung her leash over one
of the dock's poles. Blinking, Dep sat on the beach and
watched me pull my kayak and paddle out of the boathouse.
I put on my water shoes and stowed my sneakers in the compartment behind the kayak's seat.

With Dep in one of my arms and her leash connecting our
life jackets, we boarded the kayak. I pushed off. She sat up

tall on my stretched-out thighs. I imagined her wearing a captain's hat. Or a pirate's.

In the shallow water, I could see straight down to the pebble-dotted sandy bottom. Farther out, breezes blew ripples, painting the lake's surface in shimmering blue and silver. I stayed close to shore and paddled quietly. Dep peered toward the woods, probably doing the same thing I was— watching for birds and wildlife. With luck, we might catch another glimpse of the mink we'd once seen scurrying on its short little legs along the bank.

The shore scalloped in and out. I rounded rocky points of land, and then, ahead of me, was the cove where Albert's body had been. There was no yellow police tape on the ledge where he'd landed, but broken and bent brush and saplings had not completely recovered from his fall and the search. The cliffs, nearly vertical except for crannies where small plants had taken root, loomed above the ledge. The peculiar boulder I'd nicknamed The Beignet perched on top, next to the railing curving around the lookout. As far as I could tell, no one was at that lookout or on The Beignet.

Although the precarious-looking boulder was probably not about to fall, and neither was anything else, I kept my distance from that cove and eased past the second point of land that sheltered it. Ahead and slightly to my right was a larger cove, one that formed the eastern end of the lake. The shore on the north side of that cove was almost flat, with a narrow, sandy beach at the water next to a sunlit meadow gently sloping up toward treed hills. The beach and meadow curved around the bay to a steep hill that rose toward the cliffs where Albert had died.

I paddled to the shallows beside the beach and turned my kayak parallel to the golden sand. I told Dep, "This has to be the access point to the Cornflower Trail that Zachary showed me on a map. He's hoping that lots of the mushrooms he's studying will be on that trail."

As if wanting to be the first to spot some of Zachary's mushrooms, Dep leaned forward. I laid the paddle across the gunwales, looped one arm around the little cat, and braced my free hand on the paddle. Carefully, I stepped out into ankle-deep and very cold water. I waded to the beach, pulled the kayak higher on the sand, and retrieved my sneakers from the compartment. With Dep's leash still attached to my life jacket, I sat on the sun-warmed beach, peeled off the water shoes, rubbed as much sand as I could from my bare feet, and pulled on my sneakers. Finally, I stood and unfastened the handle of Dep's leash from my life jacket. I left my water shoes and life jacket to warm in the sun. Grasping the leash in one hand, I headed for a break between small bushes and wildflowers. A small, arrow-shaped sign pointed to the beginning of the Cornflower Trail.

The sun heated my back through my long-sleeved shirt. Bees buzzed among fading goldenrod, chicory, and asters. I put Dep down. From Zachary's map book, I remembered that this trail looped around and ended where it started. I suggested to Dep, "Let's start along the right-hand branch. It should head toward the base of the cliffs."

We took our time. The trail curved, following the shoreline toward the forested hill below the Clifftop Trail. Dep balked at a marshy spot. I picked her up and leaped across the narrow inlet of a stream. I batted dry and rustling leaves of cattails out of my way. Above my head, the flower heads that gave the plant its name were no longer brown, fuzzy cylinders like tails. They'd become pale and fluffy, seemingly only seconds away from dispatching their seeds into whatever wind might come along. I suspected that during the spring, most of this meadow would be wet and muddy.

Farther on, at the border between the meadow and the woods, I spotted rounded, grayish mushrooms nestled close to the trunks of trees. Zachary had said that the mushrooms he was researching weren't poisonous, but in case these weren't his cornflower-blue mushrooms and might be poisonous, I stayed away. I hoped the mushrooms were the ones he wanted to see, however, and that when he finally came over here, he wouldn't be disappointed. Then again, maybe he had made up the story about hunting for mushrooms as an excuse to spend time near Hannah, and he wouldn't care if he never saw a mushroom up here in these eerily quiet woods.

The trail didn't head directly toward the mushrooms. Still in the meadow, it ran close to the lake. Then, where it seemed to turn back toward the gentler slope of meadow and woods where the mushrooms were, Dep stopped and sniffed at a plant that resembled catnip. Judging by the aroma that even I could smell, it was spearmint.

Waiting for my cat to finish her investigation, I gazed around, and that's when I saw a narrow pathway.

Zachary's map had shown that the trail Dep and I were on was close to the Clifftop Trail, but the Cornflower Trail was low, close to the lake, while the Clifftop Trail was on top of the hill. Because of the thick woods, I couldn't see where the meager little path went. Could it possibly go all the way up to the Clifftop Trail?

I had guessed that Albert's killer had fled the murder scene in a vehicle from the parking lot, but I'd also seen a canoe that could have come from the beach where, minutes ago, I'd left my kayak, life jacket, and water shoes.

How would anyone have known, whether they arrived by vehicle or canoe, that Albert was going to be at the lookout that evening? Albert had presumably driven there in his truck, which had been in the parking area when I arrived. Had someone followed Albert in another vehicle and then escaped in that other vehicle? That was easier to imagine than someone coming from another direction in a canoe and hiking up a possibly treacherous and hard-to-find pathway in order to kill Albert.

If the rendezvous had been planned in person, there would

be no evidence. But what if it had been arranged in digital texts or on the phone? Brent and Rex would learn about it through Albert's phone records.

Or it could have been an accidental meeting, either with someone that Albert knew or with a complete stranger. If it was the latter, Brent and Rex were likely to be busy for a long time.

I picked Dep up and headed toward the narrow pathway.

Seeing where to place my feet wasn't easy. The path twisted, an animal trail that switchbacked around trees and rocks. A spindly twig touched Dep's shoulder. She hissed and struggled.

Not wanting her to leap out of my arms and tangle her leash in the undergrowth, I promised, "Okay, we'll turn around."

Back down on the Cornflower Trail, I started along the section of the loop that we had not yet hiked. This part of the trail stayed in the meadow, but meandered away from the lake and close to the wooded hillsides where scads of mushrooms were plainly visible. If even a small percentage of them were Zachary's blue-staining mushrooms, he should be ecstatic when he finally came along here. If he did.

Tiny insects flitted among grasses. The trail curved toward the lake again, and took us back to the beach. Maybe I could bring Olivia here to show her that at least one of the trails in Chicory Lake State Forest did not go close to the tops of cliffs or near boulders that no one should attempt to climb.

I sat down in the sand next to my water shoes, hooked the handle of Dep's leash to my life jacket, and muttered, "But if Olivia doesn't want Hannah to clamber around near rocks or ride on a motorcycle, she'd probably freak out about the idea of Hannah paddling a kayak or a canoe to get here. Or leaping over mud and streamlets after she arrived."

Dep was apparently too busy peering at a spider to answer.

I took off my sneakers, brushed more sand off my feet, and wiggled my toes in the sunshine.

The spider jumped. So did Dep, straight up, with a meow that resembled a yelp. The spider became indiscernible in the sand, and Dep landed on all fours. As if embarrassed by having been so obviously startled, she dug one front foot delicately into the sand, and then she pawed at the sand as if this beach were a giant kitty litter tray. Rationalizing that humans probably seldom arrived on this shore, I let her dig while I tugged on my still-damp water shoes.

The next thing I knew, Dep had abandoned what I had expected her to do and was batting around a small, balled-up piece of paper.

I reeled her in, away from the ball of paper, picked it up, and smoothed it until it was more or less flat. The two sides and the bottom edge of the piece of paper were straight, but the top was a jagged angle. It was obviously a page torn from a small notebook, approximately one and a half by three inches, a notebook that would fit into a pocket. I shook most of the sand off the torn page.

Half expecting to read someone's discarded grocery list, I moved my head to shade the white scrap from the dazzling sunlight.

Whoever had printed in pencil had started writing on the page's faint blue lines, but the printing had slanted as it crossed the page, drooping below the lines as if the writer were following the torn angle at the top of the page rather than the pale, almost invisible guidelines originally on the page.

Between the sand and the paper's soggy wrinkles, the printing was hard to decipher, but I slowly made out the words.

Sorry about yesterday. I have what you need. Meet me at the lookout at six thirty.

There was no signature.

Chapter 18

Despite the dampness and wrinkles, the paper was in decent shape, barely yellowed in patches where the outer surface of the wadded-up ball had come in contact with wet sand. I doubted that the page had been buried longer than a month. It could have been buried for only a few days.

Like maybe since Friday evening after a six thirty rendezvous . . .

Had Albert sent this note to someone, and after that person killed Albert, had he or she attempted to hide the note, perhaps forever, by burying it?

Essie had told me that she'd seen Albert take what could have been a note from his picnic table, so if this note had anything to do with Albert, it seemed likely that Albert had been the recipient, not the sender.

I stared at the note until I was sure I had deciphered all of the words correctly.

Sorry about yesterday.

Would Joshua have written "yesterday" about an argument that had occurred during the night? I didn't think Hannah should choose Joshua as a life partner, but I didn't want one of her friends to be a murderer.

Kevin Lunnion had dissolved his partnership with Albert

the day before someone had killed Albert and tossed him off the cliff.

I have what you need. What would that have been—tax or other important paperwork from Kevin Lunnion?

Meet me at the lookout at six thirty. I wasn't sure when I'd heard that scream on Friday evening, but it had been around six forty.

It seemed possible, and maybe even likely, that I—rather, Dep—had unearthed evidence in Albert's murder.

But if the note had been given or sent to Albert, how had it ended up buried on this isolated beach? Presumably, Albert was the one who had driven his truck to the parking area at the entry of the Clifftop Trail. I doubted that he had come down to this beach and buried the note before returning to the Clifftop Trail.

According to Brent, if cash had been in Albert's wallet, it had been removed.

My imagination took a new turn. Maybe the person who had printed the message had killed Albert, taken the note and Albert's cash, and then escaped down that narrow, switch-backing pathway to the Cornflower Trail. And then he could have run to the beach, quickly buried the note where he figured no one would find it, and clambered into the canoe that he'd taken to the beach. If so, I must have seen the killer paddling away.

For the note to be acceptable evidence in court, a law enforcement officer should have found it, not a civilian, or worse, a civilian's cat. But re-burying it and directing Brent to this spot would have been ludicrous. I would have to take it to Brent.

In the hope that phone service might be available at this end of the lake, I pulled my phone out of a pocket in my life jacket.

No service.

Sighing, I carefully tucked the phone and the note into pockets.

Undaunted by the loss of one potential toy, Dep had nudged a twig of charred driftwood out of the sand. I picked her up, and took her, without her new toy, back to my kayak. Holding her close, I got in.

Although I wanted to return quickly to our house for phone service, I was curious about how our side of the lake would have looked to the person I'd seen in a canoe on Friday evening. Had he been heading toward Chicanery? Keeping the shore to my right, I angled toward Barney's place. At first, I couldn't see Barney's dock or ours. A few minutes later, I made out the lake end of Barney's dock, but our dock was still hidden by rocky cliffs jutting out into the lake. I kept paddling until our dock, beach, and boathouse were visible, and I had to be about where the canoe had been when I'd spotted it. I had not been able to make out much about the canoe and its occupant, and someone out here rocking on ripples would have had trouble identifying me. But I had waved, and my red kayak would have stood out against the beach more than his possibly aluminum canoe had shown up in water that was about the same shade as aging aluminum, either unpainted or painted so long ago that much of the color had worn off.

The county road that passed our place went down into the valley beside Chicanery's beach and then crossed a bridge over part of the lake. Canoes and kayaks would easily fit underneath that bridge. Barney had said that no canoes had gone missing from Chicanery. Maybe the canoer I'd seen had paddled underneath the bridge into the west end of the lake.

How far did the lake extend west of the bridge? Were there more water-access trails, and campgrounds? Roads into the state forest might run all over the wooded hills above that part of the lake. Maybe Zachary would let me look at his map booklet. Or Brent and I could explore the west end of the lake together. Had he and Rex already looked there for signs of the person I'd seen in the canoe shortly after I'd heard that scream?

Ahead, a fish that was about the length of Dep's tail jumped partway out of the water. Dep tried to leap forward. Her leash was fastened to my life jacket, but I grabbed the leash in one hand and held it tightly until, still muttering, my excited little cat settled down again.

I paddled farther until I could see more of Barney's dock but none of ours. Was this the route that the mysterious canoer had taken Friday evening?

Needing to get home where I had phone service and would be able to call Brent, I was about to turn toward our beach.

Barney was standing near his row of overturned canoes. He beckoned to me in an unusually urgent way for such a laidback man.

I paddled almost up to his beach. "Hey, Barney!" With my paddle, I held the kayak steady in the water.

"Hey, Emily, and who's that with you?" He was again in camouflage pants and leather bedroom slippers, but this time he wore a faded gray sweatshirt with white but no-longer-legible words on the front.

"My cat, Dep. She already likes kayaking, but a few minutes ago, she saw a fish jump. Now she'll probably expect me to take her kayaking every day."

Barney laughed. "Cats kayaking. That's a new one to me, and I've seen a lot." He frowned down at his hands and then held up a large padlock with two short lengths of chain dangling from its closed shackle. "Remember, I told you that no one had rented a canoe on Friday, and all my canoes were here and chained together?"

"Yes."

"Well, they're all here, and chained together, more or less, but someone cut the chain. In two places, of all things, when one would have done the trick. I guess someone was too flustered to think clearly. They borrowed a canoe, brought it back, and then made it look just the same as it had, that is until someone carefully inspected it all. Which I did only just now. I hate to bother Brent about someone cutting my chain, but . . ." He glanced toward the eastern end of the lake. "You can't see it from here, but way over there is the spot where someone fell to his death on Friday night, and didn't you say you saw a canoe that night that could have been one of mine?"

"I did say that. And for sure, call Brent. He would want to know. Do you have cell phone reception down here?"

"People say I don't, or it's only speckly. I wouldn't know. I have my old-fashioned phone. It has always worked here and always will, as long as I'm alive."

"Do you have Brent's number?"

"Yep. We traded numbers when he bought that place. It's good to have neighbors like him. Like both of you, I mean. Three, including your kayaking cat."

I pointed toward the bridge. "Are there any boat launches on the west side of the lake?"

"Over there's all state forest land, so I think there are some, like on beaches near campgrounds that people can drive to and others near water-access campsites. Sometimes people park near the bridge and scramble down to the lake from there, but I don't recommend it, especially carrying a canoe or even a loaf of bread. And then, on this side of the lake, mine's the only launch besides your and Brent's beach."

"Do you know if anyone parked a vehicle here for a while on Friday evening, maybe between about five and seven? Those times are approximate."

"I don't know. I don't have those snoopy cameras and such, so I don't know if whoever cut the chains drove up close to the canoes or what. Probably not, if it meant leaving their vehicle here while they paddled around on a grand tour of the lake. More likely, if someone came in here and 'borrowed' one of my canoes for a while, he would tuck his vehicle in among brush on one side of the road or the other, somewhere nearby but not visible from my place. Then they could have walked in."

"Do you know what day someone cut the chains to your padlock?"

Looking out across the lake, Barney scratched his head. "No idea. I mean, it was since last Sunday evening when I locked everything up, but other than that, I don't know." He took his pipe out of his mouth and pointed the stem toward the far shore. "There's another boat launch over there, one you can't get to by road, well, not a launch as such, but a beach where you can pull up a canoe. The only place you can go from that beach is to a trail where people wax eloquent over plants they'd uproot and burn if they invaded their precious lawns, but we can't see any of that from here. Those hills and cliffs east of your property hide it from us."

"I just kayaked to that beach, and Dep and I explored the trail. I think it's called the Cornflower Trail."

"Don't ask me why it's called that. We have plenty of chicory here, but that's not the same as cornflowers, last I knew. But that young chap I told you about, he was looking for mushrooms with a name something like cornflower, so I guess anything's possible."

"Has he been back to rent a canoe?"

"Not when I've been here." Barney jingled the padlock and its trailing chains. "Unless he has a peculiar way of 'renting.'"

Although we couldn't see the Cornflower Trail, I pointed toward it. "Is there a path connecting the Cornflower Trail to the Clifftop Trail?"

"Not an official trail, but I've been up and down that hill a few times, when I was a daredevil youngster not much older than you. It's only an animal trail. I don't know how many people would know about it now." The usual humor and warmth in those watered-blue eyes sharpened to speculation. "Do you think someone might have used the canoe you saw and that path to come and go to the Clifftop Trail on Friday night and perhaps cause some mischief? What am I saying? Mischief? Murder, maybe."

Dep was becoming restless. I placed one hand on her back. "It seems like a possibility."

"Sure does."

"Can you think of anyone else who knows about that trail?"

"My wife and probably my kids, though the youngest is over fifty, and all of us are too old to go jauntering up and down rocky hillsides. And my grandkids. And probably anyone else who grew up around here or has explored the state forest. That would narrow it down to several thousand, at a guess, enough to keep your husband busy. I'm going to go inside and call him right this minute." Carrying his padlock and the rattling sections of chain, he headed toward the building housing both his business and the apartment where he and his wife and some of their offspring spent most of their summers, plus spring and fall weekends.

I returned to Brent's and my dock and put the kayak and paddle away in the boathouse. In a hurry, I carried Dep up the trail to the chalet. I let her enjoy her catio while I left a phone message for Brent and put a small roast into the oven.

An hour later, I put a couple of potatoes into the oven. Brent called back. I could tell by background noises that he was in his car. He talked hands-free while driving.

I repeated my earlier message that I'd found a note that might interest him.

"Sorry, I didn't pick up your message until after I left the office. I'm on my way home."

"I'll show it to you when you get here."

"Barney called me. I'm going to see him first and collect his cut-off chains and padlock as possible evidence, and then he's going to show me some places near his property where someone could have parked a vehicle behind trees and brush. See you in about forty minutes." We disconnected.

I lined a baking tray with parchment paper, stirred small-diced butternut squash and larger pieces of red pepper and onion in a bowl with garlic-infused olive oil, and spread them over the parchment paper. I slid the tray into the oven.

Brent arrived home as I took the roast and potatoes out of the oven.

Chapter 19

I left the veggies in the oven to caramelize and ran to kiss Brent. He went up to our bedroom in the loft to change. I made gravy.

He returned in jeans and a sweatshirt. "I hear that you convinced Barney to call me about the cut-off padlock."

Brent looked so cuddly that I had to hug him again. "He probably would have called you without my encouragement."

"That cut-off padlock might be our first, best break in the case. That, and you noticing the canoe across the lake on Friday evening. Barney showed me a couple of spots where people park alongside the road and walk down to the lake and to his place. One of them is big enough, and tucked behind enough bushes and weeds, to conceal a vehicle."

"Are there recent tire tracks?"

Brent tightened his arms around me. "It looked that way to me. We'll get the forensic investigators to check. Can you show me the note that you and Dep found?"

I led him to one of the glass-topped tables in the great room where I'd left the damp note. It was curling as it dried. "Dep and I explored the Cornflower Trail today. She dug this out of the sand on the beach where I left my kayak. The note was wadded into a ball when she found it."

Brent threw a smile toward our cute little cat. "And you thought it was put there especially for you to play with, right, Dep?"

She licked a front paw.

Brent switched on the lamp above the note and bent over. Without touching the note, he studied it for a long time. He straightened and gazed down at me. His eyes were serious.

I apologized for not leaving the note where we'd found it. "I know I've disrupted the chain of evidence."

"You couldn't have left it there. Something could have moved it. You said Dep dug it up. Was it buried?"

"Yes, probably less than two inches deep."

"Maybe it's unrelated, but between it, Essie's story, the cut-off padlock, and the canoe you saw, I'm beginning to suspect that the killer left this note on Albert's picnic table, canoed across the lake, met Albert at the lookout, killed him, took the note from him, and went back the way he or she had come, stopping to bury the note before getting into the canoe." Brent glanced toward one of the windows next to the fireplace. "It's too dark now to search that beach, but since you have tomorrow off, can you spare time from the preparations for Samantha's baby shower to go kayaking with me first thing in the morning and show me where you found the note?"

"I'd be glad to, and I'm nearly ready for her shower. Have you found the keys to Albert's truck yet?"

"No."

"Maybe they're also on the beach."

"We'll look."

I went into the kitchen section of the great room, and Brent called Rex. I heard him read the note aloud to Rex, bring him up to date on what Barney and I had said, and tell him about the unofficial, off-road parking spots near Chicanery.

Brent disconnected the call and joined me in the kitchen. "Rex and other DCI investigators will launch a motorboat from Chicanery tomorrow morning. They'll bring metal detectors and other equipment. I'll meet them on the beach near the Cornflower Trail at seven thirty. When we're done there, we'll search for tire tracks in those parking spots Barney showed me."

"While Dep and I were on the Cornflower Trail, I noticed that there could be a narrow animal trail going from it up to the Clifftop Trail. Barney confirmed that he used to run up and down that path there when he was younger."

Brent got out the carving set and stuck the fork into the roast. "The path is treacherous but still navigable. When we investigated it, there was no recent litter and no damage like bent-back branches and torn-off leaves, and the trail's too stony for complete footprints, but we might have found some partials."

I took the veggies out of the oven. "The Cornflower Trail has some damp spots, but even though I'm short, I was easily able to jump over them, and I didn't notice any footprints. But that note might have nothing to do with Albert's murder. Scheming ahead of time to escape by a peculiar route involving a 'borrowed' canoe seems unlikely."

Brent looked up from the roast and gave me an even stare, as if willing me to continue my thoughts.

With a sigh, I added, "And so does following his truck to the parking area near the Clifftop Trail. A random encounter seems even less possible, but maybe I'm thinking that way because a random murder would take you longer to solve, and I like having you home with me more."

Brent walked around to my side of the kitchen island, kissed the back of my neck, and then returned to the roast.

Spooning veggies onto our plates, I asked, "Can you tell from Albert's phone records whether he made plans with someone to meet on or near the Clifftop Trail on Friday evening?"

Brent cut neat, thin slices from the roast. "No texts. He talked to Kevin Lunnion on the phone that day, and then immediately afterward, he called Dawn. That was about an hour before he and Dawn met Kevin at Deputy Donut. Kevin and Dawn claim that those conversations were about when and where to meet. Kevin's the one who suggested getting together at Deputy Donut. Somewhere 'neutral,' he explained to me."

"Dawn could tell you if a rendezvous later at the Clifftop Trail was planned while they were in Deputy Donut. None of the three of them looked like they were making future plans for another get-together, certainly not a friendly one."

Brent slipped slices of beef onto our plates. "Dawn suspects Kevin, but she admitted that while they were all in Deputy Donut, there was no discussion about Kevin and Albert getting together the next evening."

I served the potatoes. Moving our plates to placemats in front of our kitchen island stools, I confessed, "I wanted some things for Samantha's shower, so I shopped in Dawn's store today."

"Em . . ."

"I know." I sat down and patted the stool beside me. "Dawn couldn't have harmed me without turning herself into a suspect in her husband's murder."

Brent sat beside me and squeezed my hand. "Tell me what you learned."

"She made it clear that she suspects Kevin."

Brent nodded.

I ladled gravy onto my beef. "She theorized that Kevin could have murdered Albert in order to take Albert's place in Dawn's life."

Brent's eyes widened. "She didn't make the barest hint of that to Rex and me."

"Maybe she came up with the idea after she talked to you. Naturally, I wondered if it was the other way around. She got rid of her husband because she thought that Kevin would be a better match for her, like maybe a better provider. I wonder how much Dawn can make from that store. I'd hoped to find crafts and gifts, but she mostly sells gimmicky things. I ended up going to Summer's shop for the baby hat I wanted."

"Rex asked me if Summer was still single. I told him she is."

"Rex has her phone number."

"I'm sure he'll call her when we get a moment. Maybe the note and the cut-off padlock will help us solve this. Meanwhile, who else do you have on your radar as Albert's possible killers?"

I said firmly, "Not Hannah or Zachary."

"But you're not sure about Joshua?"

"I don't know him. I know Hannah, and I feel like I know Zachary."

"There's something I haven't told you, Em. Joshua's and Hannah's stories of where they were that night differ."

My fork clattered onto the granite counter. "How?"

"Hannah said that she and Joshua went grocery shopping, and then she went home without Joshua, ate with Olivia, and went out to the campsite by herself. Joshua, however, says that right after Hannah finished work, he took Hannah on his motorcycle to a kids' football game that ended, conveniently, around six fifty, which is ten minutes after you reported hearing that scream. And then they went to the campsite. For that trip, he rode his motorcycle, and Hannah drove Olivia's car."

I picked up my fork and poked at my potato. "Hannah walked away from Deputy Donut after work that night. She was with Olivia. When I left our parking lot, Joshua was standing by his bike, apparently texting, so I know he didn't take Hannah anywhere right after work. And Laura said that Hannah shopped in the grocery store that evening about the time that Hannah said she was going there, but Laura didn't notice anyone fitting Joshua's description in the store. So, Joshua's tale sounds suspect, and so does Hannah's. But if Joshua can provide an alibi for more of Hannah's time, she's not taking advantage of it. Maybe that's because she doesn't want Olivia to know she rode on a motorcycle. Because of Laura's remembering talking to Hannah in the grocery store, I'm more inclined to believe Hannah than Joshua. But I would anyway." I popped a morsel of gravy-covered potato into my mouth.

"Obviously, we'll question everyone as many times as we need to."

I reminded him, "And then there's that couple at the campground, Harv and Essie. They have a motive."

"They've decamped."

"Oh."

"On schedule. They'd been there for two weeks."

I repeated, "Oh."

Brent moved his stool close to mine, hugged me with one arm, and said into my hair, "They live west of Fallingbrook. We talked to them at home. Rather, we mostly listened to Essie. You know, there are lots other people in the world besides the few you've mentioned."

"I know. Who else are you considering?"

He laughed and tightened his arm around me. "You know I wouldn't tell you."

I heaved a big, phony sigh. "I know."

"Even if we had other suspects at the moment."

"Does that mean that you don't?"

"I'm not saying."

I snuggled my cheek against his shoulder. "Then that means you don't. But don't worry. I won't go looking for more."

"You just stay safe."

"You, too."

"Do you need me to do anything for Samantha's baby shower?"

"Everything's done except little last-minute things. I'm sure that Dep will help me with them tomorrow after I come back from showing you where she found that note."

Chapter 20

At first light the next morning, Brent and I left Dep at home and walked down the trail through the woods. The only sounds were the sighing of the pines above us, the whispers of the stream cascading over miniature waterfalls beside us, and our sneakered feet landing softly on the leaf-strewn earth. On our beach, we launched our kayaks into the nearly silent lake. Patchy mist drifted across water that was almost the color of mercury.

We edged past the first headland defining our little bay and then took the straightest route to the narrow beach near the Cornflower Trail. The sky lightened to pearly gray-blue with orange tints near the eastern horizon. I ran my kayak onto the sand farthest from where Dep had dug up the note. Brent put his kayak next to mine, and we both waded through cold water onto shore.

From the direction of Chicanery, an outboard motor coughed and started. Fingers of mist writhed up from the lake. I shivered.

Brent put an arm around me. "Cold?"

"Not now."

He handed me his powerful flashlight. "Can you find where the note was?"

It didn't take me long to pinpoint an indentation beside a

small mound of sand. "There." The charred driftwood twig was still where I'd tossed it after I removed it from Dep's clutches.

"Okay, thanks." He gently removed the flashlight from my hand. "You can go home, now."

I teased, "Do I have to?"

"You'd be a good detective, you and your sidekick Dep." He kissed me hard, helped me into my kayak, and gave it a little push into deeper water. I waved my paddle and started back across the lake.

With its running lights on, a small motorboat emerged between fingers of mist. The boat put-putted toward Brent, standing alone in his life jacket on the beach and waving his flashlight. Although I'd teased Brent about having to leave the site, part of me wished I could have stayed and helped search for clues. Paddling quickly warmed me up. I disembarked on our beach and put my kayak and paddle away.

As I'd said she would, Dep did help prepare for the party, sort of, by inspecting streamers as I tried, mostly successfully, to hang them. Having had an unnerving experience with a balloon when she was a kitten, Dep avoided the balloons. I arranged some of them to resemble pillars flanking the great room's fireplace, and then I confidently set big pink and blue letters spelling B-A-B-Y on the mantel. Dep might have wanted to figure out how to leap to the mantel to knock the letters onto the hearth, but I hoped she wouldn't go near those balloons.

Brent came home at lunchtime. "We didn't find anything else."

"Not even the keys to Albert's truck?"

"No."

"That's disappointing."

"They could be anywhere. In the woods, in the lake, thrown out of a vehicle on a road miles away. We never find everything we'd like to." He glanced around the decorated great room. "Pink, blue, and silver. Samantha and Hooligan are still not letting us know whether they're expecting a boy or a girl, are they?"

"They want it to be a surprise, for them, too."

With Dep supervising from one of her balconies, we ate sandwiches on the catio. Too soon, Brent went upstairs and changed into his suit. He kissed me and opened the front door. "Have a great time at the shower."

"I will. I'm going out for a little while this afternoon to make a Deputy Donut delivery."

Shortly after two, I changed into my Deputy Donut polo shirt and black jeans, and then I brought Dep in from the catio and closed the door. "I won't be long. Try not to re-arrange our decorating."

She hopped onto a couch and turned her back on me.

Driving past the turnoff to Lunnion's Lawns and Order, I clenched my hands on the steering wheel. I pictured Kevin careening out and running me off the road, but no one appeared. I relaxed and drove into Fallingbrook.

At Deputy Donut, Tom, Hannah, and Olivia had packed the donut bites for Ira's party into large flat boxes but had not closed the lids. Hannah explained, "We wanted you to see them before the kids eat them, Emily."

Tom beamed.

As always, Hannah and Olivia had been creative. Some of the donut bites resembled footballs. Others looked like football helmets. Many were covered with thicker frosting than most adults would like, and liberally coated with sprinkles, multicolored and chocolate.

I put on my Deputy Donut hat, and then Hannah and I loaded the boxes of donut bites into the trunk of our delivery car, a 1950 four-door Ford sedan painted black with white front doors, like a vintage police car. Instead of a light on top, a giant plastic donut lay flat on the roof. Fake white frosting dripped down the sides of the donut. Sprinkles embedded

in the frosting were actually tiny lights that could be programmed to twinkle, dance, and change colors. Our Deputy
Donut logo was on the car's front doors.

Hannah ran back inside to wait on customers. Hoping
that the lights in the car's donut would show up despite the
autumn-hazed sunshine, I set them to flash simultaneously in
their most vibrant colors.

Surrounded by fields, the high school was south of downtown Fallingbrook. As soon as I'd driven past the houses
closest to the school's grounds, I turned on a recording that
resembled the eerie rising and falling tones of a 1950s police
siren.

The football field was surrounded by chain-link fencing.
On the other side of the fence, a man who appeared to be in
his sixties stood facing a lineup of about twenty boys. The
man's hand was on a gate. Two couples, probably parents of
some of the boys, waited on the other side of the kids, who
appeared to range in age from about six to ten. Apparently,
the boys hadn't been practicing football that afternoon. They
were dressed for Ira's party, in jeans, T-shirts, hoodies, and
sneakers. The sight and sound of the donut car seemed to en-
ergize them. They hooted, jumped up and down, and waved
their arms above their heads.

I pulled up near the gate and switched off the siren sounds
but left the lights flashing. Straightening my Deputy Donut
hat, I stepped out of the car.

The older man called, "Hi, Emily!"

"Ira?" I had talked to the Jolly Cops over the phone, but
unlike Tom, I hadn't actually met them. I was never at
Deputy Donut in the wee hours when the Jolly Cops cleaned,
and they probably slept during most of the time we were
open.

"In the flesh," Ira said. "It's not even ten p.m., and I'm
awake." He looked familiar. Maybe I'd seen him years before
in his police uniform, maybe when Alec was still alive and I'd

met his police officer colleagues. Ira told the kids, "Stay there in line," and gestured to me. We walked on opposite sides of the fence until we were out of earshot of the kids, who weren't exactly quiet and wouldn't have heard what we said. Ira asked, "How do you want to organize this, Emily?"

"Would the kids like to sit in our pretend cruiser?"

"They'd love it, but I haven't suggested it to them. They didn't know that you and your antique Ford were coming. They don't know about the donut bites, either. We can put them at that table beside the bleachers. The coolers of juice and milk are already there."

"The donut bites are in the trunk. Maybe two of the parents can keep the kids in line while the other two carry the boxes of donut bites to the table. You could supervise the kids while they come out of the field and climb into the car from the front passenger side. Then they can slide across the bench seat, have a turn behind the wheel, and get out. I'll answer questions on the driver's side, help the kids out of the car, and then direct them to the refreshment table."

"Perfect. Exactly how I'd have planned it." He turned a keen look on me. "The keys aren't in the ignition, are they?"

I patted my front pants pocket. "I've got them."

"I figured you would. You're Tom's, um, you were married to Alec, weren't you?"

"Yes."

"A fine officer, and a terrible tragedy for us all when he was taken. You have excellent taste in husbands. Everyone knows that Brent Fyne is also a, pardon the pun, fine officer."

I agreed.

Still on opposite sides of the fence, we started back toward the kids. Some of them were getting fidgety.

Ira put fingers in his mouth and whistled. I was sorry I'd stayed close to the fence.

The kids quieted. Without mentioning donut bites, Ira told them that they would get a tour of the Ford's front seat, and then they could run back into the field for refreshments. "One at a time into the passenger seat, please. Be polite and respectful. The car is older than your grandparents." Still leaving the gate closed, he spoke briefly to the two couples.

I opened the donut car's trunk.

The couples looked at me, then back at Ira. They nodded, and one couple came through the gate to the back of the car.

Leaving those two people to look after the boxes of goodies and close the trunk, I opened the front passenger door and then went around, opened the driver's door, and moved the bench seat all the way back. Maybe none of those jeans-clad legs would be long enough to reach the pedals. I stood beside the open door.

Ira warned me, "I'm opening the floodgates." He cautioned the kids to wait until he signaled them, and then he strode to the car and beckoned toward the line of kids.

Their eyes wide with excitement, they filed toward the car.

Ira helped them into the passenger seat. They scooted across it, and then most of them leaned forward and put their hands on the steering wheel. The younger kids made car noises.

And they asked me questions.

"Where do you put the bad guys?"

"I'm not a police officer and this is not a real police car, but they would go back there, and there would be a barrier to keep them from touching anyone in front."

"Why do you have three pedals? One's for the gas and one's for the brake, but what's that third one for?"

"It's called a clutch. They were needed in old cars to change gears."

"Why do you keep a toy donut on your hat?"

"A real one might start smelling funny."

"Do you ever arrest kids?"

"Never."

"Is this how you beep the horn?" He pounded on various

parts of the wheel, discovered the horn ring, and the car loudly answered his question.

"Why do you have a couch instead of a front seat?"

"That's how they made most cars in 1950."

The last kid asked, "Why is a picture of a cat on your car doors?"

"The cat is a deputy. Her name's Deputy Donut."

Giving me a skeptical look, the boy jumped out of the car and ran toward the refreshments.

Ira and I shut the car doors. He thanked me. "They loved that."

I gazed toward the kids milling around the refreshment table. "They're not dressed for practice or a game."

"Our last game was Friday evening. This is our celebration of a great season."

"At that last game, did you notice a tall young woman with long, straight blond hair, maybe in a ponytail, among the spectators? She was probably with a man about the same age—college kids—in a black leather jacket. They could have arrived and departed by motorcycle."

"Sorry, I focus on my players. I never look toward the bleachers, and I don't remember hearing a motorcycle. That was the night that Albert McGoss was killed, right?"

"Yes, and the young woman is one of our assistants at Deputy Donut. She didn't say she was here, but the young man said they both were."

"Can't help you there."

"How do people find out about your games?"

"Most of our fans are parents and other family and friends, but we have our schedule posted in various places, like the library and the post office. Also, the local radio station and weekly newspaper announce the times of the games."

"Do you remember when Friday night's game ended and the fans left?"

"It was about six forty-five." Ira pierced me with a look. "That was about the time that McGoss died, wasn't it?"

"As far as I know, yes."

"Sorry I can't say that your assistant was here."

"It's all complicated. She never said she was here."

"So, you're wondering about the boyfriend, right?"

"Yes."

"Y'know, Emily, you're good at asking questions, but since you're not in law enforcement, don't ask just anybody."

"I know." I smiled. "You guys and Tom always say things like that."

"Why aren't you in law enforcement?"

I touched the faux-fur donut on my whimsical fake police hat. "Maybe Deputy Donut is close enough for me."

He laughed. "We certainly appreciate the donuts you leave out for us."

"Plus, I seem to have this tendency to marry police officers. One in the family is probably enough."

"I worked with your late husband on a couple of cases. That was before Alec became a detective. I retired before Brent came to Fallingbrook. Like you, Alec knew what questions to ask. As I said before, Alec was a good officer. And a good and kind man. What a loss." As if to hide his emotions or avoid seeing mine, he looked away from me and toward the kids. "I guess I should go join the party. You be careful, Emily. Stay out of trouble, and don't ask too many questions."

"I have one more for you."

"What?"

"Did your team win on Friday?"

"We maintained our perfect losing streak."

"You said it was a great season."

He winked. "I didn't say it was a winning season."

Chapter 21

Driving back to Deputy Donut, I was frustrated because I couldn't remember exactly when and where I'd met Ira. I stopped in the lot behind Deputy Donut and cleaned fingerprints off the donut car, and then I parked it in its garage.

I ran into the shop and told Tom, Olivia, and Hannah about the kids' excitement.

Hannah's smile was huge. "That must have been fun."

"It was. Supervising them as they sat in the donut car was great, but I didn't stay long enough to see their reaction to the donut bites."

"They liked them," Tom stated. "I can guarantee it."

We all agreed, and I went back outside. Before I started my own car, I left Brent a phone message about what Ira had said about not paying attention to the fans at his kids' football games and not remembering hearing a motorcycle at Friday night's game. Discouraged about not being able to actually talk to Brent, I disconnected and drove back to the house on Chicory Lake.

I gave Dep the attention she demanded, set plates, platters, and utensils on the kitchen island, and then changed into black capris, a white top printed in black flowers, and silver ballet flats. In the great room, I lit a fire in the wood-burning fireplace, and then I was ready to enjoy Samantha's shower.

At six, Misty arrived with Hannah and Samantha. Obviously pregnant, Samantha beamed with maternal contentment. I gave Hannah a tour of the kitchen, and we began heating appetizers.

Misty's mother and Samantha's mother arrived together. They teased me for not kidnapping my mother from Florida and bringing her to the party. Misty, Samantha, and I first met way back in junior high. We spent so much time in one another's homes that our parents treated all of us like three nearly inseparable daughters, and the six parents became close friends, too.

Samantha's mother took Dep to the catio so we could open the front door for more guests. Dep's leash wouldn't let Dep climb to her perches, but Samantha's mother would be able to help herself to a drink from the bar I'd set up, enjoy the twinkly-light ambience, chat with other guests, and help them find drinks for themselves.

A surprising number of Samantha's, Misty's, and my friends from high school attended. Gifts wrapped in pretty pastels overflowed from tables onto the floor.

Finally, all of the guests arrived, and we wouldn't be opening the front door again for a while. I removed Dep's harness and leash. She trotted to the gifts and began nosing at ribbons and bows. Betsy, one of our high school friends, was also Dep's veterinarian. She appointed herself to prevent Dep from nibbling on the packages, and Dep decided that cuddling on Betsy's lap was a perfect activity.

I quickly forgot not to say "baby" and lost my clothespin to Misty's mother.

She and Samantha turned out to be experts at collecting clothespins from the rest of us. We tried to trick them into saying "baby," but they didn't fall for it, even during our baby animal game. Betsy won that game. No one else remembered that a baby hare was a leveret. One woman tapped her sheet of paper with the answers she'd written. "I still stay it should be hareling."

Next we played the name game. Samantha's mother pulled a B from the turquoise baby hat. We held our breaths when she started saying a name starting with B for the infant. "Bay," she started. Looking strangely apprehensive, Samantha glanced at the mantel. Grinning, Samantha's mother said "Bayberry." Everyone except Samantha laughed, but after a second's delay, she laughed, too, and I wondered if I'd only imagined that brief twinge of apparent concern.

I pulled out an F. "First," I announced. The others booed.

I held my breath when it was Samantha's turn to draw a letter. Maybe she would accidentally or on purpose divulge one of the names that she and Hooligan were planning to give their baby. She pulled out a D. She glanced at my cat, content on Betsy's lap, and said, "Deputy." People complained that she hadn't suggested a name that she and Hooligan might actually be considering. With an innocent expression on her face, she asked, "How can you be sure?"

Misty's mother pulled out the H. "Ha!" She quickly waved her hand in front of her face. "No, *Ha* is not the name I choose. It's Hooliganette."

Samantha winked and gave her a thumbs-up.

Offering appetizers, Hannah wandered among the guests. She was near me with a platter of savory shortbreads and crackers topped with slices of cheese log when a high school friend asked me, "Isn't this near where that man died from falling off a cliff in the state forest?"

Hannah turned pale, quickly set the platter onto the nearest table, and gasped, "Oven!" She hurried toward the kitchen end of the great room. I suspected that her rushing away had more to do with the conversation she'd overheard than with the oven. What had she and Joshua really been doing around the time that McGoss died? Could I convince her to tell Brent or Rex the true story before she became enmeshed in something she couldn't escape?

I gave the woman a terse answer. "Yes, Chicory Lake is just down the hill from here, but I don't want to discuss it during Samantha's shower."

The woman patted my knee. "I understand. Did you know the man?"

I shook my head, picked up the platter that Hannah had left behind, and offered the woman a snack. She took one. I excused myself and mingled among other guests. At my urging, they emptied the platter. I took it to the kitchen.

Hannah was arranging mini quiches on another serving dish. She looked up toward me but didn't quite meet my gaze. "I caught them before they burned."

To me, the mini quiches looked far from burned, and the timer on the oven still had a minute left. "You're handling this all very well, Hannah."

She mumbled, "Thanks."

I added, "I knew you would."

Samantha opened gifts while the rest of us admired them. Samantha's mother made notes, nearly everyone took pictures, and Misty's mother corralled ribbons and wrapping paper. At least, she tried to. Dep seemed to believe that every piece of wrapping paper on the floor had to be tested as a possible bed, and then, before any of us could stop her, she twisted several ribbons around her body and was happily kicking at them with her back feet. Betsy and I kept a close watch. Dep wasn't trying to eat any ribbons, and none of them were looped around her neck. We let her play for a few minutes, and then we unwrapped her. Tail puffed and held upright in a question mark, she skated across the floor to the catio, where she would undoubtedly climb to one of the cute little shelves and stare out into the night.

The baby gifts that Samantha received were adorable. Samantha's mother glowed almost as much as Samantha did. Misty's mother, Misty, and I smiled almost constantly. My face hurt.

Misty's mother won the clothespin game. I ended up with no clothespins and a lot of IOUs, and so did Misty and Samantha.

With a big grin, Hooligan arrived. He scooped up a couple of snacks, grinned at the decorations on the mantel, and then gathered the gifts and took them to his car. After thanking everyone, he and Samantha left, and the other guests left, too.

Misty helped Hannah and me wash dishes, put everything away, and take down the decorations. Dep kept her distance from the balloons but not from the streamers, and we had to rescue them from her. Or her from them. I spread out the fire's last embers, and they quickly dimmed from pale orange to gray.

Misty offered to take Hannah home, but I said, "It's out of your way. I'll take her if she doesn't mind Dep's caterwauling. I'm planning to spend the night in our Fallingbrook house. With any luck, Brent will already be there."

Misty and I again thanked Hannah for her help and gave her the pay we'd promised for her evening's work. Dep did not want to go into her carrier. I told her, "You'd have to stay here alone until tomorrow after work." I didn't know if it was that threat or Hannah's gentle smile that persuaded Dep to relax her outstretched legs enough for us to put her into her carrier.

Cooing to the indignant cat, Hannah took the carrier out to the porch. Misty watched me make certain that I locked all of the chalet's doors and windows and armed the building's alarms. I teased, "Always the police officer, Misty."

"I can't help it. And you can be sure that I watched you end any threat of the fire rekindling itself in your fireplace, too."

The three of us walked out to Misty's and my cars. Hannah asked to sit in back with Dep. "Maybe she'll be calmer." I fastened Dep's carrier to the seat belt. "Good luck. Maybe you should have brought earplugs."

Laughing, Hannah slid in beside Dep. She said, over Dep's yowls, "It's okay, Dep. I'm here with you."

In her car, Misty followed us down the driveway. Since she was accomplished at fast but safe driving, I thought she might pass us after we turned onto the county road, but she stayed a nice distance behind us. I joked to Hannah, "I can't speed while Misty's driving behind us. She might pull me over and give me a ticket."

Hannah called over the seat, "She probably trusts you. She doesn't trust me."

"Why do you think that?"

"She's nice and everything, and on the way out to your place, she didn't say a word about not trusting me, but she watches me like she's waiting for me to do something horrible. Or to confess to a murder or something. I had nothing to do with that man's death."

"I'm sure you didn't. I'm also sure that other campers had to have mentioned to the police what you told us in Deputy Donut on Friday—that Albert quarreled with you three Thursday night. So, it was inevitable that the police would be interested in all three of you, along with lots of other people. Police officers work on maintaining neutral expressions that can be misinterpreted as suspicion. Don't take Misty's behavior personally."

"Easier said than done. We were honest with Brent about that argument. It's not like we hid it."

"I've been meaning to ask you—on Friday after work, did

Joshua go into the grocery store with you?" I kept having to yell for Hannah to hear me.

She didn't answer right away. She again attempted to reassure Dep, and then she countered my question with one of her own. "What do you mean?"

"Was Joshua actually in the grocery store at the same time you were? I mentioned to Laura that you'd brought a handsome man shopping with you, and she said she would have noticed that, and you were alone."

Hannah shouted over Dep's attempts to yodel, "I'm trying to remember. But yes, I think what Laura said must be right. I went to the shop by myself, and when I came out, Joshua was in front, with his motorcycle. He offered to take me and my groceries to our apartment, but Olivia would've had a panic attack. I turned him down, and I don't know where he went after that. I thought he was going into the shop, but maybe he didn't. I went home, and Olivia cooked us a nice dinner, and then I borrowed her car and went up to the state forest."

"How did you get Dep to be quiet?"

"I unzipped her carrier enough to worm my hand in. I'm scratching her chin."

I couldn't help laughing. "Thank you. I'm going to have to start bringing you along whenever I need to take her in the car."

"She's a darling. So cute with her purring and complaints at the same time. She's both rumbling and grumbling, aren't you, honey?"

I agreed, "She is a darling." But I wasn't about to be sidetracked. I asked Hannah, "When you got to Joshua and Zachary's campsite on Friday evening, were they both there?"

"Yes, why?"

"I saw the tracks from a motorcycle in the parking area for the Clifftop Trail."

"Why did you go up there?"

"I was kayaking below the lookout and heard a scream. I knew there was some possibility that you might be in the state forest that evening, and I got scared that it was you or one of your friends who had screamed."

"I didn't."

"Also, shortly after I heard the scream, I caught a glimpse, maybe, of someone backing away from the railing next to that big balancing boulder at the lookout. I'm not positive that I saw anyone." *And Brent had said that Albert was dead before he landed, so after I saw or imagined someone backing away from the railing, the killer must have returned to push Albert's body over the cliff. And hadn't I heard something like branches snapping after I started paddling away?*

"It wasn't us." Hannah sounded tense.

Dep made a plaintive cry.

I reminded Hannah, "I found a hairclip up there that matched the pair you wore that day. Brent took it as evidence. A forensics lab can get fingerprints or even DNA from it."

"Okay, okay." Hannah was beginning to sound cross. "The three of us were up there that evening after dinner, and I did lose a hairclip, but I don't know where or when it fell out. But I didn't hear a scream, or if I did, it didn't register. We didn't get all the way to the lookout. Joshua was nervous about going out of sight of his motorcycle, and I thought I saw someone lurking in the woods, and I got scared, so I said we should turn around."

I glanced at the rearview mirror. Misty's headlights still shined behind us. "Did you tell Brent about the person you thought you saw?"

"I didn't tell Brent I was up there, so, no. None of us told him. But we should have, because we were together, and none of the three of us went out of the others' sight. We have alibis for one another, but no one's going to believe us now."

"I do."

"Police officers won't."

"Withholding information from the police doesn't help." I tried not to sound judgmental and probably did not succeed.

"It never occurred to us that it would matter. If we'd known how important it was, we would have told the truth. We just didn't want Olivia to know I went up there, even though I didn't get into the sort of danger that scares her. I wasn't climbing rocks or anything. But I guess there was still danger if a murderer was up there." I heard a slight tremor in Hannah's voice. "And now, we could be suspected of murder. Arrested, even, maybe. And end up spending our lives in jail!" That last word was so loud that it must have startled Dep. She meowed. Hannah apologized, and Dep subsided into moaning.

I told Hannah, "Other people had stronger motives to kill Albert McGoss than you three did."

"Are you sure?"

"Positive. Can you describe the person you saw? Was it a man or a woman?"

"I didn't see enough to tell. I'm not sure, but I think the person was wearing jeans, dark ones, at least that's how I picture him or her. And maybe a black hoodie? Something like that. My gut feeling says it was a man, but really, I'm not even sure I saw anyone. Thanks to Olivia and her forebodings, the whole place gave me the creeps, so maybe I just imagined that someone who might want to harm us was lurking up there."

"Did you see other vehicles in the parking lot?"

"I didn't pay attention, but I think there were a couple when we first got there, and for sure there was at least one after we ended our hike. Our attempt at a hike. I saw a pickup truck, I think, probably black or charcoal or maybe navy."

I'd seen a black one that Brent had said was registered to

Albert McGoss, but I didn't think I was supposed to tell anyone else about that. Instead, I asked, "Did you ride to and from the campground on Joshua's motorcycle?"

"I didn't have to." She sounded peeved. "Zachary had his pickup truck."

It did not quite answer my question. Several car lengths back, Misty flashed her lights and turned off Wisconsin Street toward Scott's and her home.

Hannah offered, "Joshua rides that motorcycle too fast. He roared into the parking lot and out again. That could be why none of us heard anything else, like screams."

"Do you remember when you left the parking area?"

"No, but Zachary took me straight back to the campground. I don't know when we got there."

I pulled up in front of the building where Olivia and Hannah had shared an apartment ever since their parents' death.

Hannah said, "Sorry, Dep honey, but I'm going now, and I'll have to zip you inside this nice little cocoon that you seem to think is a torture chamber."

I still had lots that I wanted to say to Hannah, but I thanked her for looking after Dep, who was accelerating her shrieks. I couldn't help reminding Hannah, "As the old saying goes, honesty is the best policy, especially when talking to law enforcement." Again, I sounded much too stern.

Hannah opened the car door. "Do you think I don't know that?" But she didn't get out. She asked in a small voice, "I should tell the detectives what I just told you, shouldn't I?"

"What do you think?"

"I should. Do you think, well, could I go talk to Brent this evening? I don't want him coming to our place and scaring Olivia."

"Talking to him this evening is a good idea. I'll call and ask if he's available."

Brent answered right away. He was already in our house

on Maple Street. I told him, "I'm bringing Hannah over. She wants to talk to you about where she and her friends were Friday evening."

"Okay." His voice was even and unsurprised. "I'm mulling cider. I'll add enough for another person."

"We're only a few blocks away."

"The cider will be ready."

Chapter 22

Brent's SUV was parked on Maple Street in front of our house.

I pulled into the driveway. Murmuring to Dep, Hannah wrapped her arms around the carrier and followed me into the house. We let Dep out of her carrier. Dep darted toward the kitchen.

Smiling, Brent brought three mugs of warm, spiced cider into the living room. He asked Hannah, "Would you like Emily to sit in on our discussion?"

"Yes, please, if she has time. She already knows everything I have to say." Hannah turned toward me. Her eyes seemed bigger and bluer than usual, maybe with anxiety, and perhaps a few tears.

Brent set the mugs on the coffee table. "Can you stay, Emily?"

"Yes." I sat on the couch and gestured to Hannah. She edged onto the seat farthest from me. Dep skittered into the room and leaped onto my lap.

Brent chose his favorite chair, picked up the notebook and pen he must have put on the table beside the chair after I called him, and gave Hannah an encouraging look. "Hannah, do your friends Joshua and Zachary know what you're about to tell me?"

"They know what really happened, but they don't know I'm going to tell you what it was."

Brent retained his nonjudgmental expression. "Please don't tell them that you're talking to me."

Hannah took her phone out of her pocket and set it on the coffee table where we could all see it. "I won't."

Brent thanked her. "My colleague from the state, Detective Rex Clobar, is on his way to their campsite now to ask them if they have anything to add to what they already told us about that evening." He gave Hannah another friendly look. "What's up?"

Hannah sipped at her cider. "Thank you for the cider. It's delicious."

Her new statement was identical to what she'd told me in the car. I was almost certain she was telling the truth.

Brent seemed particularly interested in the details of the person she might or might not have seen in the woods near the trail. He asked Hannah, "Could the person have been Albert McGoss?"

She clenched her hands on her lap. Her knuckles whitened. "Possibly. I didn't get a perfect look at Albert McGoss while he was in Deputy Donut. He was sitting down, and he didn't look up at me, not even when I took his order."

Brent set his mug down. "Do you have a sense of which direction the person was moving, Hannah?"

"Not really, but I didn't feel like he was coming closer to us. Maybe he wasn't moving, or he was going away, like toward the lookout while we were still near the parking lot. It was more like a spidey sense that someone was in the woods, a feeling like being watched, you know? Maybe no one was there. I was already creeped out. Those woods are really dense and dark, even before the sun goes down. Also, Olivia's not the only one who's petrified at the thought that cliffs might be nearby. The word *lookout* is even scary. To me, it means, 'Look out!' " She shouted it like a warning.

I sipped the warm, perfectly seasoned cider. I'd also thought I'd seen someone up near the lookout on Friday evening. That had been after I'd heard the scream, so, if I saw anyone, it most likely was not Albert. The person I might have seen was moving quickly away from the lookout, but I hadn't been able to see all the way to the trail on the far side of the lookout, so I didn't know which direction he or she went. The Clifftop Trail was an almost perfect circle. No matter which direction someone went on that trail after they left the lookout, the trail would take them back to the parking area.

But they might not have stayed on the Clifftop Trail. They could have faded into the woods or navigated that narrow, twisty pathway down the hill to the Cornflower Trail, and from there to the sandy beach where they'd left a canoe. Nothing seemed to make sense.

Brent asked Hannah, "Did you hear anyone scream?"

"No." She scooted even farther forward on the edge of the couch cushion, as if she were considering falling off the couch and trying to hide underneath the coffee table like I had when I was about six years old with this very same furniture in my grandmother's house. Hannah's voice came out softly. "Maybe the scream was when Zachary and I were in his pickup truck with the windows closed, and Joshua was still nearby, maybe starting up his motorcycle. That bike can be loud."

"Who left the parking area first?" Brent asked. "Joshua on his motorcycle or you and Zachary in Zachary's pickup truck?"

"Joshua, and he got way ahead of us. Zachary is careful with his truck, especially on dirt and gravel roads." Poor Zachary. Hannah made caution sound like a deal-breaker in a boyfriend.

Brent asked her, "Was Joshua in his and Zachary's campsite when you and Zachary got there?"

Hannah became still. "No. Joshua didn't arrive for about

a half hour after we did. He said he'd been exploring the state forest."

"Was it dark out?" Sipping his cider, Brent watched her over the rim of his mug.

"Not when we left the entrance to the Clifftop Trail, but it was by the time Joshua made it to their site. Zachary's good at building campfires, and Joshua isn't. I figured he was too embarrassed to try it again when I was there, so he stayed away until he figured Zachary had the fire going."

Brent wrote in his notebook and asked if there was anything else she wanted to tell him.

She twisted her fingers together in her lap. "Not that I can think of at the moment, but if I remember anything else, I'll let you know."

"I'll have a new statement typed for you to sign. Are you working at Deputy Donut tomorrow, Hannah?"

"Yes."

Brent looked at me. "Will Olivia be there, too, Emily?"

I stroked the soft fur between Dep's shoulder blades. "According to our schedule, yes."

Brent turned his attention back to Hannah. "So, you would probably rather I didn't bring your statement there for you to sign."

She bowed her head. "That would be best."

I suggested, "How about if I send her out on an errand, like to Freeze for some ice cream. What would be a good time?"

Brent asked Hannah, "How does eleven sound?"

"Fine." Her one-syllable answer was clipped, as if she could hardly wait to get away from us.

I eased Dep onto the cushion beside me, stood, and told Brent, "I'll send her out at five minutes to. Come on, Hannah. I'll take you home."

"I can walk."

I opened the front door. "But I won't let you. And you can

even ride in front. We won't subject Dep to the car again tonight."

Hannah breathed out a laugh but was quiet during the short ride. I pulled up to the curb in front of the building where she and Olivia lived.

Hannah opened the car door. "Thanks, Emily, for everything." She said it softly, and scrambled out. I watched until she was safely inside the entryway to the steps to the second-floor apartment.

At home, I parked my car in the garage and then put Brent's SUV in the driveway.

Brent was still in the wing chair. Dep was purring on his lap.

I sat on the couch. Brent brought Dep and sat next to me. He put one arm around me. "Thanks for encouraging Hannah to tell the truth."

"Do you think it is the truth?" Dep rolled from Brent's lap onto mine.

"Could be. Rex hasn't called me yet, but he's barely had time to get up there, let alone interview the two men to see if they're sticking to what they told us earlier."

I buried my fingers in Dep's fur. "I hope that at least one of them can describe the person lurking in the woods."

"That would be a lucky break. Do you have anything with Hannah's printing on it?"

"I think she filled out her job application by hand. I didn't pay it much attention because I was certain that, since Olivia raised her, she'd be a great employee. Want me to go get it from Deputy Donut now?"

"It will wait. When you get a chance tomorrow, can you scan it and email it to me? And might you have anything that Dawn McGoss, Kevin Lunnion, or Laura at the grocery store printed?"

"Not from Kevin or Laura, but I think that Dawn wrote *Thank you* on my receipt. Next time I'm at the lake, I'll dig it out of the trash. The printing on the note Dep found looked wobbly, like someone was trying to print differently than usual. Dawn has artistic talent. I can imagine her crafting a note that wouldn't look anything like her normal handwriting. I guess that anyone intending to lure someone to their death might do that."

A phone rang. Brent looked at me. "Is that yours?"

"Hannah must have left it behind." I moved our cider mugs. Hannah's phone was still on the coffee table. I told Brent, "The caller ID says *Joshua.*"

We didn't touch the phone. "I'm glad she forgot to take it with her," Brent said. "She might have thought that Rex had already talked to Joshua, and she would be free to tell him about the new info she gave me." Brent checked his watch. "But Rex might not have talked to both of those boys yet."

"He won't talk to them together, will he?"

"No way."

"I didn't think so. I like Zachary, and according to what Hannah just said, there's a time gap when Joshua was supposedly riding around in the state forest on his motorcycle. It might have been after I heard that scream, but no one is sure of the timing."

Brent collected the mugs from the coffee table. "I need to go meet Rex at the office to discuss it all." He nodded at the phone on the table. "You can take that to her in the morning. I hope she won't want it before then. You deserve a few hours of sleep before you have to get up for work."

"So do you."

He took the mugs to the kitchen, came back, and kissed me. "Don't wait up."

Chapter 23

Just before dawn the next morning, I put Dep's harness around her and fastened her leash to it. The air was above freezing but crisp, and I was glad I was wearing my Deputy Donut black jeans with a jacket over my long-sleeved uniform shirt. Dep, who was undoubtedly relieved that I hadn't put her into the car, was especially frisky.

Walking to work, I still couldn't figure out why Ira had looked familiar. It was embarrassing to have probably met him before and not acknowledged it. He had known who I was immediately, but the donut car had given him a substantial hint. Maybe I'd met him when Alec and I were first dating. I'd been barely aware of anyone besides Alec.

I shook my head and concentrated on more pressing matters.

Hannah.

Because I liked her and Olivia, I wanted to believe that she'd lied at first only because she didn't want to worry Olivia.

I hadn't talked to Brent after he returned from the police station. I wondered if Joshua and Zachary had admitted to Rex that they'd been on the trail Friday night. Had either of them described the shadowy person that Hannah had sensed in the woods nearby?

Was it the same person I'd thought I'd seen but couldn't identify?

That person could have murdered Albert. Had he learned enough about Hannah, Joshua, and Zachary or their vehicles to track them down and prevent them from ever identifying him?

In the kitchen at Deputy Donut, I handed Hannah her phone. "You left this behind."

She put a hand over her heart. "Thank you."

Olivia's comment was not quite snarky. "That's not like you." She turned to me. "How was the shower?"

"Fun. Busy. Hannah's help was greatly appreciated." I didn't let on that Hannah had not left the phone at the shower or that she had come to Brent's and my other house to talk to Brent. "We were lucky that she could help us, just like we're lucky that she's working here. I can speak for Tom, too." Tom had Wednesdays and Thursdays off.

While Olivia started frying donuts and Hannah prepared the dining tables, I made an excuse about wanting to check an account and returned to the office. I pulled Hannah's job application out of the file. The printing was girly, and nearly all of it was in lowercase letters. She had also printed on the lines, but these lines were darker than the faint lines on the page torn from a small notebook. I scanned Hannah's application into the computer, emailed it to Brent, and then returned to the kitchen.

Later, after all of the Knitpickers, the retired men, and our other morning customers had been served, and Olivia was frying donuts in bubbling oil, I found a chance to speak to Hannah near our serving counter when no one else was nearby or could hear us. Keeping an eye on our customers in case we were needed, I suggested, "You, Joshua, and Zachary need to be cautious. If Albert's murderer saw you three in the woods Friday night, he might know who you are, and he'll want to make certain that none of you will be able to describe him to anyone."

"Okay, and you should be careful, too, out there at that lake, especially when Brent's not around."

I couldn't help biting my lips and probably displaying the anxiety that I'd been trying to hide from Brent. "I know."

Hannah reminded me, "As I told Brent, I'm not even sure I saw anyone."

"I hope you didn't!" I became a little less heated. "Or maybe I hope that you did, and you'll be able to identify him before he identifies you three."

For the first time that morning, she relaxed into a natural-sounding laugh. "Good idea."

The front door opened. I glanced past Hannah and had to prevent myself from gasping.

Kevin Lunnion came in.

Hannah had her back to the front door. I took advantage of my lack of height. Positioning myself so that Hannah was between Kevin and me, and he wouldn't be able to see my face, I muttered, "Don't turn around. I'll serve the latest customer." I could tell that Hannah was tempted to try to see who I was talking about, so I added, "Maybe you should go into the storeroom."

She held up the empty coffee pot in her hand and said loudly, "I'll go wash this." Without looking back, she walked behind the serving counter and around the half-wall into the kitchen. I hoped she'd go directly from the kitchen to the storeroom without taking a peek into the dining room and possibly allowing Kevin to see her face.

Again I was almost surprised that Kevin was wandering around in public. Either he was innocent, or he brazenly expected to get away with Albert's murder. He sat near the Knitpickers' table.

I strolled to him in what I hoped was a casually business-like way, but I was too self-conscious, making my movements jerky. I asked, "Did you bring me the bill for sharpening my mower's blades?"

Frowning, he pulled a folded piece of paper out of the chest pocket of his green polo shirt. "Yes. I almost forgot. Here you go. No rush."

I unfolded the paper. As I'd hoped, he had printed the invoice by hand. He'd used both upper and lowercase letters. I was no expert on handwriting, but the capital letters looked similar to what I remembered of the note I'd found. I said, "You didn't charge as much as you said you would."

"Your mower was a piece of cake. Besides, I usually finish a job when I say I will. You get a discount for my lateness."

"I wasn't in a hurry. Grass doesn't grow quickly this time of year."

"True, but I'm sure you'll want to mow at least one last time before it snows."

I slipped the bill into my apron pocket. "We're not even going to mention that word. What can I bring you? Is it early enough in the day for you to try some of our coffee? Today's special coffee is a lightly fruity but well-balanced medium roast, a single-origin from Papua New Guinea. And we also have the rich and flavorful Colombian coffee that we serve every day."

"One of you used the term 'single-origin' the other day. Does that mean what it sounds like?"

"It can mean a single coffee plantation, but in many cases, like this one, it's from a certain geographical region."

"Papua New Guinea," he repeated. "That sounds interesting. I'd like to try it. And also a couple of your donuts. Do you have beignets again today?"

"We do."

"They're big. One of those, then, and . . . any suggestions?"

"Would you like to try one of our pear-ginger fritters?"

"That sounds good."

I hurried into the kitchen. The clock on the wall said it was ten thirty. In twenty-five minutes, I needed to send Hannah to Freeze so she could stop in at the police station and sign the statement Brent was having prepared for her.

I was in a dilemma. Workers on break typically took up to a half hour in Deputy Donut. Kevin could easily recognize Hannah and her long blond hair tied back in a ponytail. That would be fine if he merely remembered noticing her in the shop when he was here before. But what if he'd seen her while he was lurking in the woods, before or after confronting his former partner? Hannah's hair might have shined like a beacon in the shadowy forest, especially after she lost her hairclip.

Maybe he kept returning here to figure out if she was the woman he'd seen on the Clifftop Trail that day. Even if he hadn't recognized her by her height and her hair, he could have remembered Zachary and Joshua letting Gigi and Dep into the shop.

And he knew that Hannah worked in Deputy Donut.

I popped my head into the storeroom and told her quietly, "If he's still here at five to eleven, go out through the loading dock and walk up through the parking lots. You can cut through the drugstore and cross Wisconsin Street to Oak." A short street, Oak ended at Wisconsin Street. The police station was on Oak, in the municipal building, just past the fire station and across the street from the southern end of the village square. Freeze was farther east.

"Okay." She was drying the coffee carafe.

In the kitchen, Olivia lifted a basket of beignets out of the deep fryer. I poured Kevin's coffee and put his beignet and fritter on a plate and carried the plate and mug into the dining room. Behind me, Olivia called, "Hannah!" She sounded annoyed.

Kevin seemed to be eavesdropping on the Knitpickers. Their gossip must have amused him. Still smiling, he thanked me and picked up the mug. He looked beyond me, and his eyes opened wider. "Well, hello there!"

I turned around. To my dismay, Hannah was carrying a fresh pot of coffee and heading toward the Knitpickers. She gave a resigned shrug and glanced for a second up toward the ceiling.

Striding behind Hannah, Olivia took another pot of coffee toward the table where the retired men were joking and laughing. I should have warned Olivia that Hannah needed to stay hidden from Kevin.

It was no wonder that Olivia wanted to make certain that our regulars didn't have to wait for refills. The Knitpickers and retired men were some of our favorite customers. And while they obviously liked Tom, Olivia, and me, they all treated Hannah like a beloved granddaughter.

Kevin looked over the top of his mug, set the mug down carefully, and called to Hannah, "How did you like riding a motorcycle?"

Hannah stopped walking. With a stunned expression on her face, she shook her head slightly, pointed toward her throat, and squeaked, "Me?"

Olivia had also halted. Obviously struggling between pain and anger, she stared at the back of Hannah's Deputy Donut hat.

Hannah got control of her voice and said loudly, "I've never ridden one."

I wasn't sure she convinced her older sister. Olivia still looked worried.

I also didn't think she changed Kevin's mind. He argued, "I was sure I saw you on the back of one. Your hair is un-mistakable."

Hannah's laugh sounded forced. "Lots of us buy the same shade of blond at the drugstore."

Kevin didn't let it go. "I could have sworn it was you." He tore off a piece of beignet and put it into his mouth. Why hadn't he asked her about the motorcycle the previous time he'd been in Deputy Donut? Was he hoping to put extra time between now and the previous Friday?

I asked Kevin as innocently as I could, "When did you think you saw her?"

He began to look uneasy. "I'm not sure. Late last week?"

Hannah again denied it. "Not me."

Olivia frowned.

Then I remembered that the second time that Kevin had come to Deputy Donut, Hannah had been on her lunch break, and Kevin hadn't had a chance to talk to her. Knowing that I might cause more trouble between the sisters, I asked Kevin, "Where did you see the motorcycle with the blond woman?"

Kevin glanced at my face and away again. "I don't remember for sure. North of my place, I think." Maybe he'd been intentionally vague. He might have realized that if Hannah had ridden on Joshua's motorcycle only once, if it had been the night that Albert McGoss died, and if Kevin admitted seeing her in or near the state forest, Kevin could have placed himself near the scene of the crime. He shook his head like someone surprised at ever having gotten anything wrong. "It must have been someone else."

Hannah sent him another insincere smile. "Had to be." She bent toward the Knitpickers. "Who needs a refill of Colombian?"

Stiff and straight, Olivia stalked to the retired men and started topping up their mugs.

Kevin must have been thinking about Friday evening and what happened in Chicory Lake State Forest. He picked up his mug again and held it between both hands without lifting it to his mouth. "Tell me," he said so quietly that only I would be able to hear him, "have you heard any more about the investigation into the death, the probable murder, of my friend and former partner?"

I almost demanded, *So, now he was your friend?* Instead, I merely responded, "I haven't heard of any arrests. Have you?"

"Not a one. I can't imagine why they haven't nabbed his wife yet. I mean, the guy assaulted her, made her do all the work, and there's something else, too, something that's a little embarrassing. I'm single. Divorced, and Dawn has often hinted, strongly, that she'd be interested in, well, in me. But I made it clear that I believe marriage vows are sacred. So, what I'm afraid of is that she found an easier way than divorce, which, believe me, can get messy, to free herself from her marriage vows." He sat up straighter. "But offing your spouse in order to latch onto a new one is not exactly a great way of attracting a new one, if you know what I mean." Again, the twinkle in his eye could have fooled me into thinking he was mostly a nice person, but with a warped sense of humor. And then there was his self-serving definition of *sacred*.

I suspected that my returning smile looked as forced as it felt. "Maybe you should tell the police your theory."

The corners of his mouth turned down. "They wouldn't listen to me. They might, to you."

"Or you could call their tip line."

His eyes shifted to the side. "I might do that."

"Did you ever see Albert and Dawn's setup at the campground in the state forest?"

He didn't seem to notice that I'd eased the conversation into a different direction. "They never invited me. Which was like them. Like him, I mean. Dawn might have asked me up there if Albert was ever gone. Not that I'd have accepted an invitation to visit only her."

"The state forest is huge, and has lots of lakes, hills, and hiking trails."

He tore his beignet into bits. "I've never been interested in hiking. Never had time for it, really, with working and everything. My landscaping business gives me more than enough outdoor time." Muscles on his thick forearms bunched up.

"Did Albert like hiking?"

Kevin gulped at his coffee. "I don't know, but I doubt it. Hey, your coffee's good, by the way."

I thanked him.

"Really good. But do you want to know why I'm sure that Albert didn't like hiking?" Kevin answered his question. "He didn't like expending energy."

"What about Dawn?"

Kevin started tearing the fritter apart. "She's probably like me—too busy."

I aimed for a chatty tone. "I wonder what made Albert go hiking on the Clifftop Trail on Friday night, if it wasn't something he would normally do."

"Probably to get out of doing real work that Dawn asked him to do. I never heard of that trail until Albert's death was in the papers. With all the state forests and parks that Wisconsin has, it would be impossible to know about all of the trails, unless you were a real keener for hiking. What about you. Are you a hiker?" Finally, he put a chunk of ginger-infused pear into his mouth.

I twisted my face into what I hoped would pass as a rueful expression. "It would be time-consuming. And I probably wouldn't take the rugged, difficult trails. I prefer nice, gentle woods."

"The Clifftop Trail isn't dangerous." He quickly amended his statement. "Or so they say. Unless you're like Albert and . . ." He swooped one hand down the other arm like someone going down a slide. "And slip off a cliff."

I couldn't help a queasy grimace.

"There's a railing," Kevin said. "Supposedly." He shoved a piece of his torn-up beignet into his mouth. "And there's a big rock up there. Maybe he climbed on it and slid off." For someone who had only recently heard of the Clifftop Trail, he seemed to know a lot about it.

It was getting close to eleven. Kevin hadn't finished his coffee, and most of his beignet and his fritter were in fragments in the powdered sugar on his plate. I hoped that meant he was planning to stay longer. I needed to send Hannah on her errand before Kevin finished and might also go outside.

I glanced through the front windows. People were out on the sidewalks in the autumn sunshine. Even if Kevin followed Hannah, she wouldn't be alone. But he wouldn't follow her, would he? It would be too obvious.

I excused myself and went to the Knitpickers' table. Hannah had refilled everyone's coffee. Empty carafe in hand, she stood with her other hand on her hip, joking with the five ladies. Olivia had returned to the kitchen.

"Hannah," I said quietly, "sorry to interrupt, but could you go to Freeze and pick up a quart of vanilla bean ice cream and a quart of coffee ice cream, too, please?"

"Sure."

"I'll look after the coffee pot and your apron and hat."

"Okay." She handed them to me.

I took them to the kitchen. When I turned around, Hannah was striding north along Wisconsin Street. She held her phone against her ear. I wondered if she was returning the call from Joshua that she'd missed because of forgetting her phone the night before.

Scowling, Kevin threw bills onto his table. In five quick steps, he was at the front door. He slapped it open with one hand and hurried through our empty patio to the sidewalk.

He turned north, the same direction Hannah had gone.

Chapter 24

I didn't take time to think. I rushed through the dining area, pushed the front door open, and ran out onto the patio.

Hannah was walking quickly, but Kevin was catching up.

Olivia brushed past me and headed north. "Nothing's in the deep fryers."

I already had my phone in my hand. "I'll text her to go into the police station and tell them she's being followed."

Without slowing down, Olivia called over shoulder, "You don't have to. I taught her to do that."

Behind me, I heard footsteps. All five of the Knitpickers and all six of the retired men had followed us out onto the patio. A Knitpicker muttered, "A man his age!"

One of the retired men answered indignantly, "Following a young girl like that."

Knowing that Hannah was supposed to talk to Brent at the police station, and that she'd probably go there before picking up the ice cream, I didn't text her. Instead I called Brent. To my relief, he answered right away.

I blurted, "Hannah's on her way, but Kevin Lunnion is following her."

"I'll find her." The line went silent.

Kevin slowed and looked over his shoulder. I couldn't tell

if he saw Olivia storming up the sidewalk toward him. He sped up again.

Behind me, a dog yapped.

A Knitpicker cooed, "Oh, look! How cute!"

I whirled to see what she was excited about. How did I guess it would be Gigi? The little dog trotted onto the patio and danced around on her hind feet. Apparently, she was a bridesmaid this time, in aqua chiffon ruffles and frills with a bouquet of fabric flowers on her wrist and a tiny circlet of matching flowers fastened around the ponytail on top of her head. Where was Madame Monique?

The tiny dog pawed at my shins. I picked her up and cooed, "Did you get lost again, Gigi?"

Cheryl, the most grandmotherly Knitpicker, asked me, "Do you know where she belongs?"

I pointed. "Across the driveway, at Thrills and Frills."

Cheryl held out her arms. "You're busy. I'll take her."

I relinquished the little doggy and looked north again. Hannah was crossing Wisconsin Street onto the sidewalk on Oak.

Without turning his head toward where Hannah had gone, Kevin strode north beyond the intersection. Olivia was still a half block behind him.

"Gigi! Gigi!" Madame Monique's voice boomed out.

I turned around. Like little Gigi, Madame Monique wore a frilly aqua gown. She reached out her arms. Madame Monique's voice became soft and loving. "There you are, you naughty darling!"

Cheryl handed Gigi to her. Madame Monique covered the dog's little snout with kisses.

North of us, Olivia reached the intersection of Wisconsin and Oak. She stopped, turned, and stared east, the direction that her younger sister had gone. I could no longer see Hannah. Behind me, Madame Monique cooed to Gigi, telling her in the sweetest tones never to run out of Thrills and Frills again.

Kevin continued north.

Olivia started back. Madame Monique carried Gigi toward Thrills and Frills. I went into Deputy Donut.

From the back of the office couch, Dep gazed toward the front window. Her eyes were huge. She must have seen me cradling Gigi in my arms.

The Knitpickers and retired men followed me inside. Talking in excited voices, they sat down.

I began clearing Kevin's table.

Olivia opened the front door and came in. Knitpickers applauded her. "Our hero!"

Olivia stomped past me. I understood her annoyance. I was angry at myself.

I took Kevin's dirty dishes into the kitchen and apologized. "I'm sorry about sending Hannah on an errand when that man was still here. He hadn't finished his beignet and fritter, so I thought he would stay inside until Hannah was gone. It's a good thing that you went after them so quickly. When Hannah crossed Wisconsin Street to Oak, he looked over his shoulder. He might have seen you, and maybe that's why he continued up Wisconsin instead of following Hannah onto Oak. But maybe he knew the police station is on Oak, and he didn't want police officers seeing him near her."

"He definitely saw me. And the face I was making was probably enough to fry his hair." She lowered a basket of donuts into boiling oil. "I shouldn't have sent her out into the dining area to refill the Knitpickers' cups. I didn't understand why she was in the storeroom doing basically nothing when customers needed coffee."

"My fault. I should have explained it to you."

"I should have figured out that you'd sent her to the storeroom because of that man."

"I called Brent. Did he come out of the police station and make certain that Hannah was okay?"

"A tall man in a dark suit met her on the sidewalk in front of the police station. I guess it was Brent. By then, the danger, if any, had ended, so I came back." She began removing beignets from the basket she'd hooked over the deep fryer before she went outside. I wondered if Olivia had watched long enough to see Hannah go into the police station, and if so, whether she'd guessed that my errand for her little sister was a ruse to keep Olivia from knowing that Hannah had needed to revise her original statement about Friday evening. Maybe it wouldn't matter. By now, Olivia's suspicion that Hannah had ridden on the back of Joshua's motorcycle had probably strengthened.

I commented, "That man, Kevin Lunnion, seemed too interested in Hannah and where she'd been. He did backtrack and admit that he probably didn't see her riding a motorcycle." I added gently, "But if Hannah did ride on the back of Joshua's motorcycle, nothing bad happened."

"Not this time." Then Olivia looked up at me. "I know. We have to let them make their own mistakes, but it's killing me."

"I understand." I pointed out, "Whether Kevin Lunnion saw Hannah or not, he said he wasn't sure, but he thought it might have been north of his place. Also, he was noncommittal about which day it was. I wonder if he nearly admitted to being in Chicory Lake State Forest about the time that his ex-partner was killed there."

Olivia must have learned too much from Tom. She demanded, "But you weren't about to pursue that line of questioning with him, were you, Emily?"

"I took it as far as I dared."

She said slowly, "Maybe that's why Kevin looked so angry when he left. He could have been angry at you, Emily, not at Hannah, and maybe he wasn't following her."

"Maybe, but we couldn't take that chance. And neither could our customers. Almost everyone inside Deputy Donut went outside to watch Hannah. Even Gigi ran out of Thrills and Frills and joined us. She was wearing a bridesmaid's gown this time."

Finally, I got a laugh from Olivia.

I glanced through the window to the office, and through the office window to the brick wall on the driveway side of Thrills and Frills. "And Madame Monique wore a matching gown. They were aqua and frothy. Gigi had a bouquet on her wrist, but Madame Monique did not."

In our office, Dep was no longer sitting up straight, but her head was still turned toward our dining room and front windows. I couldn't see her eyes. Her tail had shrunk to almost its normal circumference.

Again, Olivia laughed. "I'm not sure that anyone else in the whole world has as much fun as Madame Monique." Sobering, Olivia glanced toward the front door. "Shouldn't Hannah be back by now? Freeze isn't that far away."

I picked up the tray of donuts I'd finished decorating. "I told Brent that Kevin Lunnion was following her. I'm sure he had some questions to ask Hannah about that."

Olivia asked me, "Does Brent suspect Kevin Lunnion?"

I slid the tray into the display case. "Officially? I'm not sure, but I suspect Kevin. I've told Brent about Kevin complaining about Albert McGoss."

Olivia pointed out, "But Kevin dealt with that, right? Didn't you say that when they were in here, Kevin ended their partnership? Shouldn't that have been enough?"

"Criminals have been known to justify their actions in odd ways. And there's something else. I was supposed to pick up my lawn mower from Kevin on Friday after work. He'd said that he would call me if he had to postpone. He didn't call, and he wasn't there. That was over an hour before I heard a scream while I was kayaking on Chicory Lake. I have no idea where Kevin was or when he returned to his repair shop. He lives above it."

"We all need to be wary of him, then. He could be dangerous. Maybe I should go to Freeze and walk back with Hannah."

Uh-oh, I thought. *Maybe not.*

Outside, a large black SUV pulled up to the curb.

Chapter 25

Dashing out of the kitchen, I called over my shoulder to Olivia, "That's Brent's car." Hannah opened the front passenger door.

I ran outside. Hannah hopped out of the car. I called to her, "Ask Brent to wait!"

Leaving the door open, Hannah poked her head inside the front of Brent's SUV. She turned around and smiled at me. Shopping bags in hand, she headed into Deputy Donut.

I hurried to the car, pulled Kevin's bill from my apron pocket, put it on the dashboard, and told Brent, "Kevin gave me this. It's handprinted, and the printing is similar to the printing on the note Dep dug up. It even droops down toward the right side of the paper."

Brent's warm gray eyes were as gentle and perceptive as always. "Did you see Kevin print the bill?"

My smile faded. "No, but who else could have?"

"Don't worry, Em. Rex and I will figure it out. And thanks for emailing me a sample of Hannah's printing."

"I didn't think it looked much like the printing on the note."

"Neither did I, but I'm not an expert. Talk to you later." He blew me a kiss.

I shut the door and waved goodbye through the closed passenger window.

In the kitchen, Hannah was stowing the ice cream in the freezer.

Hands on hips, Olivia commented, "The police brought you back, Hannah." Her smile showed that she was merely trying to sound stern.

Hannah closed the freezer door. "Emily noticed that Kevin Lunnion might have been following me. She called Brent. He came out of the police station and found me. Then he wanted me to tell him all about Kevin's latest visit here and why Kevin might have been following me. By the time I finished, we were certain that Kevin was no longer nearby, but Brent took me to Freeze, waited for me to buy the ice cream, and dropped me off here. Brent's nice."

Grinning, I touched the rings on my left hand. "I noticed." I wondered why Hannah had been holding her phone to her ear after she left Deputy Donut. It had been before Kevin lunged out of his chair and started up the street behind her, so she hadn't been calling anyone about him. I hoped she hadn't been trying to coordinate stories with Joshua and Zachary, but I wasn't about to ask while Olivia was nearby.

Just before noon, the Knitpickers and retired men vacated their tables and went off, still teasing one another, toward their separate vehicles.

We battered and fried smoked gouda, parmesan-coated eggplant slices, and zucchini spears to serve at lunch. Olivia was the first of the three of us to take a lunch break. She returned and took over the frying while Hannah continued serving customers.

We didn't have a large lunch crowd, so I took off my Deputy Donut hat and apron and went outside.

I enjoyed a walk through the midday warmth to the grocery store. Although I toured the store, Laura didn't seem to be there, and I had to give up on talking to her again. I chose a roasted-veggie wrap and took it to the checkout in front.

The woman at the counter muttered sourly, "Afternoon."

My pleasant greeting failed to cheer her. I paid and asked, "Is Laura on her lunch break?"

"I don't know where she is, and I don't care. She'd better show up here in the next couple of days with a good excuse, or she's out of a job. Would you believe she just walked out of here in the middle of her shift last Friday without a word of explanation?"

"That's strange." I had seen Laura in the grocery store on Saturday. She'd said she hadn't felt well Friday afternoon and had left after serving Hannah. Curious whether this woman would tell the truth about Saturday, I asked, "Has Laura been gone ever since?"

"She was back the next day with some tale about a sick sister, and then she did it again. She simply didn't show up for work on Monday. She's taking advantage of my good nature, not to mention the difficulty of finding good workers to replace her. You wouldn't be looking for a job, would you? I can tell by your eyes that you're honest and would make a good employee."

Maybe she hadn't noticed the Deputy Donut logo on my shirt. Besides, I hadn't known that she was one of the people who had recently acquired this grocery store, so I couldn't expect her to know I was one of Deputy Donut's proprietors. I had never seen her in our shop. I kept my expression serious. "I'm sorry, but I'm not looking for a job."

She wiped the counter. "Just my luck."

"You mentioned honesty. Did anything disappear when Laura did?"

"I counted every penny and went over the accounts. Not a cent was missing, so I can't claim that she stole from me, unless she's the one who took the chocolate bar last month. She just didn't have the courtesy to ask if it was okay to take days off work. Must be nice." She nodded at the bag in my hand. "Enjoy your lunch."

"Thank you. Your wraps are delicious."

"That's the best thing I've heard since I started here. I make them myself."

"I'll be back another day for more." I headed for the door. She called to me, "Tell your friends about my wraps and sandwiches. I make soups and salads, too, from scratch."

"Okay!"

I hurried back to Deputy Donut's office. Dep purred on my lap while I ate. Again, the wrap was excellent. The red peppers and onions had been roasted in oregano-infused olive oil, with enough balsamic vinegar sprinkled over them for a refreshing tang.

I finished the lunch, washed my hands, and joined Hannah and Olivia in the kitchen. Hannah went into the office with a plate of the day's savory lunch treats.

I took cold-brew coffee from the fridge and poured it over scoops of the ice cream that Hannah had brought back from Freeze.

Everyone who tried the coffee floats loved them, and coffee fans especially liked the floats made with coffee ice cream. The day had warmed and turned sunny, and the sky was brilliant blue. One customer commented that we were making summer seem to last longer, but no one seemed to think we were serving the treat out of season. And Olivia didn't need to know my real reason for sending Hannah out for ice cream.

Hannah returned from her lunch and suggested, "We should get chocolate ice cream to try in some of those cold-brew coffee floats."

"Next time," I said.

After work, Dep and I visited our Maple Street home. Everything was in order, so I drove us to the house on Chicory Lake. Dep protested all the way.

Fortunately, I'd thrown the receipt from Dawn's gift shop

into our bedroom wastebasket and didn't have to sort through all of the garbage from Samantha's baby shower. The receipt had been machine-printed, but Dawn had written *Thank You!* on a slant across the bottom. The slant appeared deliberate, low at the T and high at the exclamation point, the exact opposite of the drooping ends of the lines on Kevin's invoice and on the note that Dep dug up. Although only two words, Dawn's printing was flowing and embellished. The exclamation point was puffy, outlined in shapes similar to balloons. It didn't look much like the printing I remembered on the note, but as I'd said to Brent, Dawn had artistic talent. She could have drawn childlike letters on the rendezvous note on purpose.

Brent made it home shortly after I took a chicken pot pie out of the freezer and started reheating it. We traded hugs that, of course, included Dep. Brent told me, "Rex and I are taking the evening off."

I gave him Dawn's receipt. He agreed that the two words did not resemble the printing on the note, but he put the receipt into an evidence envelope to take to work the next day.

I asked him, "What did you think of the printing on Kevin Lunnion's invoice?"

"Rex and I thought it looks similar to the printing on the note Dep found. We've sent it to an expert. I made a copy for you and me, and then I dropped off a check at Lunnion's Lawns and Order."

"Thank you."

"Maybe he won't have an excuse to visit Deputy Donut again so he can follow any of you around."

I tried to look as huffy as Dep at her most disgruntled. "We do serve good food."

Grinning, Brent placed his forefinger against my lips. "Agreed."

I gently nipped his finger and pushed it aside. "Was Kevin at his shop when you were there?"

"No, and his peacocks were complaining about it. I put the check in his mailbox." Brent headed upstairs to change out of his suit and tie.

I got out salad vegetables, cutting boards, and knives. Looking totally huggable in jeans and his white dress shirt, now untucked, Brent joined me in the kitchen. We poured drinks, and he began chopping a cucumber. "Hannah's two friends changed their stories."

"After the three of them discussed it with one another?"

"The other two didn't have a chance to discuss it with Hannah before Rex talked to them at their campsite. Joshua admitted that he did not take Hannah to a kids' football game. He'd only heard about the game on the radio. Joshua claimed he went from the parking lot behind Deputy Donut to the campsite and arrived there shortly after Zachary did, and Zachary agreed about the time of Joshua's arrival. The two men ate a quick dinner and waited for Hannah. She arrived in Olivia's car. All three stated independently that they all went to the parking area at the beginning of the Clifftop Trail. There's a discrepancy in their descriptions of how they got there. Hannah claims she rode with Zachary in his pickup, but Zachary and Joshua both say she went there on the back of Joshua's motorcycle. The two men said the same thing that Hannah said about how she returned to the campsite. She rode in Zachary's truck."

I removed the stem and seeds from a green pepper. "Kevin Lunnion said that he saw Hannah on the back of a motorcycle. She said she'd never ridden one. I asked him where, and he said he thought it was north of his place. He claimed that he didn't remember which day it was. But . . . if he saw her Friday evening between Herbgrove Lake Campground and the Clifftop Trail, then he just neatly placed himself in the area."

"Hang on a second." Brent left the kitchen and came back with his notebook. "Tell me all of that again?"

I did. When he stopped writing, I asked him, "When did Hannah and the two guys say they got to the Clifftop Trail's entry point?"

"None of them were sure, but their guesses were between six and six thirty-five. They all said they didn't go far. As Hannah told us last night, she got scared, partly because of the woods and the cliffs, even though she hadn't gone near the cliffs, and partly because she thought someone might have been lurking in the woods. She wanted to leave. Joshua also thought someone else might be around, and he became concerned about leaving his motorcycle unguarded. Zachary didn't notice anyone, but he was looking at the ground, checking for mushrooms. They all agree that Joshua got ahead of the other two on the way back to the parking area. Joshua claimed at first that he waited for the other two, but then he admitted that he left the parking area first. He was annoyed because after that one ride on the motorcycle, Hannah wanted to return to the campsite in Zachary's truck. Hannah and Zachary went straight back to Joshua and Zachary's campsite. Joshua claimed he was right behind them when they drove into the campground, but Zachary said the same thing that Hannah told us last night, that Joshua showed up about a half hour later."

"Aha."

"Exactly."

I tapped out a rhythm with my knife on my cutting board. "Did Joshua or Zachary remember hearing a scream?"

Brent scraped chopped-up cucumber into the salad bowl. "No, but you thought you heard it around six forty, and that's about when Joshua says he drove his motorcycle out of the parking area. You and I could both tell that he drove out of there fast, scattering dirt and gravel. Hannah and Zachary said he revved the motor, and it was very loud. You heard it, too, didn't you?"

"Yes, but later than that, after I paddled back to our shore, and that time the motorcycle sounded like it was near the top of the hill"—I pointed toward the hill behind our house— "like on the state forest road, the one that enters the forest at the county road. Or the motorcycle I heard could have been accelerating on the county road. It's hard to tell where sounds come from out here. They seem to bounce from hill to hill." I added diced pepper to the salad. "Did Zachary and Joshua explain why they didn't tell you the truth when you first asked what really happened?"

Brent started cutting up a red beefsteak tomato. "It was what Hannah said. They didn't want Olivia to find out that Hannah had gone to that trail after Olivia told her not to, and although Hannah did drive Olivia's car to the state forest, Hannah and her friends didn't want Olivia to know that Hannah rode even once for a short distance on the back of Joshua's motorcycle. Zachary drove behind them and kept them in sight." Brent put the juicy pieces of tomato into our salad. "When I talked to Hannah this morning, she confessed that she had ridden on Joshua's motorcycle. Olivia would be glad to hear that Hannah didn't think much of motorcycle riding. For one thing, she wasn't wearing a helmet or even a scarf. Her hair got blown and tangled."

I whisked olive oil with lemon juice, lemon zest, and Greek spices. "And her hairclip started slipping out, but she didn't notice."

"Probably. So, assuming that Hannah and Zachary are telling the truth, the two of them were together the entire evening after Hannah arrived at the men's campsite, or at least Zachary could see Hannah ahead of him on the motorcycle."

I put the salad dressing aside. "Joshua's whereabouts for about a half hour are in question, but the scream I heard might have happened while he was gunning his motorcycle out of the parking area, which would mean he is innocent."

Brent reminded me, "We still don't know if it was Albert

who screamed, and you're not positive about when you heard it."

"True. But if the roar of the motorcycle kept any of those three from hearing the scream, they weren't close to the lookout when the person screamed. That doesn't explain why I heard the scream but not Joshua's motorcycle."

"Although the Clifftop Trail is mostly level, a tall rock formation is between the parking area and the lake, and sounds probably don't carry through that wall of rock. Also, you were close to whoever screamed. Screams are compelling. They can prevent people from noticing other sounds."

"None of it can exactly prove that Hannah and her two friends are innocent, can it?"

"Not conclusively. What is conclusive is that other people in the campground saw Harv and Essie in Herbgrove Lake Campground that afternoon and evening, and if the campers are correct about their timing, neither Harv nor Essie was away from the campground around six forty, at least not long enough to drive their enormous pickup truck to the lookout on the Clifftop Trail and return, let alone do anything while they were there. And Essie claims that she can't drive their pickup truck, which she fondly refers to as The Whale."

I repeated, "If the campers are correct about their timing."

"There is that. However, one woman was positive that at five thirty Friday evening, she went to Harv and Essie's site to ask to borrow salt, and Essie talked until nearly six thirty. Harv wasn't part of the conversation, but he was puttering around their firepit off and on that entire time, and The Whale stayed where it was."

I laughed. "That does sound believable, but Essie told me they drove out to check after they heard sirens and saw police cars and fire trucks near the Clifftop Trail."

"Essie didn't tell us about that bit of snooping, but she told a reporter and at least one pair of campers about it, and the campers saw The Whale leave around seven thirty or eight and come back a few minutes later. Harv and Essie wouldn't have heard the sirens before seven thirty."

"So, those two are very likely in the clear, and we have a 'maybe' for Joshua and a 'probably not' for both Hannah and Zachary, though if we're sure that the killer borrowed a canoe and took a convoluted route to and from the murder, we can rule out Hannah and her two friends. Dawn told me she was home alone that evening, and isn't that what Kevin said about himself? He was home alone and didn't have an alibi?"

"Yes. He said he must have just missed you."

"Do you agree that we still have a 'possibly' for Albert's widow Dawn and maybe even a 'probably' for his former partner Kevin?"

My darling detective husband was noncommittal. "Maybe."

"And then there's Laura, who had to close Cheese It after disastrous renovations that we think Albert did. I bought my lunch at the grocery store today. The woman who seems to own or at least manage it complained that Laura left Friday evening during her shift, returned Saturday, but then didn't show up on Monday and hasn't been back since."

Brent stared into his nearly empty wineglass. "We've talked to that woman. She's one of the owners of the store."

"Do you know where Laura is?"

"We know where she's not. She's not in her apartment, and her car is gone."

"So, would you agree that Laura is another possible suspect in Albert's murder?"

"We might have others that you haven't met or thought of yet."

I frowned. "And you're not going to enlighten me."

"Certainly not. Can I pour you another glass of Chardonnay?"

"Sure. While you change the subject."

He poured us more of the nearly clear liquid. "I won't

completely change the subject. We're concerned about Laura's disappearance. No one has reported her missing besides her boss, who seems to think that Laura chose to go off on her own, but we're not ruling out that she might also have met with foul play."

I took a sip of wine and set my glass down. "The obvious connection between Laura and Albert is Kevin." I shuddered. "I shouldn't have sent Hannah out of Deputy Donut while he was there. I expected him to finish his fritter and beignet before he left the shop. I should have kept her there until after he left, and then I should have told you she would be delayed. Thank you for looking after her."

"As you know, I needed her to sign her statement, and then, because of Kevin's possibly following her, I needed to ask her more questions. She deserved rides after all of that. Was Olivia concerned that Hannah took too much time?"

"She was mainly worried about what Kevin might do to Hannah if he caught up with her."

"All of you should stay out of his way. Serve him if he comes in, but be cautious."

"We will. Tom was off today and has tomorrow off, too, but I don't think we need to call him to babysit us."

"I don't think so, either, as long as none of you get into situations where Kevin Lunnion could be alone with you."

"We won't."

Together, we set the table on the catio. Dep went out with us and clambered around on her ramps and stairways. She selected a perch and sat on it while I went inside again, took the chicken pot pie out of the oven, and drizzled the dressing over the salad. I carried the salad out to the catio.

Brent brought the steaming pot pie out and set it on a trivet. "Aren't you going to ask me what Rex is doing tonight?"

"I wasn't, but . . ." Suddenly understanding Brent's grin, I couldn't help a big smile and a little dance. "What's he doing?"

"He left work at five to go kayaking on Deepwish Lake, and a barbecue afterward."

"With Summer, I hope."

"With Summer."

I managed not to knock over my wine.

And we dug into the pot pie before it became completely cold.

Chapter 26

✻

In the morning, I asked Brent, "Do you think you and Rex can take time off again tomorrow evening? You should get some Friday evenings off, plus you do need to eat. We could invite him and Summer for dinner, and maybe some kayaking, too, if the weather's decent."

"Let's try for it and hope nothing comes up to prevent it. I'll ask Rex."

"I'll ask Summer."

"And I'll reserve a couple of kayaks or a canoe from Barney for the evening."

I kissed Brent, put our softly grumbling cat into my car, and drove to work.

As soon as I thought that Summer would be at The Craft Croft, I called and invited her to dinner and possibly kayaking on Chicory Lake the next evening. "Brent hopes that he and Rex can make it."

"I'd love to. I spent last evening with Rex at my parents' place, and he's even more wonderful than I remembered." She hiccuped a little laugh, quieter but more contented than her usual laugh. "And I'm sure he won't turn down Brent's invitation because I'm coming. On the contrary."

I couldn't help a big smile. "This sounds promising."

"I think it is. I hope so."

"Want to show up about six?" I gave her the directions.

Halfway through the morning, Dawn McGoss came into Deputy Donut. She sat where she'd been with her late husband and Kevin almost exactly a week before. I asked her, "Do you have an assistant running Proceeds of Craft when you're not there?"

"No, but I deserve a coffee break, and Thursday mornings are never busy. Also, I really like your beignets, and although Albert brought some home, I never got any of those, only the one I ate here. The other two ate the others. Could I have three this time and a big mug of coffee?"

"Would you like our special coffee today? It's a lively and almost sweet medium roast from Rwanda."

"Does it go with beignets?"

"Everything does!"

A shadow of a smile crossed her face. "I'd like to try that."

When I took her the coffee and beignets, her smile was again gone, and her entire face seemed to droop. "I remembered something about the night my husband died." Even her voice sounded dreary. "After they told me about him, I was so devastated that I forgot that I'd been with my late husband's partner Kevin that evening."

I didn't say anything, but I thought, *Where? On the Clifftop Trail murdering your husband and then, after the two of you buried that note on the beach, in a canoe?* That canoe had been too far away for me to have been positive that only one person was in it. Dawn could have been in the bow. If, for some reason, she'd ducked down, I wouldn't have noticed her.

She said slowly, as if she were reciting a speech she had not completely memorized, "Kevin came over to my shop on Friday afternoon. We sat and drank tea and ate cookies, and then I made some chili, and we had that. He stayed until, oh, probably seven or eight o'clock."

"Did you tell the police?"

"Not yet. I thought of it just now while I was sitting here

remembering being in the same spot, like, the day before that horrid day."

"If Kevin corroborates that you two were together Friday evening, you both have alibis."

Dawn's careworn face seemed to turn grayer. "I didn't think of that." She blew powdered sugar off a beignet. A cloud of sugar rose and then settled onto her plate, the table, and her coffee.

I hesitated beside her, but she gazed at her plate and seemed to have nothing more to say, so I went to the next table. The Knitpickers were discussing what gown Gigi the dog might be wearing that day.

"She doesn't have to wear a gown," Cheryl pointed out. "I mean, she's a dog. No one would complain if she wore a tux, and she'd be cute in any costume. Or none at all."

We all agreed that Gigi couldn't help being cute. And we also hoped that she wouldn't keep escaping from Thrills and Frills.

"Though," Priscilla said darkly, "who can blame her? She might be afraid of having to wear an even more outrageous gown. Animals should be allowed their dignity, and not be dressed up like dolls."

I glanced toward the office. Dep sat up straight on the back of the couch. "I often put poor Dep into a harness."

Cheryl gave me an approving smile. "That's to keep her safe."

"And that's not all," I admitted. "She has her own cat-sized life jacket. She actually likes riding in a kayak."

Priscilla could look sterner than she actually seemed to be. "Safety has to be a priority for pets. I don't see why that poor little dog has to wear silly, frilly gowns. It's just because she's tiny with frou-frou looks. You wouldn't dress a rottweiler like that."

When our laughter died down, Cheryl confessed with a wicked twinkle in her eyes, "I might."

Smiling, I headed to the kitchen for another pot of coffee. But I wasn't thinking—much—about which breeds of dogs might look comical in poufy chiffon dresses. I was wondering how Dawn could even pretend to forget who she was with in the hours before she was informed that her husband had died. And whether it had occurred to Dawn, before she alleged just now that Kevin was with her, that she was destroying the theory she'd suggested to me before, that Kevin had killed Albert.

Either Kevin had killed Albert, or he was with Dawn in her shop the entire time and couldn't have killed him.

Or Dawn had killed Albert and was making up an alibi for herself that also provided, perhaps accidentally, Kevin with one.

Or Dawn and Kevin had killed Albert together.

I sighed. Or none of the above.

A few minutes later, Dawn quietly left. Her head down, she walked north.

Lots of people came in to try our lunch treats—sweet potato fries, battered and fried mini bocconcinis, and battered and fried green tomatoes. Hannah, Olivia, and I waited until one in the afternoon to take our lunch breaks. Hannah went first, and then Olivia. When I was ready for lunch, only one mini bocconcini was left. Naturally, I ate it. "Delicious," I said.

Olivia said, "If you can wait, I'll make more."

"No, we might need donuts, crullers, fritters, and beignets this afternoon, so it would be better if you started frying them. I'll go see if the grocery store has more of their delicious wraps. It's a pleasant walk on a sunny day like this."

Olivia warned, "You might want to wear your jacket."

She was right. Outside, despite the bright sunshine, the air was crisp, the sort of day that could make me want to kick through piles of fallen leaves.

As if she'd never been gone, Laura was talking to a customer at the checkout counter. Wondering where she'd been, why she'd returned, and if she'd played a part in Albert's murder, I waved and headed to the back of the store. Few choices for lunch remained that late in the afternoon. I chose a Caesar salad topped with a chunk of grilled salmon, slices of hard-boiled egg, and a sprinkling of capers.

I didn't see the woman who claimed she made the wraps, sandwiches, salads, and soups. I returned to the front and placed the salad container on the checkout counter. The other customer had left.

Laura looked less harassed than she had on Saturday. Her frizzy perm was still untamed, but her face seemed less lined and more colorful. And her blouse was neatly tucked in. I stated the obvious. "You're back."

"So are you."

"The food here is good. I bought lunch here yesterday, too, but you weren't here."

"I got called away for an emergency."

"I hope you're feeling better." I also hoped that my prodding came across as empathy.

"I was in shock! I'm a little better now. My sister was admitted to the hospital Friday afternoon. I got the call only about a minute after Hannah left here. I drove straight down there. My sister was stabilized, and there was nothing I could do then, so I came back and worked on Saturday, but the hospital released her, and there was no one to look after her. I rushed off again."

"Is she okay?"

"She will be. Another sister took over. She's a retired nurse, so she's more qualified than I am, and I could come back here."

"That's lucky."

"It sure is. I nearly lost this job, but after I explained, everything's okay here, too. Not that I couldn't have found a job close to my sister's place. Do you know what really freaked me out, though?"

"What?" I braced myself to hear uncomfortable details of her sister's medical condition.

"While I was gone, some detective, or maybe more than one, has been coming in here asking where I was Friday night. I guess it's no secret that I was angry at some guy who ended up dead on Friday, but I had nothing to do with that. I was long gone." She pressed keys on the old-fashioned cash register. "With both of my sisters getting older—I'm the baby of the family—I'm going to try to convince them that we should all move closer together. We get along. Sisters are the best. Like Olivia and Hannah. Such nice girls." She stared off into the distance and then looked back at me. "You just gave me an idea." She lowered her voice. "I'm tired of this town, tired of this job, and if I don't quit, I'll probably get fired. Why should I wait?" She snapped her fingers. "I'll give my notice today and go live with my sister, find a job there, and try to convince the retired sister to move in with us."

I paid for the salad. "That should make your sick sister—and all of you—happy."

"It will." She nodded her head up and down so vigorously that I was afraid she'd get a sore neck. "I can hardly wait. And who says I need to give notice? My boss will probably be happiest if I just leave. Thanks for the idea."

I couldn't help a teensy, non-amused laugh. "It wasn't my idea. I would say to give notice."

"Spoilsport." But she was smiling. "Maybe I will."

I figured that was my cue to leave.

The sidewalk in front of the library was out of sight of the grocery store. I called Brent and quickly told him, "I found out two things today. One, and probably the most crucial, is that Laura is back at the grocery store, but she's thinking of leaving again without giving her boss any notice. On Saturday, she told me she left because she hadn't felt well, but today, she said she rushed away because a sister was admitted to the hospital. She kind of tied the two ideas together by saying that she was in shock after she got the call, but I wondered if she forgot what she'd told me on Saturday. Maybe none of what she said is true."

"Thanks. I'll go see her if she's still there. What's the other thing?"

"Dawn McGoss came into Deputy Donut this morning. She said she just remembered that she wasn't alone Friday evening, after all. She said that Kevin Lunnion came over in the afternoon, and then they had tea and dinner and talked, and he didn't leave until seven or eight."

There was a silence on the other end, and then Brent repeated, "Kevin Lunnion? The man she accused of probably being her husband's murderer?"

"Yes. I suggested she should call the police and tell them. Tell you."

"When was this?"

"Around eleven. Nearly three hours ago."

"She hasn't called. Thanks, Em. Rex and I'll go see both of those women."

I returned to Deputy Donut's office and ate my salad without giving my suddenly super-attentive and affectionate cat more than a few morsels of salmon.

Later, near our closing time, Olivia, Hannah, and I were all in the kitchen. Olivia and I were making batches of dough for the next day, and Hannah was cleaning coffee makers.

Zachary and Joshua came in and sat at a table near the front windows. Hannah glanced at them and went on with what she was doing.

I told her, "I'll finish cleaning those. You can take their orders and then sit with them. We're not busy."

She shrugged in a show of disinterest. "Okay." She took

her time, stopping to talk to other customers, before going to Joshua and Zachary's table. Minutes later, she was back in the kitchen putting donuts on plates and pouring coffee. I pointed at the tray. "Only two mugs and two plates? You can have some, too, you know."

"I'm not hungry."

She set the men's plates and mugs in front of them and brought the tray back to the kitchen. She started toward the coffee makers.

I repeated, "I'll clean them. Go talk to your friends."

Hannah didn't answer, but she did join Zachary and Joshua at their table. I couldn't hear what they said to one another, but all of them looked stiff and constrained, which wasn't too surprising considering that they were probably embarrassed about revising their descriptions of the previous Friday evening, contradicting themselves and one another.

A tall man who looked familiar was across the street, standing with his back to Deputy Donut and peering into the front window of a bookkeeper's office. He turned slowly and looked up and down Wisconsin Street. Traffic cleared, and he sauntered across in the middle of the block. Eyeing our building, he slowly approached, and I recognized Forrest Callic, the man who had tried to interest us in investments that would supposedly yield impossible returns.

On a different day, he had peeked inside but had not come in. I hoped he would avoid us again. Joshua, Zachary, and Hannah, who had refused to listen to him before, were again in plain sight. Maybe he would notice them through our large front windows, decide they were too hostile to his schemes, and go away.

He came up the walkway between the two sides of our closed-for-the-season patio, inched the door open, and peeked inside.

Still standing in the doorway behind the partially opened

door, he glanced around the dining room. His gaze lingered on Hannah, Zachary, and Joshua. They were all tensely staring down at the table and didn't appear to be talking. Forrest glanced toward the office, and then he seemed to notice Olivia and me in the kitchen. I did not look forward to having to send him away if he started bothering us and our clients, but I would if I had to. I often missed Tom on his days off, and this was one of those times. My expression was far from welcoming.

It didn't deter Forrest. He opened the door all the way and strode inside.

Chapter 27

I sidled to Olivia and muttered, "I wonder what that so-called investment counselor is selling today."

She snickered. "Shoelaces, maybe, or a pill that reverses aging, and we'll all go back to being babies."

As I'd feared he might, Forrest stopped at the table where Hannah sat with her two friends. Unable to stop my lips from thinning into something resembling a frown, I started toward Forrest. I caught the tail end of his question: ". . . thought more about investments?"

Hannah shook her head.

Joshua sighed, leaned back from the table, and crossed his arms over his chest. "No."

Only Zachary met the man's eyes. "Sorry, we're not interested."

The hint was more than a hint, but Forrest didn't take it. "How about if I sit with you, then?"

Joshua leaned forward. "We're in a private meeting."

Raising his palms in a gesture of surrender, Forrest backed away. "Okay, I can take a hint."

I almost felt sorry for him. Almost. I pointed toward the corner table near the office. "There's a clean table back there."

Actually, all of the tables that weren't occupied were clean, but I wanted to isolate him so he couldn't easily harass other customers with his pitches. No one else was sitting near the office.

Forrest laughed. "That cat looks mean."

Dep sat up almost straight. She had stopped in the middle of licking a paw and was staring toward us with one front leg angled toward her mouth, her tongue sticking out, and her eyes slightly crossed. She looked adorable. "She's not mean, and she's locked inside our office. You're safe."

"Just the same, I think I'll sit here, nice and far from it. Cats can't be trusted."

I opened my mouth but decided not to argue.

Forrest sat at the table next to Hannah, Zachary, and Joshua. Facing them, he could see Hannah's and Joshua's faces from the side and Zachary's from the front. I asked him, "What can I get you?"

"Just a coffee. Not a fancy one, a normal one."

I brought him a mug of our delicious Colombian coffee and then purposely placed myself between him and his view of Hannah. Her youthful beauty was attracting too many men who were creepily too old for a college girl. I asked Forrest, "How's it going?"

"Great. You should have gotten in on the ground floor when I did, but it's not too late. My investment has been doubling every day."

"That sounds too good to be true."

His laugh seemed uneasy. "In this case, it is true."

Behind me, a chair scraped back, and Zachary said, "I'm off to hunt mushrooms. See you two later."

I couldn't see Hannah, but out of the corner of my eye, I saw Joshua smirk, like he'd just won a competition. "Yeah."

I heard Zachary walk toward the front door and heard it close behind him.

I barely paid attention to Forrest's list of the benefits of a miracle drug, but Olivia's age-reversing guess seemed to have been close.

Behind me, Hannah told Joshua, "I need to get back to work."

Forrest said loudly, "Soon, this start-up company will be the only thing in the news that people will pay attention to."

Joshua stood. "Okay, Hannah, see you tomorrow after work." He glanced toward the kitchen and Olivia. "I guess you don't want to ride on the back of my bike."

"You guess right."

Joshua asked her, "Do you know where the canoe rental place is?"

"Sure. What's a good time?"

"How about dinner first at our campsite? Zachary will probably heat beans in their cans on the fire and cook wieners on sticks again."

Hannah laughed. "Okay."

Looking intently into my face, Forrest said in urgent tones, "As soon as word gets out, everyone will compete to invest in the company. The guys who run it are geniuses. They're inventors, and they're good at more than just medicines. It's all hush-hush now, but they're working on affordable personal hovercrafts. The company's stock will zoom upward even faster than it's been. Are you sure you don't want to get in on this exciting opportunity?"

"I'm sure. And while we appreciate your coming here to enjoy our coffee, please don't give sales pitches to our customers. That's not why they're here."

His smile lacked sincerity. "I wouldn't do that, but I wanted to give you waitresses a chance to lift yourselves up." He leaned toward me. "I thought I saw Tom Westhill here. Does he work here?"

"Yes, and he would say the same thing I did. Our customers come here to relax."

"Westhill was a detective for a while, right?"

"Yes."

"So, he has pensions plus the income from this place. I'd

rather help his employees, you know, waitresses, cleaning staff, clerical help, and people like that, than business owners with pensions from other jobs."

I wasn't about to tell this man that I was Tom's business partner. Forrest seemed happy believing that I was an employee. I wasn't keen on making customers unhappy.

"Tom had a son," Forrest said, "who was also a policeman. I heard that he died."

"Yes." My one-word answer sounded as tense as I felt.

Forrest shook his head slowly. "What a pity."

Afraid of displaying my grief, I glanced away. Across the room, a woman held up her mug and called, "Is it too late for more coffee, Emily?"

"Not at all. I'll go get you some." Suddenly I could breathe again.

In the kitchen, I said to Hannah and Olivia, "I don't trust that man. Stay away from him."

Hannah shuddered. "Me, neither. I think we were all right the first time. He's not a real investment counselor. Besides, I hate being stared at."

"We all do," Olivia said.

Forrest didn't stay long. Hannah cleared his table and came back laughing. "Look what he left instead of a tip." She held up one of Forrest's business cards.

I made a face of fake horror. "I guess he didn't like me telling him not to give our customers sales pitches."

With a flourish, Hannah threw the card in the trash. "I hope he doesn't come back."

Olivia and I agreed.

After work, walking with Dep toward our Maple Street house, I heard distorted band music. The high school marching band must have been practicing at the field, and the breezes were blowing just right, bringing snippets of tunes all the way to this part of Wisconsin Street and then wafting them away again. Remembering the fun of showing Ira's team our donut car on Tuesday, I pictured Ira's face and suddenly realized why he had looked familiar.

Although it was possible that I had seen him around town when he was a policeman, he resembled an older version of Albert McGoss.

What if Albert McGoss had been killed because someone had mistaken him for Ira?

Why would anyone want to kill a cheerful retired police officer who coached kids' football and celebrated a losing season with his team?

Had someone wanted revenge for something Ira had done when he was a police officer?

Ira had been retired for at least ten years. Where had the imaginary revenge-seeker been in the meantime? Prison? That would have been a motive for harming someone.

Maybe it was a gigantic leap of logic, but I'd just been talking to a possible con man in Deputy Donut, so I naturally pictured Forrest Callic as a potential suspect for other crimes besides encouraging people to invest in phony investment schemes.

Other crimes—like murder.

Forrest had been in Deputy Donut the previous Thursday, already a week ago, when Albert had been there with Dawn and Kevin. Forrest had left the shop with Kevin. While I'd been watching, Forrest had appeared to be doing all of the talking, but what if Forrest had gleaned enough information from Kevin to connect with Albert, a man Forrest mistakenly thought was Ira?

Watching Dep's cautious approach to a fallen maple leaf tap-dancing along the sidewalk in a breeze, the ends of its curled-down leaf tips acting as tiny feet, I muttered, "Emily, your ideas can be ridiculous. A convicted criminal would not return to the scene of his earlier crimes and try to again con people, much less commit murder."

Dep flattened the leaf. Tail straight up in proud victory, she led me home.

It wasn't too early in the evening to call Ira and try out my theories on him.

But they were far-fetched.

There might be another way of testing them without embarrassing myself by sharing them.

Ira had said he'd worked with Alec on cases.

Alec had kept diaries.

Alec's diaries were still in the basement of Brent's and my Maple Street home, the one that Alec and I had bought together. And I was almost at the front porch of that house.

I ran up the steps and let Dep trot ahead of me into the living room. Barely thinking about my soft little cat, I took off her leash and harness.

Alec had told me that his journals didn't contain police secrets, and I should feel free to read them. While he was alive, I'd simply enjoyed being with him. After his death, I hadn't been able to face his journals. Even though I was now married to Alec's detective partner and best friend, I had not been able to part with the diaries and their connection, however limited, with my first husband.

Some of Alec's diaries probably mentioned meeting me and our first dates. I wasn't strong enough to look at those, but he had also kept journals before I met him.

I texted Brent that I would probably spend the night at Maple Street.

He texted back that he expected to work late but would go out to the lake afterward and stay there for whatever was left of the night. Also, he had learned from Rex that Summer had accepted our invitation. Rex had accepted, also. Brent would get steaks out of the freezer to thaw in the fridge for the next evening.

I told Dep, "He's perfect."

"Meow!" I wasn't sure if Dep's enthusiastic statement was

her agreement with what I'd said about Brent or a reminder that she had not yet eaten dinner. I fed her and then cooked one serving of bowtie pasta, stirred a tablespoon of the summer's homemade basil pesto into it, and grated parmesan cheese over it. Garlicky, cheesy, basil goodness.

After I ate, I cleaned the kitchen and told Dep, "I'm going down to the basement. You can come along if you want to."

She wanted to.

The basement was still unfinished, but it was dry. I opened the filing cabinet where Alec had kept his diaries, neatly labeled and in chronological order. Guessing when Ira might have retired from the Fallingbrook police, I walked my fingers along the journals' spines until I reached that year. I pulled out a half dozen journals, carried them upstairs to the living room, and plunked them and myself onto the couch. Dep jumped into my lap. Okay, fine, I would look at the books by opening them on the cushion beside my thigh. I skimmed through a few pages of the first book. I wasn't sure what I was looking for.

Alec hadn't written every day, but when he did, he entered the date. Sometimes there was very little information. Other times, he described a party or a meeting in detail. He referred to people by their initials or by code names that I suspected he'd made up. I also suspected that he never told anyone who those code names stood for.

I hoped that if Alec mentioned Ira, he hadn't simply abbreviated the name to *I*. Alec referred to himself as *I*, and skimming every page for a capital *I* by itself would probably take more time than I'd be able to stand, especially considering that I was merely attempting to test a theory that possibly did not make sense.

Ira's last name was Purcils. Looking for *IP*, I quickly turned pages.

By the fourth diary, I was about to give up and put the books away, but then, halfway down a page, I spotted an *IP*.

I read the passage several times. *IP and I disappointed. About to arrest Schemer, but he had skipped town.*

Halfway through the fifth diary, I found another reference to Schemer. *All in the department relieved. Schemer apprehended selling fake "investments" in Brainerd. To be tried there. We'll provide evidence.*

Brainerd wasn't in Wisconsin. It was in Minnesota, northwest of Minneapolis. Alec had written nothing that might identify Schemer, nothing to prove my sudden and rather tentative guess that he could be Forrest Callic, now trying to sell fake investments in Fallingbrook.

I closed the book and told Dep, who had moved off my lap onto the still-open fourth journal, "But there's nothing in there that proves that Forrest Callic is *not* the same man, back in Fallingbrook, unrehabilitated, and attempting more scams similar to his original ones."

"Meow."

"I agree. It would be a stupid thing for anyone to do."

Looking smug, Dep tucked her front paws underneath her chest.

I scratched the top of her head. "You would never do such a thing, would you?"

"Mewp."

I again checked the date on the journal. It was before Alec and I met and before Brent joined the Fallingbrook police force. I moved Dep aside and rechecked the journal that had been written previous to the one referring to IP. Those initials weren't mentioned in that older one. I checked for Schemer, too, and didn't find it.

Tom would have been a Fallingbrook detective or perhaps police chief when Alec and Ira were participating in the investigation into Schemer.

Forrest Callic had peeked into Deputy Donut one day and had backed out. Was that because Tom had been there? And then today, he'd gazed inside when Tom wasn't there, and after checking everything he could see of our shop from the door, he had come in and again started trying to sell investments. Talking to me, he had made it obvious that he'd recognized Tom when he'd peeked in the previous time. He also knew that Tom had been a policeman, and that Tom's son Alec had died. And he'd mentioned that cleaning staff might be interested in his investment schemes. Had he already figured out that Ira was still alive, cleaning businesses at night with the other Jolly Cops?

Had Forrest come in this afternoon merely because Hannah was a pretty girl? Or because he'd seen one or more of us on the Clifftop Trail on Friday evening and wanted to learn more about us, like whether we seemed to have seen him around the time of the murder?

I muttered to myself, "A few hours ago, you were almost convinced that Kevin, maybe with Dawn's help, had murdered Albert. And now you've built a case, based entirely on guesses, against Forrest."

I could have called Ira and asked him about Schemer. I could have called Brent and told him about my leaping to possibly false conclusions. I was too tired to think straight. Maybe in the morning, everything would seem clearer.

Chapter 28

I was wrong. When I woke up, nothing seemed clearer.

I dressed and walked with Dep to work. We were the first to arrive. An envelope addressed to Tom and me was propped up against the computer on our desk.

I released Dep. She clambered up her ramps and staircases to catwalks near the ceiling.

I opened the envelope. A business card fell out and landed face down on the desk. The note said: *I don't know how the enclosed card got into the trash in Deputy Donut's kitchen. Tom, remember this guy? If not, call me ASAP. Don't worry about waking me up. This could be important. I don't know what Callic is doing back in town, if it really is him, but he should be watched. You might want to alert Brent and explain it to him.*

The note was signed *Ira Purcils.*

Ira might never have seen Albert McGoss, and even if he had, he might not have noticed that Albert could have resembled Ira ten or more years ago. If my possibly outlandish theory about Forrest's having mistaken Albert for Ira was right, Ira could be in danger.

And he might not know it.

One of the sentences in the unsigned note that Dep found was *I have what you need.* If that note had been meant for

Ira, what would Forrest Callic have that Ira might need? Probably not a scam investment idea, but Forrest could have thought the hint would tantalize a policeman to meet him to possibly learn details about crimes or criminals.

I was almost certain that Ira had not buried that note on the beach near the Cornflower Trail. Ira had probably never received the note. Essie had seen Albert pick up a piece of paper from his picnic table. Maybe Forrest had driven to Herbgrove Lake Campground in the noisy car that Essie heard, and had left the note for the person he thought was Ira to find.

The promise of *what you need* could have been enough to cause the suddenly unemployed Albert to give up his usual indolence and go hiking shortly before sunset on a nearly deserted trail.

Ira might have finished work only a couple of hours before I opened the envelope he'd left us. Although reluctant to disrupt his sleep, I tried reaching him. He didn't answer. I couldn't blame him. I left a message explaining my mistaken identity theory. Some people were insulted when told they looked like someone else, but I hoped that Ira wouldn't be. I ended the message with, "Be careful, Ira. If Forrest Callic was trying to kill you, you'll be in danger when he realizes he killed the wrong man." I added, "But I really don't know if my theory makes sense. Meanwhile, I'll tell Brent about it."

Tom came in, and I showed him Ira's note and Forrest's business card. Tom recognized Forrest Callic's name. "We nearly nabbed him, but he got away. They caught him in Minnesota and charged him there. Our evidence helped put him in jail. Maybe the man who left that business card is using Callic's identity. Can you describe the man who was in here?"

"I guess he's in his fifties. He's not conventionally handsome, but he's nice-looking. He's about six feet tall, with a slender build and a roundish face. His brown hair is very short. I'm not sure, but I think his eyes are brown. Both times he was in here, and the time he peeked in, he wore a blue blazer, khakis, a white polo shirt, and orange-ish, pointy-toed shoes. The outfit looks nearly brand new. He walks with his shoulders back and his chest out, which made me think he was a salesman. Well, he is, but he's more of a scammer, trying to sell so-called investments that supposedly skyrocket in value."

Tom rubbed his thumb against the edge of Ira's note. "None of that rules out the Forrest Callic we investigated. It sounds like Callic's up to his old tricks. He scammed a lot of money out of his victims before he was finally arrested."

I was about to tell Tom what else I thought Forrest Callic might have done, but Olivia and Hannah arrived. Tom told us all that if Forrest Callic came in again, Tom would wait on him.

I tapped my fingers on the computer monitor. "Forrest probably won't come in again if you're here, Tom."

"Then the rest of you, don't let that man near you, and for sure don't give him money or personal information."

I warned all three of them, "It might be worse than investment scams. I have a theory, and I know it sounds weird. When Forrest Callic was in here the first time, he definitely saw Albert McGoss, who looked kind of like a younger version of one of the Jolly Cops, Ira Purcils. Ira helped put Forrest Callic in prison for his earlier crimes. What if Forrest came back here to get revenge on Ira, Tom, and everyone else who testified against him? Yesterday when Forrest was in here, he knew that Tom had been a detective. Forrest also mentioned that Alec had died, and according to Alec's diaries, Alec and Ira both participated in investigating Forrest."

"They did," Tom said. "We all worked on that."

I suggested, "What if, the first time Forrest was in here, he mistook Albert for Ira? Forrest could have followed Albert or arranged a meeting with him, and killed him, believing that he had killed Ira. What a shock it must have been when Albert's name was reported."

Hannah shuddered. "No wonder Forrest Callic gave me the creeps."

Olivia added, "Be careful, Tom."

"Don't worry." He turned to me. "Emily, let's call Brent."

Without being asked, Olivia and Hannah left the office so they could start making donuts and preparing tables.

Tom and I reached Brent by phone while he was still at home at Chicory Lake. Brent thanked us and said he'd find out if Forrest Callic had left prison, legitimately or not. He would also call the number we read to him from Forrest's business card and arrange to go talk to him. "With Rex and maybe some other backup. Save that business card for me, okay?"

We said we would, and the three of us reminded one another to be careful. Tom and I disconnected and went into the storeroom and put on our Deputy Donut hats and aprons. With Olivia and Hannah's help, we began filling our display case with decorated sweet fried treats.

Later, when Olivia wasn't around, I asked Hannah, "Could Forrest Callic have been the person who could have been lurking in the woods?"

Hannah gave me a mischievous grin. "Impossible. He would have given up his murderous intentions and strutted out in his new clothes to try to sell us a diamond mine or something. This person, if there was one, stayed hidden, probably on purpose."

"I'm still afraid that it could have been Forrest Callic, and that he saw the three of you that evening. He might not know that you can't positively identify him, and he might try to prevent you from telling the police about him."

"If he didn't want us to recognize him, he shouldn't have come back to Deputy Donut. That makes no sense."

"Just in case, can you warn Joshua and Zachary? They'd probably be safest if they packed up and left the campsite. Left the area, really. And if you have somewhere you can go, maybe you should leave for a while, too."

"Zachary will stay as long as he wants to look at mushrooms. And Joshua and I are canoeing this evening. And I don't want to go anywhere except maybe back to school, but I'm still not sure if that's what I really want to do."

Her mention of the canoeing date reminded me to warn her, "Joshua might not know that Chicanery, the canoe rental place on Chicory Lake, is not open except Saturdays and Sundays during daylight hours at this time of year. You can call the owner and make an appointment." I gave Hannah Barney's phone number.

Hannah thanked me, and then customers began arriving, and we were busy serving breakfast. At nine, the Knitpickers and retired men came in. They all wanted donuts and hot drinks. The Knitpickers finished their donuts and headed to the ladies' room to wash their hands before they took their knitting projects out of bags and baskets.

Brent came in through the front. I met him, took him to the office, and gave him Forrest Callic's card. Dep purred around Brent's ankles.

Brent compared Forrest's card to a page in his notebook. "No one answered at the number you and Tom gave me for Forrest this morning. I thought I might have written it down incorrectly, but I didn't."

I grinned. "Of course you didn't."

He smiled back. "And of course you read it aloud correctly." He slipped the card into an evidence envelope. "After he exhausted all possible appeals, Forrest Callic ended up in prison. He was released a month ago. Did you happen to see what vehicle he drives?"

"No."

Brent turned the page in his notebook. "He might be driving his mother's car, a low-mileage black Camaro that's about twenty years old. She no longer drives, but the car has always been in her name, and she's kept it licensed. She lives near Indianapolis. We could ask Indiana law enforcement to interview her, but at the moment, we don't have a good enough reason."

"Essie might have heard a car with a noisy engine last Thursday night or early Friday morning, and later, she saw Albert take a scrap of paper off his picnic table. Would a twenty-year-old Camaro be noisy?"

"Could be."

"I'll tell the others to beware of Camaros."

Brent picked up our demanding cat, kissed the top of her head, and told her, "That's for both you and Em." He set her gently on the floor. "I should get back. See you tonight." He went out into the parking lot.

When I got a chance to speak quietly to the others, I told them what Brent had said about Forrest and the car he might be driving.

Tom reminded us all that Forrest might not be a murderer.

Hannah glanced toward the table where Albert McGoss had sat with Dawn and Kevin. "The man who died was in here with his wife and also with that lawn mower repairman, and they all seemed angry. I'm guessing that one of those two might have knocked him off."

I agreed. "We need to be careful around all of them."

Olivia added, "We need to be careful, period. Always."

Shortly before noon, the Knitpickers and retired men left.

Zachary and Joshua came in for lunch, and the rest of us told Hannah to take her lunch break and eat with them.

In the kitchen, Olivia muttered to me, "Even Zachary must get tired of wieners and beans once in a while." I couldn't control a loud laugh.

Hannah took deep-fried chicken and French fries to Joshua and Zachary and sat down with them. For herself, she took a small serving of the day's salad—baby greens, dried cranberries, and mandarin orange segments with an orange marmalade vinaigrette, all of it topped with slivered almonds.

A few minutes later, I served salads and fried chicken to diners at the table next to Hannah, Joshua, and Zachary.

I couldn't hear everything Hannah said, but she finished with, "Maybe you two should go home and come back after all this is over."

Joshua reminded Hannah, "We're going canoeing tonight, and you just gave me the number to call to reserve a canoe." His voice seemed deeper than usual.

Zachary said, "I can't leave the area. I'm supposed to be hunting and observing mushrooms for my thesis."

I turned to their table. "Zachary, I'm sorry I didn't think of this before, but my husband and I have property on Chicory Lake. I don't know if we have the sort of mushrooms you're looking for, but if we do, you can gather as many as you like from our property, since you can't pick them in the state forest."

"They grow best near the edge of woods where they get shade and moisture, but not too much. Thank you. Collecting specimens would be helpful."

Behind me, the front door opened. I told Zachary, "Here's the easiest way to explain how to get to our place. Park at Chicanery and walk east, along the shore and close to it. Barney can explain where our property begins. Knowing him, he'll also let you gather mushrooms from his place."

Hannah stared at me with a concerned expression on her face and shook her head slightly. Her hands on the table clenched and unclenched. She was probably horrified that I might be causing Zachary to insert himself in her canoeing date with Joshua. I quickly added, "Feel free to look for mushrooms at our place any time."

The person who had just come in walked past me.

Kevin Lunnion. Had he heard me? If so, he now knew how to find Brent's and my property.

And for all we knew, he, and not Forrest Callic, had killed Albert.

He might have recognized Zachary, Joshua, and Hannah as the three people he'd seen in the woods near the outlook on Friday evening. And he might have recognized me when I was kayaking below the cliffs. Had Dawn overheard me telling the Knitpickers that Dep liked kayaking, and had she told Kevin? I doubted that any other cats rode around in kayaks on Chicory Lake.

No wonder Hannah looked worried.

Chapter 29

Before I could reach Kevin's table and distract him with offers of coffee and beignets, Joshua pushed his chair back and said, much too loudly, "See you around six at Chicanery, Hannah."

I nearly tripped over my feet in my rush to Kevin's table. He was watching Joshua leave, but he turned his attention to me. "Hey, thanks for the quick payment, at least I guess it was from you. The check was signed by Brent Fyne."

"Brent's my husband."

Kevin opened his mouth, closed it again, cleared his throat, and finally asked, "The detective?"

"Yes."

All of a sudden, Kevin became super-sociable, with a smile too broad to look sincere. "He seems like a great guy."

I thought, *What an odd thing for someone to say about a detective who pulled him from watching TV at night to question him about his whereabouts when his former business partner was killed.* I said, "I think so. What can I get you, Kevin?"

"Today's special coffee, whatever it is. I'm enjoying trying these new types."

"It's a complex, rich, slightly chocolatey medium roast from Sumatra."

"Sounds good, and I think I'm addicted to your beignets. Do you have some today?"

"They've become so popular that we almost have to make them every day. Dawn likes them, too. The last time she was in here, she ordered three."

My ploy to cause Kevin to talk about Dawn must have been too obvious. Kevin said only, "Then I'll have four."

I brought him his coffee and four chubby, sugar-covered beignets, and he did what I'd hoped he'd do earlier. He turned the conversation toward Dawn. "Poor Dawn." He shook his head in exaggerated sadness. "The police—including your husband—came around yesterday asking if I was with anyone around the time that Albert died. I told them I wished I had an alibi, but I don't. The only reason I can think of for them asking me that question is if someone said I was with them. And I'm guessing that person would be Dawn. It's like she's desperate to come up with an alibi, and I can think of only one reason—maybe she didn't do it on purpose, but whether it was an accident or intentional, she killed Albert."

"Or she knows that spouses are nearly always scrutinized, often for good reason." Kevin had told me he was divorced. I wondered where his ex was now, and if Brent knew anything about her, like why she and Kevin broke up. Maybe Kevin had a history of violence.

He bit into a beignet and ignored the puff of powdered sugar. "I wish I could say I was with Dawn or someone, but I was by myself, and as far as I know, no one has come forward to say they saw a plain white panel van driving around south of Fallingbrook that afternoon with me at the wheel. Lots of people know me, of course, because of my business, but who pays attention to the drivers of vans? To make matters worse, my windows are tinted."

"Maybe the police will find videos from people's security cameras."

"That's all I can hope for. Or that they find out who actually killed Albert." He took an almost savage bite of a beignet. "Such a waste. He could have made something of himself if he'd tried. It's not up to me to psychoanalyze anyone, but with Albert, I think it was more than laziness. It was like he didn't want to do well—don't ask me why—and kept sabotaging himself. One good thing, anyway, if you can call it good, is he didn't live long enough to fall for a scam that could have wiped him out financially, not that he and Dawn had much to begin with, but whatever is left, Dawn can't afford to lose it."

Watching me, Kevin sipped at his coffee. I tried not to hyperventilate. Maybe Kevin would answer questions about Forrest without my having to reveal my latest suspicions of Forrest. And I also still suspected Kevin. And Dawn. And I was not about to trust any of them. "Scam?" My voice came out sounding almost normal and not as excited as I was beginning to feel.

"A man came in here last Thursday, dressed nicely. I think he talked to you, too. You warned me about him when you dropped off your mower."

"I know who you mean. He made ridiculous claims about investments."

Kevin set down his mug. "That's the man. He left when I did and walked down the street with me, trying to get me to invest. It sounded like a scam to me, and I refused. Then he asked me about the couple I'd been with. I told him that they couldn't—shouldn't—engage in risky investments, couldn't afford it, and they did volunteer work in a campground to give themselves somewhere to stay besides a stuffy, one-room apartment during the summers."

"Did you name the campground?"

Kevin gave me a thoughtful look. "I think I see where you're going with this."

"I can't help wondering." *And also wondering if Kevin was making this up to cover for his own actions, like deliver-*

ing a note to Albert in the middle of the night, a note that might have enticed Albert to a deadly rendezvous.

"The so-called investment counselor asked me which campground, and I probably said I thought it was Herbgrove Lake, up in the state forest." Kevin must have realized that knowing which campground Albert hosted could make Kevin himself appear to be an even more likely candidate as a murderer. He backtracked and added, "I'm not sure that's the name of the campground."

I kept a neutral, almost Brent-like face. "Have you told the police any of this?"

"I didn't guess that it could be relevant, but maybe it is, and I should talk to your husband about it."

"I think you should."

"Maybe it could get me off the hook. Or they—the police—will think I'm making up tales to distract them from suspecting me."

It was similar to what I'd been thinking, but I merely suggested, "It's worth a try."

"Yeah." Kevin didn't sound convinced. He shifted the conversation in a different direction. "Here's the funny thing. The investment scammer said that Albert was a policeman. 'Deep undercover,' he said, with a new identity. He also said that the woman with Albert was not really his wife but was probably also an undercover cop, and they must have had scads of money in bank accounts under their real names."

I couldn't help opening my eyes really wide. *Ira*, I thought, and *I have what you need.* Had Forrest believed that Albert was Ira, and that Ira had gone "deep undercover?" Did Forrest believe that this so-called Ira would jump at the chance of receiving information he could use in an investigation? And that an undercover cop would not warn a colleague that he planned to go alone to meet an anonymous note-sender at the top of a cliff? Also, wouldn't it have occurred to Forrest that an undercover cop should be able to defend himself and might possibly re-arrest Forrest if Forrest attacked him?

Kevin's smile could have been read as consoling. "Don't look so worried, Emily. I'm sure that Albert was not an undercover cop. I just thought it was funny—funny ha-ha and funny peculiar—for this complete stranger to come up with a theory like that about Albert, of all people."

"How long did you know Albert?"

"About five years." Kevin thought for a second. "No, probably more like seven. If Albert was deep undercover as a police officer, which I can't believe, he's been using that identity for at least seven years." He shook his head. "I just don't see it, but I suppose it could explain why Albert accomplished so little, if policing was his actual job, and the work he did for me and up at the campground was merely a cover." Kevin gazed out toward Wisconsin Street. "It could be true, but if so, he was really good at pretending to be just a regular, not terribly smart, guy." Kevin looked at me again. "So, do the police have a suspect, besides Dawn and me?"

"They probably have lots of them, or lots of people of interest. Brent doesn't tell me about his cases."

Again, Kevin gave me that quick, wide smile that I couldn't quite trust. "Of course not, if he's a good police officer. Anyway, I didn't kill Albert. I don't know about Dawn, though. Or that investment scammer."

"Would you like me to call Brent and ask when you can go talk to him?"

"I'll do it. He gave me his number in case I thought of anything, and thanks to you, maybe I just did." Kevin paid me and got up. "I need to rush off to an appointment. See you later."

Leaving torn beignet remains on his plate, he walked out and headed north. Would he contact Brent?

It didn't matter. Later, during my lunch break, I called

Brent and told him what Kevin had said about Forrest, including Forrest's statement that Albert was an undercover cop. "So, that leaves Dawn McGoss, Kevin Lunnion, and Forrest Callic as my prime suspects. And Laura from the grocery store."

"Laura's alibi checked out. She arrived at the hospital to visit her sister about the time that you heard the scream."

"Good. She doesn't seem like a murderer, but . . ."

"I'm still trying to learn more about Forrest and his movements that night. Dawn hasn't told me the tale she told you about Kevin being with her the evening of the murder. And Kevin has not yet contacted me about possibly telling Forrest where the McGoss's campsite was."

I also told Brent, "Kevin overheard me give Zachary directions to our place so he could look for and maybe collect some of the mushrooms he's researching. Kevin was also here when Joshua told Hannah he would meet her at Chicanery this evening. And when Forrest was here yesterday, he might have overheard Hannah and Joshua talking about meeting at the canoe rental place this evening after they eat dinner at Joshua and Zachary's campsite."

Brent let out a low whistle. "Rex and I will definitely rent kayaks at Chicanery this evening. My kayak and paddle should fit Summer. She can use them, and you two can get out onto the lake if we're late or don't make it."

I thanked him and added, "Joshua and Hannah are meeting at Chicanery around six. I told Summer we'd eat at six, but maybe we should go kayaking first and have a late dinner on our romantic catio with the twinkly lights."

"Rex and I will try to be on the lake around six. If not, you'll see us at the chalet later."

"Great!" Smiling, I returned to the dining room and our customers.

The afternoon seemed to go slowly. When we closed, we

still had freshly made beignets. We each decided to take some home to re-warm and coat with powdered sugar for dessert that night.

Although Dep was leashed and harnessed, I carried her, along with the paper bag of beignets, to our Maple Street house.

I unlocked the front door and set Dep down. My phone rang.

Ira.

He warned me, "Stay clear of Forrest Callic. Alec and Tom helped with the investigation that enabled us to testify against him at his trial, and Forrest might be looking for revenge against Tom and anyone in Tom and Alec's family. Like you."

"And you, Ira. I found out something else today. Forrest told Kevin Lunnion that Albert was an undercover cop."

Ira nearly exploded over the phone. "What?" He quickly reached the conclusion I did. "He thought I'd stopped aging and had gone undercover?"

"It seems like a reasonable guess. You'll be careful, won't you?"

He chuckled. "What a preposterous notion. But yes, I'll keep my eyes open for Forrest to come creeping up behind me, and I won't agree to any assignations with him. I might be safe, anyway, if he thinks he already killed me."

I said slowly, "He might have realized that he didn't. An undercover cop might have been able to defend himself better than Albert McGoss did."

"Not necessarily. Cops can be taken unawares, even ambushed."

I felt like my heart had gotten caught in my throat. *Alec.* I managed a one-word answer. "True."

"Sorry, Emily, that was insensitive."

"It's okay, and it's true about retired cops, also. Forrest said he'd like Tom's employees to benefit from his so-called investments, and he specifically mentioned not only waitresses and clerical staff, but also cleaning staff. He might have already figured out that you work with the Jolly Cops."

Ira exhaled loudly. "I see."

"Were any of the other Jolly Cops part of that earlier investigation into Callic?"

"Yes, but Callic might not have known who they were. I'll tell them, and we'll watch one another's backs. We do lock ourselves in when we're cleaning."

We reminded each other to be careful and then disconnected.

Dep and I quickly toured the house. I double-checked the locks on windows and doors. Everything was the way we'd left it.

I put Dep into her carrier and drove north. Passing the turnoff to Lunnion's Lawns and Order, I wondered again whether my theory about Forrest Callic was wrong. As far as I knew, neither Kevin nor Albert's widow Dawn had an alibi.

Dep sang her version of opera all the way to our chalet at Chicory Lake.

Chapter 30

In the chalet, I changed into stretchy shorts, put on a warm sweater, and adjusted my life jacket to fit over the sweater.

Dep ended her post-car-ride sulk and perked up. "Okay," I told my suddenly attentive kitty. "I'm sure Summer won't mind if I add you to our party."

"Mew."

"And I hope that Rex and Brent can make it." I tucked Dep's life jacket around her.

Footsteps sounded on the front porch, and someone knocked on the door. Wearing shorts and a sweatshirt and dangling a life jacket from one hand, Summer smiled. Her glorious, ruby-red wavy hair curled around her shoulders. "You look happy," I told her.

"It's been wonderful getting to know Rex better and discovering that he is every bit as marvelous as I thought. Hi, there, Dep. Don't you look cute! Are you going kayaking, too?"

Life jacket and all, Dep rubbed against Summer's bare ankles.

In case that answer wasn't enough, I explained, "She likes kayaking. How about if we do it now? A couple of men who could be murder suspects might have overheard one of my assistants and her friend planning a canoe outing on Chicory Lake this evening. Brent and I would like to keep an eye on the young couple."

"Rex told me. Let's go now."

"Would you like anything to tide you over? A snack or a drink?"

"No. Let's make the best of this gorgeous fall weather while it lasts. And daylight, too." She put on her life jacket.

I told her, "I wear my sneakers down the trail and change into water shoes on the dock."

"I wade in with my sneakers on and let them get wet. I have slippers in the car. I can change into them when we get back up here."

I snapped Dep's leash onto her life jacket. "We're ready." On the way down through the woods, I asked Summer, "Did Rex tell you that if he and Brent make it to the lake, they're going to rent kayaks or a canoe, and you're borrowing Brent's kayak and paddle?"

"He did, and I appreciate it. Who wants to spend time tying a kayak on a car and taking it off again when we could be out there paddling instead?"

At the dock, I looped Dep's leash over a pole. Summer and I took the kayaks and paddles out of the boathouse.

Without being asked, Summer did the same thing that Brent did when Dep went kayaking with us. Summer picked up Dep and held her until I was just barely afloat in my kayak, and then she splashed into the water in her sneakers and gently placed the purring kitty on my lap. Thanking her, I attached the loop end of Dep's leash to one of the clasps on my life jacket.

Summer launched her own kayak and turned toward me. "Which way?"

"Wherever you like. The county road and the canoe rental place where Brent and Rex will rent kayaks or a canoe, if they get here in time, are to the left, about a quarter mile away. The state forest borders the rest of the lake."

"So, civilization and maybe a couple of yummy detectives are to the left, and wilderness is everywhere else?"

I laughed. It was great to be floating in the kayak with nothing urgent to do besides enjoy myself and look after my cat, who would likely be content whichever way we went, especially if there was a chance that a fish might leap out of the water for a second. "More or less."

"Wilderness, then." Summer aimed her kayak to the right. I followed, moving my paddle in a gentle rhythm matching hers. The hazy late afternoon, with the setting sun slanting beams to the opposite shore, had a dreamlike, relaxing quality. There was no need to hurry. And I was as giddy about knowing I might see Brent soon as I was about Summer and Rex possibly spending another evening together, this time with us.

To our right, near the middle of the lake, a canoe also headed toward the east end of the lake, where the steep cliffs and rocky bluffs were. Joshua was in the canoe's stern, and Hannah, wearing a bright orange life jacket, was in the bow. With those sunbeams shining softened, golden light over the pair, they made a romantic scene. Hannah should have been wearing a broad-brimmed hat and a feminine white dress, both trimmed in blue ribbons . . .

Hannah broke the spell. She yelped, pointed ahead, and started paddling furiously.

Across the water came one single word. Hannah shouted, "No!"

Joshua also began paddling faster, and Hannah yelled something else. It sounded like, "Help!"

Summer must have thought so, too. She sped toward Hannah and Joshua.

Was something moving in the water toward the couple in the canoe? Not a monster or a moose, but something small. A mink? A fish?

Whatever it was, it was alarming Hannah. She must have spotted me coming toward her. I clearly understood her next scream. "Emily!" The canoe scooted toward the creature swimming furiously enough to create a small bow wave in front of it and a wake behind it.

I paddled as hard as I could. Summer stayed ahead of me. Both of us veered toward the swiftly moving canoe.

Our kayaks were light, fast, and maneuverable. Constantly adjusting our direction, Summer and I remained more or less perpendicular to the canoe as we closed in on it. I could easily see both Joshua and Hannah, pushing hard with their paddles. The small animal was almost beside Hannah. She jammed her paddle into the canoe, leaned over the gunwale, and dipped her right hand into the water. She leaned farther.

I shouted, "Careful!"

Hannah inched all the way to the right gunwale, half stood, and bent toward the water.

The canoe tilted toward us. With a cry, Hannah tumbled into the lake.

The canoe continued its roll. It overturned, dumping Joshua.

I didn't know if Hannah could swim, but at least she was wearing a life jacket. She came up spluttering. Treading water, she shook strands of hair out of her face and held a tiny brown animal up out of the water. It did resemble a mink, a soaked, long-haired one. The hair on top of its head was tied into a topknot that now resembled a half-dead palm tree.

The animal barked a pathetic little yap and leaned into Hannah's face.

Gigi.

Muttering a kitty version of a growl, Dep dug her claws into my legs.

What was Gigi doing miles from Thrills and Frills, and how did she end up struggling to stay afloat in Chicory Lake?

Beside the capsized canoe, Joshua hollered, "I can't swim!"

Chapter 31

✿

The life jacket that Joshua should have worn was drifting away from the canoe. And from Joshua. Water frothed around his flailing arms and legs.

Hannah hollered, "Joshua! Hang onto the canoe!" Still clutching the little dog next to her face, she bobbed toward her faltering friend.

With one blade of my paddle, I snagged Joshua's life jacket. I put it into my kayak, paddled to him, extended the life jacket on my paddle until it was within his reach, and ordered, "Hold the life jacket underneath your chin and chest with one hand and grab the canoe with your other hand." My loud and unusually commanding voice seemed to cut through his panic. Where had I learned to speak with such calm authority, from Brent?

Gulping for air, Joshua let the life jacket support his chin. He groped for the canoe and finally managed to flop one arm over its keel, which, instead of being underneath the canoe, was now its uppermost part.

Beside Hannah, Summer leaned over without rolling her kayak and scooped up poor, drenched little Gigi. Summer tucked the little dog inside the front of her life jacket. Gigi's head poked out. Her ears stuck up, and her shiny black eyes seemed to gaze back and forth at everything around her. Summer cooed to her.

Hampered by her life jacket, Hannah swam to Joshua. "It's okay. We'll be fine."

"Freezing." Joshua's teeth chattered.

Experts might have been able to turn the canoe right side up and help Joshua and Hannah into it. I didn't know about Summer, but I didn't have those skills. Besides, we needed to get Hannah and Joshua out of the cold water as soon as possible. I called to Summer, "Can we each tow one of them to shore?"

"Let's."

I positioned my kayak beside Hannah and told her, "Grab the line from the top of the back of my kayak"—I had coiled the rope neatly on the boat's rear deck—"and make certain that Joshua has a good hold of it. And Joshua, keep that life jacket underneath you so your head stays above the water. And use your other hand to hang onto the rope Hannah's going to give you. Don't let go of either the life jacket or the rope."

"I won't." Maybe letting Hannah see him vulnerable and not in control of the situation was making him surly.

Hannah helped him grasp the line from my kayak's stern.

Summer backed her kayak close to Hannah. Without needing instruction, Hannah reached for the line on the rear deck of Summer's kayak.

When I was certain that both Hannah and Joshua were holding the ropes, I gave Dep a gentling pat and then thrust my paddle into the water. "Let's go."

Summer began pulling ahead.

As Hannah was being towed past me, she kicked with her feet as if she were swimming and shouted a succession of words that I couldn't quite make out, but what I heard chilled me almost as if I'd also been dunked. "Dropped . . . Gigi!"

Was she saying that someone had dropped Gigi into the lake? Rising horror, panic, and anger threatened to explode my lungs, but I managed to shout back, "Who? Where?"

Without letting go of the tow rope she clutched in both hands, Hannah cocked her head slightly to the left. The Clifftop Trail was in that direction, but behind bluffs jutting into the lake. "Kayak!"

The sun had disappeared behind hills. Ahead of us, the woods, and the shallow water nearest the shore were all in deep shadow. I was higher in the water than Hannah, but I couldn't see a kayak. I twisted momentarily in hopes of catching a glimpse of the beach where Dep had found the note. The curving shoreline of Brent's and my side of the lake had already hidden that beach from me.

Glad of the strength I'd developed while carrying trays around Deputy Donut and from a summer of kayaking at almost every opportunity, I put all of my might into towing Joshua. He was heavy and seemed to have no concept of how to streamline his body or kick his feet to help me pull him through the water.

Brent's and my beach seemed very far away.

Again I scanned the shadows along our shore, and again I spotted no sign of a kayak. If someone had dropped Gigi into the water from one, that evil person could have skulked off to hide behind headlands or up inlets closer to the bluffs, the Clifftop Trail, and The Beignet.

I couldn't worry about that now. I had to try to prevent Joshua from getting hypothermia. I yelled encouragement back to him. "We're getting there!"

He didn't answer, which was fine. Under the circumstances, I didn't want him to open his mouth.

Dep's tense little body quivered on my thighs. Gigi wasn't

making a sound that I could hear, but Dep undoubtedly knew that her canine nemesis was in Summer's kayak. Ears folded almost all the way back against the top of her head, Dep stared ahead at Summer.

I powered through the strokes. Right, left, right, left. My jaw hurt. I tried to stop gritting my teeth.

Finally, Summer was beside the midpoint of our dock. She stopped paddling. Hannah stood and then stumbled out of the shallows and onto the beach. She took off her life jacket and tossed it onto the sand.

Summer beached Brent's kayak and got out. She lifted little Gigi out of her life jacket and handed the sopping bundle of fur to Hannah. Clutching Gigi to her chest, Hannah started jogging along the shoreline trail that Brent kept groomed summer, winter, and everything in between. Running should help Hannah warm up. Running might have worked for Gigi, too, if Hannah had a leash to keep the little dog safely with her. Hannah did the next best thing. She hugged Gigi. Although I didn't think the unknown person in the kayak could have gotten between our beach and Chicanery's without our noticing, I called out, "Hannah! Don't go far." Hannah must have understood my fear that the person in the kayak might be hoping to finish what he or she hadn't managed before—silencing Hannah. She turned and jogged back toward the dock. Gigi didn't seem to mind being carried around.

Summer pulled Brent's kayak up farther onto the sand and waded toward us.

I paddled. *Right side, left side, right side, left side, lean into it* . . .

Hannah started toward Chicanery again.

Thigh-deep in water, Summer grabbed the nose of my kayak and helped pull it toward shore. She told Joshua, "You can put your feet on the bottom now and let go of the rope."

Dripping and scowling, Joshua pushed past Summer, strode out of the water, and threw the life jacket he should have been wearing onto the beach beside Hannah's.

Summer shrugged and waded to the shore.

Still cuddling Gigi, Hannah jogged to Joshua. "Run back and forth with us, Joshua. You'll warm up."

Holding Dep, in her life jacket attached to her leash, which was latched to my life jacket, I clambered out of my kayak onto the beach. I pulled keys from my pocket. "Better yet, Hannah and Joshua, run up to the house and find towels. You, too, Summer. But watch the woods for anyone who shouldn't be there."

Joshua gestured toward the lake. "Hannah needs to take that canoe back to where we rented it." I could barely see the grayish canoe lying upside down and almost still in silvery water, now speckled in indigo reflected from the darkening sky.

Even in the dim light, I glimpsed tears glinting in the corners of Hannah's eyes. "I'm sorry, Joshua, I didn't mean to tip the canoe. I didn't know you weren't wearing your life jacket, and I had no idea you couldn't swim." Tendrils of wet hair lay flat on the shoulders of her oversized shirt.

Joshua growled, "Thanks to you, I have to walk back to my bike." He pointed west. "Does this trail take me there, or am I going to have to slog through the water the whole way?"

My answer came out in clipped tones. "The trail will take you there. It's about a quarter mile. But . . ."

Joshua interrupted my warning. "I can take care of myself."

Beside me, Summer mumbled so that only I could hear, "We noticed."

Hannah told Joshua, "The trail is decent for jogging."

But Joshua was already discovering that for himself. His running shoes made squishing, bubbling sounds with each running step. Fortunately, he hadn't worn motorcycle boots to go canoeing.

Biting her lips and hugging Gigi, Hannah watched him go. He was soon out of our sight and out of our hearing.

I disconnected Dep's leash from my life jacket and again hooked the handle of the leash over one of the posts supporting the dock. "We'll see that you get home, Hannah."

She raised her free arm and wiped the sopping sleeve of her shirt across her eyes. "It's okay. I parked Olivia's car at Chicanery. But Josh is right. I should go get that canoe. Do you think I could tow it behind your kayak?"

I tried to hide my shivering. "You could, but it's getting dark. That canoe can't get out of this lake by itself, and I'm sure Barney has experience retrieving overturned canoes. We'll take Gigi up the hill to where there's phone service and call Madame Monique. She must be frantic, missing Gigi. We can also call Barney about the canoe."

Summer squeezed water from the hems of her shorts. "Does that dog belong to the owner of Thrills and Frills?"

Hannah kissed the wet little head. "Yes." Gigi licked Hannah's chin.

I added, "I don't know how the dog got way up here."

Shuddering, Hannah looked out at the calm and innocuous-looking lake. "Someone—I'm not sure if was a man or a woman—was in a blue kayak. The person saw me watching and lifted Gigi up where I could see her, held her far out from the side of the kayak, and then just dropped her into the lake and paddled away."

I hoped that Hannah's anger was warming her as much as mine was warming me.

Summer asked me, "Did you see that kayak?"

"No, but it was east of you, Hannah, wasn't it? You suddenly started paddling really fast, and then you saved Gigi."

Hannah pointed east. "It was that way. I didn't see where it went. I was focusing on Gigi." Hannah gazed west along the trail. "We don't need to run up the hill to call Barney. I'll go to his place and apologize and see if he'll help me get his canoe back, but . . ." She stroked Gigi.

I offered, "I can look after the dog, but let's stay together. We can snap Dep's leash to the hook of Gigi's collar, and there must be a rope in the boathouse that we can tie to Dep's life jacket as a temporary leash, and then we can all climb up to the house together." If the person from the kayak was between the lake and the house, I didn't want my arms to be full of cat. In case I might need both hands to defend us, I would tie the rope "leash" to my life jacket.

Hannah exhaled a tremulous sigh. "Okay. Meanwhile, can you hang onto Gigi? I'll exercise to warm up."

I held out my arms. Hannah kissed Gigi again, gently gave her to me, and began running in place.

I cupped the palm of one hand around the dog's little chest. She was wet but warm. Her heart pounded. I wrapped her in the lower front half of my shirt, kissed her damp little ponytail, and felt her collar until I found the loop on it. "C'mon, sweetie, let's find a rope for Dep and put Dep's leash on you so you can run up the hill with the rest of us and warm up." I was mostly dry, but cold. The others must have felt worse. I opened the boathouse door, and Summer and I went inside.

With dusk falling outside, the interior of the boathouse was dark. Summer turned on her phone's light and flashed it around the walls.

A length of thin rope was coiled in a figure eight on a lower shelf. Still holding Gigi with one hand, I bent over and picked up the rope.

Gigi let out one sharp bark, wriggled out of my grasp, and dashed toward the boathouse door.

Chapter 32

Panicking that Gigi could become lost in the forest, I ran out of the boathouse and shouted, "Hannah! Catch Gigi!"

But Gigi didn't head to the trail where Hannah was jogging in place and flapping her arms.

Gigi darted across the dock and jumped down onto the beach.

In the dusk, I could barely make out Dep slinking away from the dock as far from the lake and the little dog as her leash would let her. Dep crept to the base of a shrub between the beach and Brent's groomed trail where Hannah was trying to warm herself.

From the lake west of us, a woman called in a loud and panicky voice, "Gigi!"

Madame Monique? On the lake?

Beside wavelets rippling up onto the sand, Gigi bounced in circles, barked in her shrillest voice, and wagged her little tail.

A canoe rounded the point at the edge of our cove.

Wearing a ruffled fuchsia chiffon evening gown, Madame Monique sat regally in the bow. Barney paddled in the stern. Neither of them wore life jackets. Madame Monique's voice was anything but regal.

Still afraid that Gigi might bolt, I ran toward her. I nearly tripped over Dep's leash, stretched tight a couple of inches above the sand between the dock and the shrub. I dashed to the water's edge and swooped down toward Gigi.

Something crashed through bushes behind the boathouse. I yelped and jumped. Gigi scooted away from me.

I turned toward the boathouse.

A dark shape burst out from beside it. A person wearing jeans and a black hoodie with the hood up over the head and hiding most of the face ran in a crouch across the narrow section of beach above the dock. Brandishing a kayak paddle like a spear, the person charged toward Hannah. She fled into the darkness between trees on Brent's mown trail.

Apparently the hood and the deepening dusk prevented the person from seeing Dep's leash. A pointy-toed tan leather shoe snagged the leash, and the person went sprawling, face down on the sand. Dep let out a startled screech. The stranger's kayak paddle landed close to me.

And to Gigi. Luckily, it didn't hit either of us.

It was enough to excite Gigi into a defensive frenzy. Yapping, she ran to the person—by now I was sure it was a man—and latched her teeth into the hem of his jeans.

The canoe's bow touched the sand. Madame Monique shouted, "Gigi!"

With fierce growls, Gigi braced her front feet in the sand, leaned back, waggled her head, and tugged at the pantleg.

I picked up the kayak paddle and dashed toward the man and the little dog.

Arms pumping, Hannah sprinted toward us and stopped near the man's head. "It's him!" she shouted.

Behind me, Madame Monique yelled, "It's him! Don't you go near my dog, you dognapping thief!"

Gigi growled and pulled at the pantleg.

Hannah stayed out of the man's reach. "He's the one who dropped Gigi into the lake."

I told the man, "Do not move."

Silently, Summer appeared beside me. She had a kayak paddle in one hand and her phone, still serving as a flashlight, in the other. She focused her light on the back of the man's hood.

He started to push up with his hands. I was afraid that if he got his feet underneath him, he would step on Gigi, who was still waging a ferocious battle with his pantleg.

Roaring, Madame Monique trundled around us. Wielding her canoe paddle in both hands like a baseball bat, she slapped the flat side of the paddle's blade across the back of the man's shoulders.

He slumped down onto the beach with his sand-dusted face turned toward the lake. Summer aimed her phone's light at his face. He scowled.

Behind me, Barney said, "It's him. It's—"

I completed Barney's sentence. "Forrest Callic." I added, "He heard Hannah and Joshua say they were going canoeing here this evening. He . . ." I didn't want to accuse Forrest of murder in front of all these people—I would leave that to the police. I couldn't explain that Forrest must have seen Hannah, Zachary, and Joshua in the woods around the time Forrest murdered Albert, and Forrest must have devised a way of putting Joshua and Hannah into danger that might silence them forever. Wondering how Forrest had planned to also prevent Zachary from identifying him, I explained, rather lamely, "He must have guessed that Hannah would not be able to resist rescuing a little creature. So, hoping she'd capsize the canoe and make herself and Joshua easy targets in the water, he brought little Gigi out onto the lake and dropped her out of his kayak."

Barney scratched his head, "That dastardly . . ."

Shifting her canoe paddle to her left hand, Madame Monique scooped Gigi up with her right. "Scum." She added

French words that I was probably glad I didn't know. "I was closing Thrills and Frills for the night. That dastardly scum opened the store's front door, grabbed Gigi, and fled. I had to leave too fast to lock up. He drove north in a black sports car, and I followed in my car."

From about a quarter mile away, near Chicanery, a motorcycle revved and roared away, up the hill, heading toward Fallingbrook, it sounded like.

Other than raising her chin, Hannah didn't noticeably react.

Forrest shoved his right hand into the front pocket of his jeans. His hand came out in a fist, not obviously holding anything, certainly not a large weapon. He flattened both hands against the sand and started another pushup. Before any of us could stop her, Madame Monique raised the canoe paddle she held in her left hand and whacked his upper back again. His shoulders fell onto his hands.

Barney said mildly, "It wasn't his kayak. It's one of the two that I tied at my dock for Emily's husband and his friend. I went inside for supper, and this nice lady in the pretty dress came pounding on our door and hollering that a man had stolen her dog and parked his car beside the road and would I help her find the dog? Of course I would, after I put a canoe in the water to replace the kayak that had gone missing while I was inside. Emily's husband reserved two kayaks. I hope he can make do with a canoe and a kayak." Barney gazed toward my hand. "Emily, is that a rope?"

"Yes."

"Then we don't have to keep paddling poor Forrest, do we." It was not a question. "If you ladies will continue to stand around him with your paddles at the ready, how about if we tie his hands behind his back? Then he won't go far while we get to the bottom of why he was taking a poor innocent little dog out in a borrowed kayak and then dumping the pup to try to get this lovely young lady to rescue it." In the dim light, I could see that Barney was wearing his leather bedroom slippers. They were wet, and so were the bottoms of his camouflage-printed pantlegs.

Madame Monique corrected him. "Her. Gigi is a girl. But this man, he is a scum." She added more harsh-sounding French words. "Dropping my sweet baby into the lake for someone else to rescue does not make sense."

Barney looked at me and thinned his lips. He knew that the previous "borrowing" of one of his canoes could have been connected to the murder of Albert McGoss. He also knew about the animal trail connecting the Clifftop Trail to the Cornflower Trail. And apparently there was more. Barney said softly, "Forrest worked for me when he was a teen. Or, I should say he was employed by me. He mostly paddled off in canoes so he could explore the lake and the woods surrounding it. He must have gotten to know every inch of everything around here. And I was mostly okay with that. He might have shirked some of his duties, but he was just a kid, right? And I thought he was maybe training himself to guide our customers through the lake and the woods, and that would be good for business. But then he grew up, and his lack of respect for other people's rules got him into trouble. When did you get out of jail, Forrest?"

Forrest spat sand out of his mouth and didn't answer. The fingers of his right hand twitched, burrowing into the sandy beach.

Hannah's eyes, wider than ever, glimmered in the light from Summer's flashlight. "Oh." She drew the word out. Only the morning before, she and I, along with Tom and Olivia, had discussed the possibility that Forrest had mistaken Albert for one of the policemen who had gathered evidence putting him in jail for his earlier scams.

"Hannah, where are you?" Zachary's concerned voice came from the shoreline trail leading to Chicanery.

"Zachary!" It came out almost like a sob. Hannah turned toward his voice.

Zachary dashed out of the darkness and stopped as if unsure what to do next.

Hannah threw herself at him. His arms closed around her.

I put down the kayak paddle that Forrest had accidentally launched toward Gigi and me, knelt in the sand, and tied Forrest's hands behind his back.

He objected, but not as strenuously as he might have if Madame Monique had not shown her willingness to slap him with a canoe paddle.

His sweatshirt hiked up in back, revealing a pinch of a fuchsia chiffon ruffle at the top of the back pocket of his jeans. Without mentioning the chiffon, which the others might not have seen, I picked up the kayak paddle and rose to my feet.

Arms around each other, Hannah and Zachary joined the group surrounding Forrest, still lying on his stomach in the sand.

Madame Monique handed her canoe paddle to Barney, who held his in his other hand. Hugging Gigi, Madame Monique pulled a phone out of a pocket in her voluminous gown and punched at the phone's screen. "No service, not even emergency." Her fuchsia satin shoes, now sopping and probably ruined, peeked out from beneath the bedraggled hem of the gown.

I asked Hannah, "Do you have your phone?"

"It got soaked. It doesn't work. Do you have yours, Zachary?"

He didn't let go of her. "Yes."

I suggested, "Can you two run up to the house where there's phone service and call the police?"

Zachary nodded, turned on his phone's light, and shined it toward the uphill trail.

Nearby on the lake, a wooden paddle gently knocked against an aluminum canoe hull. Boats scraped on sand. From the safety of Madame Monique's arms, Gigi let out several high-pitched barks. A canoe and a kayak, piloted by tall men wearing life jackets over their suits, landed on the beach.

I couldn't help smiling. "Hannah and Zachary, stick around. The police have arrived." I raised my voice. "Brent? Rex? We're over here."

Chapter 33

Brent called from the kayak, "Thanks."

From the shrub where she'd been cowering, Dep let out a pathetic mew. She was probably in the safest spot for her at the moment.

Brent and Rex shined powerful flashlights toward us. Both detectives were barefoot and carrying their loafers. Their pantlegs were rolled up almost to their knees. They waded out of the water and forced their wet feet into their shoes. Neither of them took time to roll their pantlegs down.

Rex threw his life jacket onto the beach. "What's going on?" He sounded about to laugh.

I glanced suspiciously at him. Above his flashlight's beam, his face was in darkness, and I couldn't read his expression.

We were probably a perplexing sight. Barney held a canoe paddle in each hand. Summer still had the paddle from Brent's own kayak, and I had the kayak paddle that Forrest had "borrowed." We all held the paddles upright as if we were attempting to barricade Forrest inside a picket-fenced fort.

Nearby, Hannah nestled close to Zachary, who was wearing a bulging backpack. Summer, Zachary, and I were aiming our phones' lights at Forrest, still lying on his stomach in the sand. The rope tied around his wrists glared white. The lower band of his sweatshirt again hid the fuchsia chiffon sticking out of his back pocket.

Somewhat surprisingly, the usually talkative "investment counselor" said nothing.

Still quietly surveying the scene, Rex and Brent, who had removed his life jacket also, waited for answers. I gave Hannah an encouraging smile. The first part of the story was hers to tell.

She pointed at Forrest. "That man dropped the poor little dog into the lake and paddled away in a kayak, leaving her to sink or swim."

Madame Monique hugged Gigi closer and shouted over the yapping, "That man stole my little Gigi right out of my shop and drove her up here. I followed him, me, and enlisted this oh-so-capable canoe-owning man to help me find Gigi. And we did."

Figuring that with two detectives nearby, I no longer needed a kayak paddle to encourage Forrest not to flee, I laid the paddle on the beach. "Forrest dropped this."

Barney bent over the paddle. "That's one of mine. My initials are on the shaft."

I went to the dock and removed the handle of Dep's leash from the pole and then walked over to the shrub where she was hiding and eased her out from between lower branches. Clutching the tense kitty tightly, I hoped that Madame Monique wouldn't let go of Gigi.

Madame Monique pulled a pink leash from one of her obviously capacious pockets and snapped it onto Gigi's collar. Hugging her little dog, she whispered into one tiny ear. Then she raised her head and demanded, "What did you, you thieving, dastardly, dognapping thief, do with my darling's bridesmaid's gown?" She smoothed her hand down her damp and sandy skirt. "It matches mine."

Forrest didn't answer.

I carried Dep close to the group, but not too close to Forrest. Or to Gigi. I pointed down at Forrest. "Brent and Rex, I think that Gigi's bridesmaid's dress might be in Forrest's back pocket."

Rex pushed the sweatshirt up enough to reveal the fuchsia fabric, took photos, and then pulled a miniature ruffled chiffon bridesmaid's gown out of Forrest's pocket.

Madame Monique gasped, "That's it! He had my darling's little dress. That proves he stole her."

Hannah added, "And dropped her, without her gown, into the lake."

"Cruelty to an animal," Rex announced. "I think we can book Mr. Callic for that, don't you, Detective Fyne?" I was certain from Rex's tone of voice that Brent had told him my theories about Forrest possibly believing that Albert was Ira, deep undercover, and luring the man he thought was Ira to his death.

In two steps, Brent was beside me. He put one hand on my shoulder, and the other one underneath Dep's chin. "Absolutely."

Ordinarily, Dep responded to our affection with purrs. Never taking her eyes off Gigi, she remained silent except for a tiny growl deep in her throat.

Forrest whined. "I found that pink thing in the woods where I was innocently hiking. I don't like seeing litter, so I picked it up to throw out later. I did not put the dress on the ground. I did not dump a dog out of a boat. I've been hiking. I don't own a boat."

I couldn't help being sarcastic. "Hiking," I repeated. "Carrying one of Barney's kayak paddles instead of a hiking stick."

"I saw him," Hannah said. "Wearing that black hoodie. He was in a blue kayak. He's the one who dropped Gigi into the lake."

Rex gently helped Forrest sit up. Forrest tried to rub sand off his face onto the shoulders of his black sweatshirt. Unsuccessful, his face still sandy, he asked politely, "Can you untie my wrists?"

Rex patted his arm. "Sorry, buddy, but that's the best we can do for now."

A siren came closer. It sounded like it was on the county road near the top of the hill, and then probably coming downhill past Brent's and my driveway. Seconds later, from the direction of Chicanery, the siren ended abruptly. Still beside me, Brent said, "That should be Misty and Hooligan."

I exclaimed, "Already? You two just got here, and I didn't see anyone using a radio."

Gigi had stopped barking, and Madame Monique apparently heard me. "I called the police while I was driving out of Fallingbrook, right after that scum-man stole little Gigi, the poor petite. I described the—what do you call it?—the getaway car and told them the license number."

Brent explained quietly to me, "That description and plate number were enough for Rex and me to speed here and make certain that backup officers would follow. And then Barney's wife told us about the stolen kayak, so we came out in boats to look for the kayak thief, who we guessed was Forrest."

Madame Monique loudly continued her tale. "I didn't have phone reception after I found the car on the side of the road, so I went to this nice man's house, this Barney, and he promised to help me while his wife called the police again to tell them that the car had been found, but not my poor petite Gigi. But now you're found, aren't you, my little cabbage? And you're nearly dry."

Forrest looked up at Rex. "See? No harm done."

Hannah's protests were drowned out by Madame Monique's bilingual and very loud tirade.

I asked Brent, "Do Misty and Hooligan know where we are?"

He glanced toward Madame Monique. "They probably do now."

We waited. Forrest sat with his knees drawn up, his hands behind his back, and his hood-covered head drooping, a perfect picture of despondency. If I didn't know better, I might have believed that he had never committed a crime in his life.

I asked Hannah if she'd like to go up to the chalet and borrow dry clothing.

"I'm okay. I'm nearly dry."

Zachary offered, "You can come to my campsite. I'll build a fire."

Hannah bit her lip. Finally, she repeated in a small voice, "I'm okay."

Zachary told her, "Joshua said he was going to pack up and go home. He's probably already gone."

Hannah brushed a wet strand of hair off her cheek. "A fire would be nice, but it's my fault that one of Barney's canoes is out there floating upside down in the lake. I should—"

Zachary said calmly, "I'll help. After we get you warmed up."

Barney told them, "Don't you two worry yourselves over that canoe. I've fetched many an errant canoe in my time."

Summer leaped into the conversation. "Hannah couldn't help tipping the canoe. She had to lean over, or she might not have rescued the dog."

Madame Monique gasped. "You rescued my darling Gigi from the freezing depths? You are a heroine! When you're ready for your wedding gown, you come to me, and I will make you the most gorgeous confection ever, and you won't have to pay a cent."

Hannah's eyes opened wider. "That's very generous of you, but really, it was no big thing. Any normal person would have done what I did." She sent a furious glance at Forrest and repeated, "Any *normal* person. And I won't be needing a wedding gown for a long time, probably not until after I finish my degree."

One arm still around Hannah, Zachary stared out toward the lake and didn't say a thing.

Madame Monique turned to Barney. "And I, myself, will help retrieve the canoe that this marvelous young lady overturned while saving my baby's life."

Barney raised one of his paddles like a policeman with a hand-held stop sign. "Thank you, but that will not be necessary. I will go out in the morning and get that canoe. You will need to be opening your shop about then. Going out on the lake is my job, however much it seems like play."

"I'll want to be out on the lake early, too," Brent said. "I'll help you, Barney."

Zachary said, "Hannah has to work, but I'm camping nearby, and I'd like to help."

Barney nodded. "I'll accept your help, young man. In return, you can lead me to some of your blue mushrooms."

Zachary took off his backpack and opened it. "I collected a few from Emily and Brent's property." He held the open bag so that Barney could see inside and then pointed at the trail leading toward Chicanery. "A whole bunch of them are back in there." He couldn't help sounding excited. Hannah looked at him with, I thought, appreciation.

Brent asked Barney, "How about nine in the morning?"

"Or nine thirty," Barney suggested.

Brent agreed. "It's a date."

I smiled. Brent obviously expected to spend part of the night at home.

Zachary quietly agreed. "I'll be there." He grinned at Hannah. "Maybe I shouldn't ask this in front of law enforcement, but do you still have your wallet and driver's license so you can drive yourself back into town later? If not, I'll take you."

"My wallet's safe unless someone has broken into Olivia's car." She winked toward us. "But Brent wouldn't stop me from driving without my license."

Rex continued to stand in front of Forrest. He said in a fake-stern voice, "I didn't hear that. Hannah, you're shivering. How about if you go get warmed up, and we'll take your formal statement later?"

"Okay." She looked up into Zachary's face. "Will you build a nice, hot campfire?"

"I will. And I have a sweater or two you can put on." His arm around her shoulders, he turned her toward the trail leading to Chicanery.

Brent called after them, "If you see a couple of police officers, tell them where we are."

Already jogging with Zachary behind the light of Zachary's phone, Hannah called back, "Okay!"

Breezes stirred leaves above us. Wavelets lapped on the beach.

Forrest complained, "My wrists hurt. Let me go. I didn't do anything."

Madame Monique yelled, "You stole my dog!"

Forrest came up with an excuse. "I found the dog and was looking after her when she jumped out of my kayak. That's not animal cruelty."

Madame Monique stomped one of her satin-slippered feet. "I saw you open the door of my shop and the friendly little darling went right up to you. And then you picked her up and took her, all dressed up in her hot pink bridesmaid's gown, and ran away with her. I saw it all, me."

Forrest sneered. "Your word against mine."

Barney scolded, "Forrest, you stole my kayak."

Forrest snapped, "Prove it." He struggled as if trying to get up.

Rex laid a restraining hand on his shoulder and pointed at the kayak paddle that Forrest had "borrowed." "I don't think we'll have trouble with that."

Forrest protested. "I found that paddle in the woods and

was bringing it back to Barney. Let me go, and maybe I'll find his kayak, too. And maybe even lead you to the person who did steal it."

Rex kept his hand on Forrest's shoulder and said calmly, "The car that Madame Monique saw you driving with her dog inside it does not belong to you."

Forrest stopped struggling. "It's my—I have permission to drive it. You can't hold someone for a false accusation of cruelty to an animal, an unproven allegation of a stolen kayak, or for driving a car he has permission to drive. You have to let me go."

Brent stepped away from me and toward Rex and Forrest. "We'll discuss it when we get to the police station."

From west of us beyond trees, Misty yelled, "Brent?"

He shouted, "We're near the dock and boathouse!"

Forrest snarled, "I'll sue you for police brutality. And some of these people assaulted me. That little woman there— Emily, I think her name is—tripped me, and then she tied my hands behind my back. I have rope burns to prove it. And that woman in the long pink dress, she walloped me with a canoe paddle. Several times."

Powerful flashlights bobbed along the trail from the west, and then Misty and Hooligan, both in uniforms and looking familiar and comforting, came out from between tall pines.

Rex told them, "This is Forrest Callic. We need you to take him to headquarters and book him for theft of an animal, theft of a kayak, and cruelty to an animal."

Brent added, "And he's complaining about the ropes on his wrist. Handcuffs might be more comfortable for him."

Forrest shouted, "No! I'll come along without cuffs."

Misty and Hooligan didn't question Brent and Rex. Earlier, when Brent had called for backup, he'd undoubtedly told the dispatcher that the driver of the car that Madame Monique described could be guilty of other crimes besides dognapping. Misty and Hooligan helped Forrest stand, snapped the cuffs on Forrest's wrists, and untied the rope.

"We'll have to walk back to Chicanery, I'm afraid," Misty told Forrest. "Lucky thing this trail is wide."

Brent said, "I'll go ahead and light the way."

He murmured to me, "You and Summer should eat dinner. Rex and I will grill our steaks and eat after we help Misty and Hooligan lock Forrest inside their cruiser. We'll also take time to check around Barney's place."

I asked quietly, "Are you two going to the police station tonight?"

"Not until after dinner. Callic can wait in a cell. That poor little dog must have been terrified." Brent loved animals as much as I did.

I shined my light at the disturbed sand where Forrest's right fingers had burrowed after he apparently removed something from his pocket. "Before you go, would you have a look here? I think Forrest buried something with his fingers while he was lying there. Not very deep."

Summer spoke up. "I saw that, too. He'd taken it out of his pocket, and it was small enough to be hidden in his fist."

Brent gave me a one-armed hug and then examined the sand. He pulled out something that glimmered in the light from our phones. "A key," he said. "Probably from a pickup truck."

Forrest whined, "You can't blame me for everything you find on someone's beach."

Hooligan silently handed Brent an evidence envelope.

Brent slipped the key into it. "True, but Emily and Summer thought they saw you bury something small here. We'll see who else's fingerprints might be on this one besides mine. This could be the truck key we've been looking for since last Friday."

Rex held the tiny pink dress up and gave it a little shake.

"Hooligan, do you have another evidence envelope we can put this into?"

Hooligan quirked an eyebrow up. "Sure." He gave a small paper bag to Rex, who deftly slipped the little gown into it.

Shining his flashlight ahead, Brent started on the trail toward Chicanery.

Misty and Hooligan grasped Forrest's upper arms and forearms. Positioning themselves slightly behind him, they nudged him to follow Brent. Misty said with exaggerated kindness, "Watch your step."

Rex fell into line behind them. With no restraints on his ankles, Forrest could have run, but those four police officers would not let him go far.

Madame Monique bellowed, "Officers, I need to give you my statement!"

Rex called back, "We'll meet you at Chicanery."

Barney offered her the paddle she'd brought from his canoe. "I'll take you there, if you don't mind another canoe ride."

Madame Monique held the paddle in her free hand. "I think I would love one, even though poor little Gigi might be scared. She is going to be even more scared later. As soon as I give my statement, I am taking the poor baby to a veterinarian to be checked out, even if I have to drag the vet out of bed."

Barney said gently, "My wife is a retired vet. She will be happy you have found the pup. She will thoroughly check the wee creature, and if she has any doubts, she will call our granddaughter Betsy, who is also a vet, to come right over."

"Thank you." Madame Monique's voice had become quiet and a little shaky.

I walked closer. "Dep's life jacket should fit Gigi, and it will give you more to hang onto in the canoe."

Madame Monique displayed the little pink leash. "There is no need. I'll keep her safe if Barney will paddle. Which he did on our way here." She brandished her paddle. "Luckily I had this in case I needed it. And I did. To keep that skulldugger from running away or endangering any more little animals." Madame Monique would probably be even prouder of herself when she heard about the other charge that I suspected Brent and Rex would eventually make against Forrest—the carefully planned murder of Albert McGoss.

Chapter 34

Barney took the paddle back from Madame Monique, stowed both paddles in his canoe, and then helped Madame Monique, cradling Gigi in one arm, into the bow.

I fastened Dep's leash around the pole of the dock again and warned Summer, "Don't trip over her leash."

Summer laughed. "Don't worry. I've seen how dangerous tripping over that leash can be. It brings detectives and other police officers."

"Which is not necessarily a bad thing. Brent said to eat without them. They'll be back for dinner, but it might be late."

"Do we care?"

I grinned. "Not at all."

Barney swung the bow of the canoe, with Madame Monique and Gigi now settled in it, into deeper water. The stern, where Barney would sit, barely teetered in the water, inches from dry beach. Barney was about to get his slippers wetter. I called, "Just a second, Barney. I'll help launch you."

He waved his paddle in a salute.

Summer and I ran to the canoe and steadied the stern. Barney climbed in. As far as I could tell, his slippers did not dip even a toe into the water.

Summer and I pushed the canoe out, and Barney began paddling.

I called, "Bon voyage!"

Because Gigi was vigorously shouting in her own language, I couldn't tell if Madame Monique's answer was in French or English.

Summer and I stood at the edge of the water and watched them go. Not surprisingly, Barney's paddling was efficient, with no splashing. The canoe disappeared around the point.

The evening was cloudless, with a pudgy, just-past-quarter moon that was bright enough to turn the lake into a sheet of silvery gray. I thought I could see the overturned canoe, lying unmoving, about halfway across the lake.

The volume of Gigi's yapping diminished.

In case wind and waves came up during the night, Summer and I moved Brent's and Rex's canoe and kayak farther up the beach. We put their paddles and life jackets in the boathouse and also hung up the life jackets that Hannah and Joshua had worn.

Summer pointed at the kayak paddle that Forrest had brought with him when he came crashing out from beside the boathouse. "What do we do with that? Technically, wouldn't it be evidence in the theft of the kayak?"

"Technically, but several of us touched it after Forrest dropped it, including me." I shoved it underneath the canoe. "I wonder where Forrest left the kayak he took from Barney's dock."

She gestured toward the nearly flat, pale lake. "We could look, as long as we don't touch. If Rex and Brent don't have to search for it, maybe they can spend more time with us."

"I bet it's not far from the boathouse, probably in the inlet from the stream that runs down the hill beside the trail between here and Brent's and my house." I turned toward Dep, still attached to the dock. "Would you like to go kayaking again?"

Dep didn't answer. She was probably thinking that sensible humans should be taking their kitties into warm homes. I wondered if she could still hear Gigi. I couldn't.

Summer waited until I was afloat in my kayak, and then she handed Dep, complete with her life jacket and leash, to me.

Summer got into her kayak. This time, I led the way.

Being out on the lake in the moonlight was magical, and I wished that Rex and Brent had been able to join us.

About twenty feet beyond the boathouse, where our stream entered the lake, arrowhead plants, recognizable by their arrow-shaped leaves, grew among a scattering of rocks in the shallows. I turned on my phone's light and shined it up the inlet. No kayak. I asked Summer, "Do you mind paddling a little farther along the shore?"

"Not at all, even if it means waiting to eat after Brent and Rex get to your place."

I teased, "Wouldn't that be a tragedy?" I gazed eastward. "The kayak Forrest used can't be too far away. There are no reasonable trails along the shore east of our property. Bushwacking through the undergrowth couldn't have been fast or easy."

We paddled around another headland. It curved out into the lake, forming a small, nearly hidden bay where another stream, one that tumbled down the hill through state forest land, entered the lake. I paddled several feet into the inlet and shined my light farther up the stream.

I didn't have to raise my voice for Summer to hear me in the nearly silent night. "I see the stern of a blue kayak." I paddled closer. A life jacket had been thrown onto the bank between tree trunks. I took photos and prepared them to be sent to Brent, along with a description of the kayak's location, as soon as I was again within range of cell phone service.

Warm but not purring, Dep lay almost relaxed on my lap.

I backed my kayak to the lake and said to Summer, waiting in Brent's kayak, "Go have a look and tell me what you think."

Summer paddled close to the blue kayak. Her phone's light went on, and then flashed a few times as if she were also taking pictures. She deftly steered Brent's kayak out of the creek, returned to me, and said, "That has to be it. No paddle in sight. And there could be fingerprints and some of Gigi's hair in and around that kayak. More evidence against that horrible man."

"Exactly." I turned my kayak toward our dock. "Let's go get warmed up and start dinner."

We returned to the beach and put the kayaks and paddles we'd used away. I locked the boathouse.

With her phone, Summer lit the trail up the hill. Nearly running to keep up with the tall woman, I carried Dep. She didn't protest, but conditions were not quite up to her standards, and she didn't purr, either.

Inside the chalet, I made certain that the photos I'd taken of the kayak were on their way to Brent's phone. It was a quarter to nine. My stomach growled with hunger. Summer put on her dry slippers, and then we made a salad and put frozen fries into the oven. Dep must have felt like she'd had enough of being outdoors. Instead of coming out to the catio with Summer and me while we grilled two small steaks, Dep curled up on one of the couches in the great room.

Summer and I ate our dinner, drank some lovely Beaujolais, and discussed everything we'd experienced that evening. Summer heaved a dramatic sigh. "The problem with probably having caught the murderer is that Rex will go back home. I might never see him again!"

I predicted, "He'll come back. He'll call it his vacation, but he'll really be planning to see you."

"I hope so." Then she grinned. "In fact, I think you might be right."

I put the beignets in the oven for a couple of minutes to warm, and then coated them with powdered sugar. Laughing at our attempts not to make a mess, we bit into them.

Vehicles drove close to the house and stopped. Car doors slammed. Hearing Brent's and Rex's voices, I ran to the front door and opened it.

Brent and Rex were still in their suits. Their rolled-down-again pantlegs were only slightly damp and wrinkled. I gave Brent a hug.

Rex walked around us and hugged Summer. "Thanks for the help, you two." He let her go.

Talking companionably, the two men went out to grill their steaks. I put more frozen fries into the oven and set the outdoor table for the men's supper. Summer brought the wine bottle, a pitcher of ice water, and glasses.

Dep joined the rest of us outside on the catio, but she sat on my lap instead of climbing to one of her perches. She probably enjoyed my warmth as much as I enjoyed hers. Unlike Dep, I couldn't show my appreciation by purring. I stroked her soft fur instead.

Planning to go into town and talk to Forrest, Rex and Brent drank only water. Summer and I had a little more wine. We drank a toast to Hannah for saving Gigi and to Hannah and Madame Monique for giving Rex and Brent enough information to allow them to arrest Forrest.

Brent thanked us for locating the stolen kayak. "I'll go down and take more photos in the morning before Barney, Zachary, and I retrieve the boats that ended up scattered around the lake tonight."

I held up my glass. Light streamed through the red wine. "I wonder why Forrest didn't wait and stay hidden behind the boathouse until after we all left. Chasing Hannah with a kayak paddle when Summer and I were nearby was risky. Maybe the three-against-one odds didn't faze him."

Summer raised a finger. "I think I know why he came out of hiding. We had just gone into the boathouse to look for rope. Something thumped against the outside of the boathouse. You might not have noticed the noise, Emily, because that was when Gigi started barking and escaped out the door."

I thought back. "I guess I did hear something bump into the boathouse, but I was too worried about Gigi to really notice. You were behind me. Maybe I subconsciously attributed the noise to you. So, do you think Forrest accidentally bumped against the boathouse, thought Gigi was barking at him, guessed that we knew he was back there, and decided to attack Hannah before any of us could attack him?"

Summer tilted her head to one side. "Maybe, or maybe he thought all of us were inside the boathouse, and he could be long gone before we managed to bumble outside in the dusk. As you said to me earlier, bushwhacking through the underbrush isn't easy, so going all the way back to the kayak would also have been risky for him. He had to know that Hannah, at least, had an idea of which way he'd gone after he dropped Gigi into the lake."

Brent commented, "I don't know what he might have done if you two hadn't gone out onto the lake early this evening when you did. Hannah and Joshua would have been vulnerable out there after their canoe capsized. The water's too cold for even a good swimmer to function for long. Forrest could have paddled to them and made certain they could never tell anyone what he did to Gigi or to them, or what they might have suspected or known he did to Albert McGoss in the woods near the lookout last Friday."

We all agreed that we were glad that Summer and I had decided to go kayaking at six and delay dinner.

Summer asked, "Did you two find Forrest's car?"

Rex cut a piece of steak. "His mother's Camaro was parked

off the road among trees just uphill from Chicanery. The car's being impounded. We'll check it thoroughly tomorrow."

I had another question. "Can you keep Forrest in custody based solely on the theft of a kayak, the theft of an animal, and cruelty to the animal?"

Brent squiggled a finger through the condensation on his water glass. "The earliest that a bail hearing can happen is Monday. Forrest has a record. We'll need more evidence to keep him indefinitely, but as Barney said, Forrest knows his way through these woods. With that, the cut-off padlock, the canoe you saw, Emily, after you heard the scream, and the note Dep found on a beach across the lake, we can argue that Forrest planned and premeditated McGoss's murder. I don't think the judge will grant bail. Forrest might as well get used to the accommodations. Again."

Summer sighed. "Why do people ruin their lives like that?"

Rex squeezed her hand, and then let go and cut off another piece of steak.

Summer bit her lower lip, then she raised her chin, straightened her shoulders, and obviously repressed a sigh.

Knowing she was dreading Rex's eventual departure from Fallingbrook, I made the invitation I'd been contemplating. "Tomorrow is Saturday. You two detectives will probably have to work all day, and Summer and I will put in a full day at our shops, but do you think we can go kayaking tomorrow evening? The weather's supposed to be nice, and the moon should be high again, and almost half full. We could eat around six and go kayaking in the moonlight."

Rex squeezed Summer's hand again. "Sounds good to me."

She gave him a dazzling smile. "To me, too."

Brent raised his water glass. "Let's plan on it." He reached for my hand. Apparently hand-squeezing was contagious.

After we finished the rest of the beignets I'd brought home, Summer and Rex thanked us and went outside together.

They were probably regretting having arrived in separate vehicles, since they wouldn't be able to ride back to town together. From our front porch, Brent and I watched them drive away, with Rex following Summer.

Inside again, I picked Dep up. Brent wrapped his arms around both of us. "I have a question for you, Em. Forrest said you tripped him."

"I noticed that. It wasn't me. Dep was tied to the dock, and I was in the boathouse with Gigi in one arm. She got away and ran toward Madame Monique's quite effective voice. Dep either thought that Gigi was chasing her, or Dep just wanted to escape from the yapping dog. Dep scurried to the nearest bush, which stretched her leash just above the sand. I noticed in time to hop over it, but Forrest seemed intent on aiming that kayak paddle at Hannah and apparently didn't notice the leash."

Without letting Dep and me go, Brent threw back his head and laughed. Then he looked down and murmured, "She's our little hero."

When I could talk again, I agreed. "If Dep's our little hero, why are you kissing me?"

"Just because." He opened the front door. "I'll be back, but you don't need to wait up."

Chapter 35

Taking Dep with me, I left for work the next morning before Brent was awake. By halfway through the morning, nearly everyone in Deputy Donut was talking about Forrest's arrest for the murder of Albert McGoss. Some of the Knitpickers and retired men remembered Forrest from his dubious investment schemes years before. Priscilla shook her head. "It's not surprising. That man was going to get himself into trouble after his incarceration, one way or another."

Charles agreed. "He was a smooth talker. One of my buddies lost a lot of money, thanks to him." Naturally, the other men and the Knitpickers tried to convince Charles that he was the one who had succumbed to the scam.

Charles denied it. "I certainly did not."

Halfway through the afternoon, Dawn came in. She was beginning to look less haggard. I asked her, "Want to try today's coffee? It's a rich dark roast from El Salvador."

"Sure, but none of those beignets. They might bring back bad memories."

"How about a comfort food, like an old-fashioned cake donut with chocolate frosting?"

"That sounds perfect. Listen, last time I was in here, I think I told you something that, uh, probably wasn't quite true. I thought it was, but you see, after my husband's shocking death, I wasn't myself. I was stressed, and I maybe combined some meds that might have caused me trouble, like hallucinations, you know?" She didn't wait for my response. "And then afterward, I thought those weird and vivid dreams really happened. So, ignore anything odd that I might have said. Like, um, I think I remember dreaming something about making chili. I even went looking for it where I thought I put it in the fridge, and of course it wasn't there. And the can of beans was still on the shelf. Have you ever heard of such a thing?"

I didn't answer her question, but I suggested, "Maybe you shouldn't combine those meds again."

She shuddered in a dramatic way. "I won't."

Almost certain that she was still making up stories, I went to the kitchen for her coffee and donut. She didn't stay long, and I suspected that she might never want to face me again. I probably hadn't succeeded in quite looking like I believed her.

At home after work, I made thick burger patties, sliced onions and tomatoes, shredded some lettuce, and got out condiments.

I heard a car and ran outside. Brent met me on the porch. He gave me a bear hug and confirmed the rumors. "We charged Forrest with the murder of Albert McGoss. I doubt that the judge will grant Forrest bail."

We gave each other a high-five.

Summer and Rex arrived in Summer's car. Smiling and laughing, they removed two kayaks from carriers on top of the car. Brent and Rex picked up the kayaks and paddles and headed down the trail leading to our beach.

Summer came inside, patted Dep, and asked me, "Did Brent tell you?"

"What, that you and Rex are dating?"

She slapped at me. "No, and I wouldn't quite put it that way. They charged Forrest Callic with murder, plus a bunch of other things."

"He told me about the murder charge. So, aren't you and Rex dating?"

She shrugged with one shoulder. "Not exactly, not officially, but I think it might happen."

"So do I. Shall we eat inside tonight so we can get out on the lake sooner?"

"Sounds great."

Summer and I set places at the kitchen counter, and the two men returned and helped grill the burgers to everyone's taste.

We sat down to eat. I asked Brent and Rex, "Did you find more evidence that allowed you to charge Forrest?"

Rex laid his hand over Summer's. "We did. The tires of the Camaro that Madame Monique saw drive away with her dog in it match the tracks that were near Chicanery after you and Barney alerted us to the cut-off padlock and the note. And a couple of interesting objects were inside that car." Rex picked up his glass and tilted it toward Brent in a toast that was also an invitation to speak.

Brent gave a dramatic pause and then told Summer and me, "We found a notebook with pages missing, obviously torn out. Magnifying the ragged edge of a small portion of one of the pages that's still in the notebook and also magnifying the torn top of the note that Dep found, we're certain that the note came from that notebook. Also, I'm almost certain that indentations on the next page of the notebook will match the words printed on the note."

Summer clapped her hands. "I remember a clue like that from Nancy Drew or The Hardy Boys or something."

Brent smiled at her. "Forensics will be able to confirm it all. And . . ." He nodded at Rex to continue.

Rex set his glass down. "Forrest seemed to have been carrying most of his possessions around in his mother's car. We found bolt cutters like the ones used to cut Barney's chains."

I wiped mustard off my lips. "Can you use your magnifying glass to see if they're the same bolt cutters?"

My statuesque friend Summer could giggle like a girl. "Do you wear deerstalker hats while you're at it?"

Rex spoke in serious tones. "I think someone at your shop should make us some of those hats, Summer." The skin at his temples crinkled with humor.

Brent pretended to smoke a pipe. "So far, we're limited to the magnifying glass. The forensics lab has powerful microscopes and ways of testing minute amounts of metal that might have transferred from the bolt cutters to the chain and vice versa. With only the magnifying glass, though, it appears that nicks in the bolt cutters' blades match marks on Barney's cut chains."

Rex slipped a slice of dill pickle back into his hamburger. "If the lab agrees with us about the marks in the chains, the tear in the notebook matching the tear on the note, and the indentations on the next sheet of paper, we have some pretty good evidence, and the tiny dress is evidence in the dognapping and cruelty to an animal charge."

I tried for a sad face. "Poor Madame Monique might have to make Gigi a new gown."

Eyes twinkling, Summer asked me, "Do you think Madame Monique will mind?"

I gave up on the sad-looking face. "She'll probably love the excuse. She's probably already started it."

Summer turned toward Rex. "What about the key that Emily and I saw Forrest bury with his fingers?"

The warmth in Rex's eyes when he looked at Summer made me certain that he would come back to Fallingbrook, probably many times. "It fits Albert McGoss's pickup truck, and, by wielding our trusty magnifying glass, we suspect that at least a partial of one of Forrest's fingerprints is on it."

Summer toasted Rex with her glass. And with her eyes. "It sounds like you have a good case."

"It's decent." Rex managed an almost neutral expression. "Thanks to you and Emily. And Dep. And Hannah and Barney and Barney's wife. And Madame Monique and Gigi." The smile that had been lurking behind his eyes spread over his face.

I couldn't help a spurt of laughter. "And Joshua. When Hannah overturned the canoe, he fell out. He couldn't swim and acted rather childish about it after Hannah helped him hang onto the line of my kayak and I towed him to shore. By the time the trial comes around, Joshua will probably believe that he's both the star witness and Gigi's rescuer." I became serious again. "Summer towed Hannah back to land."

Summer added, "Hannah kicked her feet and made it easy. You had the tougher job, Emily, a big man who wasn't helping."

"Both Hannah and Joshua got colder than anyone should be." Ignoring the admiring way that Brent was looking at me and Rex was looking at Summer, I suggested, "Let's leave the dishes for later and go kayaking."

We gathered life jackets, for the people only, left Dep behind to enjoy a nap, and took our time enjoying the flashlit trail down the hill through the dark, rustling woods.

A haunting whinny sounded from a nearby tree.

Rex demanded, "What's that?"

Summer tucked her hand in the crook of his elbow. "A screech owl, city boy."

The city boy asked, "Don't owls hoot?"

"Hooty owls do," she told him. "Screech owls screech. We have them out at Deepwish Lake, too."

Rex concluded, "I need to spend more time in the country."

I barely heard Summer's quiet answer. "Yes."

At the beach, Rex and Brent gallantly helped Summer and me launch our kayaks. With only a few comments about wading into cold water, the two men clambered into their kayaks.

The moon—high, almost a half circle and bright white, gleamed on the nearly flat, metallic-gray water.

Brent and I let our guests decide which way to go. They headed toward the middle of the lake and then veered right. Brent and I followed, but stayed far enough behind to give them some privacy for their own quiet conversation. Near the cliffs crowned with the boulder that I'd privately nick-named The Beignet, Summer and Rex stopped and steered their kayaks toward each other. The sides of their kayaks touched.

Without saying a thing, Brent and I turned our kayaks around so that our backs were to the other couple. We reached out with our free hands and grasped each other. Brent murmured, "Remember that other magical October night?"

"How could I forget? I was afraid you were only holding my hand to keep our kayaks from drifting too far apart in that night's mist."

"I wasn't."

"I know that now."

"Do you think if we leaned toward each other, I could steal a kiss without capsizing both of us?"

We could, and he could, but we kept it to a quick peck. We didn't want to risk tumbling into the cold water. We could do our kissing later in our nice warm home just down the lake and up the hill.

From the nearest shore, a screech owl called, and another answered. Behind us, Summer's musical laugh rang out.

Brent and I put our paddles into the water and started toward home.

RECIPES

Blameless Pumpkin Spice Swirl Beignets

(Makes about a dozen, and no one will blame you if you eat more than one . . .)

½ cup skim milk
⅛ cup granulated sugar
2 teaspoons fast-acting (instant) yeast
2 tablespoons unsalted butter, melted
1 egg (large or medium), beaten
¾ teaspoon salt
1 teaspoon your choice of vanilla, calvados, brandy, rum, or
 bourbon extract (optional)
2 cups all-purpose flour
2 teaspoons pumpkin spice (purchased or mix your own—
 see below)
vegetable oil with a smoke point of 400 degrees F or higher
 (or follow your deep fryer's instruction manual)

Grease a medium bowl thoroughly and set aside.

Warm the milk to 115 degrees F and place in your large mixer bowl if you're using an electric mixer, or a large mixing bowl if you're mixing by hand.

Add the sugar and yeast. When the mixture bubbles (be patient—this can take up to 15 minutes), add the egg, salt, and flavoring extract (if using). Add ⅓ of the flour. Mix by hand or with your mixer until the flour is incorporated. Similarly, add the next ⅓ and then the last ⅓. Mix until the dough is smooth.

Tightly cover the dough with a damp cloth and then plastic wrap and allow the dough to rise and puff up—an hour or two, depending on the warmth of the room.

Coat your hands with flour. Lightly squish the dough into a ball and place it in the greased bowl you have prepared. Move the dough ball around to grease its outside. Again, cover the bowl tightly with a damp cloth and then a layer of plastic wrap.

Allow the dough to rise again for 1–2 hours in a warm place.

You can refrigerate the dough for as much as 48 hours. Remove it from the refrigerator an hour before forming.

When you're ready to form the beignets, coat your hands with flour and lightly knead the pumpkin pie spice into the dough, not uniformly. You want to end up with swirls of spice. Don't overwork the dough.

On a lightly floured pastry cloth, roll the dough to about ¼-inch thick. If the dough has toughened too much to roll it thinly, cover it with a damp cloth and leave it alone for about 10 minutes to allow the dough to loosen, and then roll it to ¼-inch thick. Cut it in strips about 2 inches wide, and cut the strips into approximate squares. Some of them will end up as triangles, and that's fine. Cover the uncooked beignets with the damp cloth and allow them to rest while you heat the oil.

Pour 1–2 inches of oil into a deep, cast-iron skillet set on your stovetop. For safety's sake, put a lid that fits the skillet nearby in case the oil overheats and flames up—this should not happen, but if it does, extinguish the fire with the lid. Set the burner's heat to medium and slowly heat the oil to 350 degrees F. Again, be patient.

Or you can use a deep fryer, following the manufacturer's suggestions.

Using a spatula, gently slip the pieces of dough into the hot oil, being careful not to splash. Fry in small batches. Do not overcrowd, and keep an eye on the temperature of the oil, adjusting the heat as necessary. Fry for about 1½ minutes until golden brown, turn with tongs, and fry 1½ minutes.

Lift with tongs and drain on paper towels.

While the beignets are warm, press powdered sugar through a sieve onto them or shake them with powdered sugar in a clean paper bag. Some of the sugar will soak into the warm beignets. If you like, you can add more as it cools. If possible, serve the beignets while they're warm.

Pumpkin Spice

1 teaspoon ground cinnamon
1 teaspoon ground nutmeg
½ teaspoon ginger
½ teaspoon mace
½ teaspoon allspice
¼ teaspoon cloves

Mix together and store in an airtight container away from heat and light.

Chicory Coffee

Measure out about ten percent more ground coffee than you ordinarily use. Add about ⅕ as much ground chicory. Brew the coffee your favorite way without increasing the amount of water. It's supposed to be extra strong.

For café noir, serve black with sugar to taste (optional).

For café au lait, fill the cup halfway with chicory coffee and top it up with warm milk. Add sugar to taste (optional).

Savory Cheddar Shortbreads

(Makes about twenty)

¾ cup unsalted butter, room temperature
1½ cups freshly grated aged cheddar cheese—Wisconsin
  cheddar, if available
1 teaspoon lemon zest
1 teaspoon finely chopped fresh rosemary OR ½ teaspoon
  dried rosemary
¼ teaspoon salt
⅛ teaspoon ground pepper
1¼ cups all-purpose flour
Water

With your mixer, cream the butter. Mix in the cheese, lemon zest, and rosemary.

In a separate bowl, stir the salt, pepper, and flour with a fork until well blended.

Add the flour mixture, one-third at a time, to the butter and cheese mixture, and mix (a hand-held pastry blender works well for this, or use two dinner knives, scissors-style, to cut the butter mixture into the flour mixture) until evenly combined. Drop in water by the teaspoonful and mix until dough just barely holds together. Two teaspoons of water are probably enough.

Roll the dough in logs 1½ inches in diameter. Wrap the logs tightly in plastic wrap and chill for at least an hour, or up to two days.

When you're ready to bake them, preheat the oven to 325 degrees F.

Line a cookie sheet with parchment paper.

Cut the dough logs into ¼-inch slices and place on the parchment paper, leaving an inch between them.

Bake on the middle rack of your oven for 15–20 minutes or until edges just barely begin to brown. Remove from oven and let rest for 2 minutes. They will be delicate. Carefully lift them with a spatula and drain on paper towels. Serve warm or cool, and store extras (if any) in a tightly sealed container for up to two days.

Radish-Cucumber Salad

(Makes about three cups)

1 large English cucumber
6 to 8 medium radishes
2 tablespoons sesame oil
1 tablespoon rice vinegar
1 green onion
Sesame seeds—regular, toasted, or black

Thinly slice the cucumber and radishes. Add the sesame oil and rice vinegar and toss.

Allow the salad to sit for a half hour.

Top with the green part of a green onion, sliced on the diagonal.

Sprinkle the sesame seeds over the salad, and serve.

Visit our website at
KensingtonBooks.com
to sign up for our newsletters, read
more from your favorite authors, see
books by series, view reading group
guides, and more!

BOOK CLUB
BETWEEN THE CHAPTERS

Become a Part of Our
Between the Chapters Book Club
Community and Join the Conversation

Betweenthechapters.net

Submit your book review for a chance to win exclusive
Between the Chapters swag you can't get anywhere else!
https://www.kensingtonbooks.com/pages/review/